Covert-Ops:
The Golden Camel

Steve Barker

GREEN CAT BOOKS

Published in 2022 by

GREEN CAT BOOKS

19 St Christopher's Way

Pride Park

Derby DE24 8JY

ISBN: 978-1-913794-41-5

ACKNOWLEDGEMENTS

Thank you to

George James
Simon Munnery
Derek Barker
George Holland
Hadley Hatton

for their help with this book

Contents

Chapter One – Release

The time is now 06:00, and at last, been released from the police station in Shanklin after 12 hours of mind-numbing questions on some shootings that took place in America Woods a few weeks back. Of course, I denied any knowledge.

Now, this wouldn't be too bad, but this is the third time they dragged me in for questioning, not only me. The same also applies to Simon and George over on the mainland. I guess that once the local constabulary gets the slightest whiff of your previous life, they make you their first port of contact, the lazy bastards.

However, the boys and I have had several conversations regarding this since the first round of questions. Surely it can't just be the cops being too idle to come up with other suspects, so someone would have pointed the finger at us, but who?

Will give both George and Simon a call later today, but first, this fat boy needs feeding, and there is an Iranian café on the high street that makes the best Full English Breakfast, which isn't far from here.

When I arrive, a young lady no more than twenty is standing behind the counter drying cups with an old white linen cloth.

"Good morning, sir… grab a seat anywhere. Will be over in a moment," she said, grabbing a menu from the organised stack behind her under the rows of drinks that lined the wall.

"Thanks, I'll squeeze myself in here." I choose a table close to the open kitchen to watch as the chef prepared my food. While I wait, I scan the room, out of nothing more than habit, as I always did when entering any premises. Over on the other side, an older couple in their late sixties sit at one of the tables that line the opposite wall, chatting away while sipping on some kind of hot beverage.

Apart from them and myself, the place is empty, so the waitress soon appears with my morning coffee. With both hands wrapped tightly around the mug, I take a long sip while checking out the rest of the café. The walls had been painted a light red colour on which hung several photos of unrecognisable towns and villages — I guess they are somewhere in Iran.

A sound coming from the door attracts my attention, snapping me out of my mini trance. A middle-aged man whose clothes have seen far better days comes in and asks for a hot drink. From his appearance, I would say he is one of the many homeless people who live on the streets.

To my surprise, he is invited to take a seat near the door while Laura, I read her name tag, brings him over a large cup of hot beverage of some type. So I guess there is still kindness left in the world.

"Here you go, one Full English, would you like a refill of coffee?" she says, placing the plate in front of me.

I drink what remained in the cup and handed it to her, "Yes, please."

A quick glance down at Mickey on my wrist tells me time is getting on. Not that I have anything to do for the rest of the day, but being the world's worst fidget, I would end up drinking far too much just to keep my hands occupied. Better make a move.

Find my lodge in the same state as I left it yesterday, with the remains of a microwave meal sitting on the small coffee table close to the sofa along with a half-filled mug of cold coffee, which had now formed a thick crust lying across the chilly liquid beneath.

First, I need to remove the police station's stench from me and the kit I'd been wearing since last night, so I head for the bathroom. The cleaning up can wait until later.

Typical, the moment you get in the shower, the fucking telephone rings. Can't be arsed to wrap the green towel hanging from the back of the door around my waist, as I am the only one here. With water still dripping from me, walk back to the front room and pick up the phone that has, as always, now stopped ringing. Better take a gander to see who it is, I suppose.

Enter my four-digit number into the keypad to unlock the screen. The message reads, 'missed call from George'. Will call him back once I'm dressed, replacing the mobile back on the table. Lucky for me the BV970 phone is waterproof, which is a good job as the thought of drying my hands first didn't even enter my head.

A short while later, with my arse planted firmly on the sofa, I dial George's number. After several long rings, he answers the damn thing.

"Hi, George, hope everything is fine on your end?"

"Morning, yes, all good here—just got back from the cop station. More questions on the America Woods job. Do these fuckers ever give it a fucking rest!"

"Know how you feel, mate, not been back long myself from speaking with the police here on the island, and with any luck, for the last time on the matter."

"Fingers crossed, hey, Steve. The reason for my call is I have just spoken to Simon. We are getting together tomorrow around two-ish in Southampton. Believe he may have some work we might be interested in, and the best part, it isn't in the UK. Are you coming over now you have a shiny new car?"

"Of course, George, couldn't leave you two idiots to organise anything."

"To use one of Simon's expressions, Steve, the second word is off, guess the first."

"That is what I love about you, George, fuck all. Yeah, will meet you in the boozer at the end of the high street at around 14:00."

Well, that is tomorrow sorted, now what to do for the rest of today. After the police questioning on several visits to the cop station, it will seem odd if I don't show some kind of interest in what's happening over in America Woods, especially after our handy work. I will take a walk down there shortly to find out what's going on.

The cleaning up didn't take as long as I expected, so I might as well get my boots on and head for the woods. Soon reach the farmhouse and couldn't help but glance over to the treeline beyond the pond where Derek was laid up in his OP not long ago. This makes you wonder if anyone is over there watching me strolling past. If someone is there, it will be the fucking police keeping tracks on me.

The track leading up to Dennis' property is hard going as it has been pissing it down all night, and the path is now one big quagmire of sticky mud. As I approach the red brick wall surrounding the property, my mind flashes back to several documentaries I watched on television some time ago. One part, in particular, pushed itself to the front, 'all criminals at some point return to the scene of their crime'. So true... In fact, that's just what I'm doing. Better ensure I'm not seen by the boys and girls in blue.

To this end, I leave the muddy footpath and enter the trees to my right, heading to the location our IEDs blew up the vehicle on its way to assist Chad's people.

In front of me, about ten metres away, on the road leading to the gate, a wide area of scorched dirt is cordoned off by yellow and black police tape. Take up a kneeling position under some nearby undergrowth, remain motionless for several minutes, want to confirm nobody else is in the vicinity. Guess they took the car away for forensic analysis.

Only when I am convinced the place is void of people do I move forward to search the ground for any incriminating evidence we may have accidentally dropped that could lead back to us. Simon, George and I had already done this once a few days after the attack on Dennis' place, but I want peace of mind. Anyway, it never hurts to double-check.

Can't find anything here, so I cross over the track and headed through the densely packed woods and undergrowth towards our start location for the last mission. From my vantage point, the yellow tape across the entrance can be easily seen. Once more checked for dropped items but didn't expect to find any as George is far too professional.

Remove the binos hanging from my neck from under my green jumper, where they have been since leaving home and scan the area. As I observe the ground to my front, a white transit police van arrives at the main gate. The driver says something to the person I didn't notice until now and proceeds to drive up to the house's front door. One policeman is standing at the door, guessing he is standing there to control access to the house.

About to leave for my home when my mobile phone starts playing my ring tone 'High on the Hill', so loud it must be audible over on the mainland. As I fumble to cancel the call, I look up in time to witness the copper at the gate peer over in my direction. Fuck, this so-called professional forgot to turn off the bloody volume. Shit, he must have detected the sound coming from somewhere in the treeline. I observe motionless as the man examines the area looking for the source of the noise.

After a few agonisingly long minutes, he turns away and makes his way back behind the wall, likely using the small hut as a control point. Take advantage of this and start walking through the dense woods, across the track, and head home.

Time to discover who the fuck it was who nearly got me arrested by getting my telephone to sing its merry head off at the wrong time.

With the phone in my left hand, unlock the device and navigate to the missed calls, it was Lucy. Shit, forgot she was calling today.

We'd stayed together after the last mission and spent a lot of time in each other's company. Even found her first name is Lucy, not Lorna, as this is her middle name, and she always used it when working. In fact, she is moving in with me. A big step for both of us. The reason why she is not here—she's gone home to go on a planned holiday with her mates before collecting stuff from her mum's house where she's been living for the past year. Better telephone her when I'm back indoors.

After strolling back through America Woods, I eventually reach home about thirty minutes later. Right, one task completed—better move on to the next and call Lucy back. She would kill me if she discovered I referred to calling her as a task, but hopefully, that's one thing she will never find out.

Pick up my phone and dial, "Hi, honey, sorry I missed your call, I was working down the woods," she would know exactly what I meant and not push the comment. Anybody could be listening.

"Hi, Steve, not an issue, just called to say I will be staying at my mum's for a couple of extra weeks—she is not well, I need to take care of her. You OK, missing me yet?"

My voice might have replied, "Of course I miss you; I hope your mum isn't too bad and gets well soon."

But the mind is thinking, fantastic, that may keep her busy while the boys and I go on another mission. Knowing Lucy, she would want to come along, and she is a trained killer. There again, if the assignment is delayed and she is home, she will be welcome to join us.

"Thanks, Steve — I promise to be back ASAP, and if you're a good boy... I'll do something special for you!"

"Now, that is mean, Lucy. That's got my mind racing away in all directions. I love you lots. Stay safe, and I will phone you later in the week...

"OK, speak soon. I love you too."

After that call and the trek through the woods, think I need a lukewarm shower. Raise my arm and take a sniff of my armpits. Yep, shower it is. I'm planning to go down to my local pub for a few cold ones plus a meal as I managed to slip back into old habits since Lucy's been away and relying on the good old microwave.

The hands of the large grey clock hanging on the wall tell me it is now beer o'clock and who am I to argue. So grab my coat, lock the place up after placing my trusted leaf in the door, and then head for Shanklin high street and the boozer after a quick check around the lodge.

The plan is to use the same pub I've been using since before the boys came over last time. Now started to become a regular and liked the welcome with no need to ask what I wanted — they already knew.

The walk along the busy street that made its way through the middle of Shanklin is a pleasant one. Crowds of people are going about their business, darting in and out of the local shops or simply walking and chatting with others. The parked cars that line both sides of the road are starting to thin out as some stores begin to shut for the night.

This idyllic scene in the warm autumn sunshine doesn't stop my hypervigilance checking out everyone who comes too close, working out which to take down first. In case any trouble starts. Relief, time to relax again for at least a few minutes as I reach the door to the pub.

With my hand resting on the solid wooden door, I pause and take a couple of deep breaths before completing a shorter version of my breathing exercise. OK, idiot, in you go... remember, not everyone is out to hurt you.

The door groans quietly as I push it fully open and step across the threshold into the main bar. The place is quieter than my last visit, with only a small group of people to my left, all sitting around tables and happily drinking away.

Four more people occupy the tall, dark brown wooden stools at the long bar that stretches along the far wall, drinks in one hand, chatting away with the person next to them. Turn to look to my right to see if my favourite leather sofas close to the open fire are in use. It must be my lucky day, they are free. With any luck, they will stay that way until I get my beer.

Several seconds later, a voice from behind the bar shouts out, "The usual, Steve... is the missus not with you today?" It was Gary, the barman.

"Yes, please, mate, and no, she is at her mum's for several weeks."

"No problem, one John Smiths coming right up."

"Thanks, Gary."

With a pint in one hand, I walk towards the brick-clad fireplace, place the beer on the table, and warm my hand by the fire's hot red and yellow flames. Not sure why, as it isn't cold, out of habit, I suppose.

I slouch back in the soft leather seats for the next few hours and relax, trying not to scan the room for danger too often. For most of the time, I manage with my mind off to happier times and thinking of Lucy; she's been good for my mental health.

Just sat down with a fresh drink when the groaning of the front door attracts my attention. Take one gulp of beer and place it carefully down on the long two-foot-high table in front of me before looking up. Standing in the doorway is the recognisable figure of the fat bastard I dealt with when they tried in vain to jump me a while back. Not seen these arseholes in here since. For the moment, they haven't clocked on to me and continue to the main bar to order drinks.

From behind the counter, I can overhear Gary's voice, "You can come in, gents, but if we get any trouble from you, you're banned for life." The four nod to confirm they understand.

After ordering and with beers in hand, they turn to make their way to the sofas and fire. At the last moment, their brains must have kicked up a gear when they spotted me. My body tenses up, with my hands slowly starting to clench into a solid fist, ready for trouble that might come my way.

Luckily for us all, they change direction and head the opposite way, plonking their arses at tables on the other side of the bar. Thank fuck, as I didn't want to get barred as I liked the place.

The rest of the evening goes without a hitch. Apart from the occasional glance over my direction from our friends, I'm in a good mood, and I'm not going to let some dimwitted numpties change that.

A glimpse down at Mickey on my wrist informs me time is getting on, so better head home as I have an early start tomorrow, if I don't want to get ripped off by the ferry company who choose any price they like for a crossing.

13

Chapter Two – Catch Up

I started this morning early and now find myself leaning against a row of blue metal railings surrounding the car park. Not sure if it is my hypervigilance or the mixture of the vending machine coffee and the fresh sea breeze keeping me alert. That's got me looking down several rows of parked vehicles towards my own car about three-quarters of the way down the lane to my left.

While I scan the whole area, I take another long sip of lukewarm beverage while pondering what to do for the rest of the morning once the ship docks in Southampton. Perhaps a trip to several family members who live in Totton, as I've not been over to the mainland to visit them for some time. After all, the catch-up with the boys isn't until 14:00.

From the corner of my eye, spot the red and white vehicle ferry entering Cowes harbour. Better go back to my vehicle. About to move when something attracts my attention. A couple of casually dressed men, both in blue denim jeans and different colour woollen jumpers. Both are supporting short back and sides hair cuts. Their dark skinned complexion suggests they are of a Middle Eastern origin. They are now walking down the lines of vehicles before coming to a stop on each side of mine.

Stand off and observe with curiosity to find out what they do next. Would take an educated guess these people are either plainclothed cops or military, supporting one of the biggest rookie mistakes when carrying out any type of surveillance. The short hairstyle.

Reminds me of my first tour of Northern Ireland back in the early eighties, where the other drivers and myself had to educate the platoon colour sergeant that our army regulation haircut made us stick out like spare pricks at a wedding while driving undercover.

Witness one of them, after taking a quick glance around to ensure none of the half-asleep people in their vehicles aren't looking in his direction, proceed to slowly bend down and place something inside the car's front wheel arch. The idiots mustn't realise I'm watching them from my vantage point; they probably think I am still in the terminal.

Will give it a few minutes for them to vacate back to wherever they came from before going back to my vehicle. To conceal my subsequent actions from the view of anyone to the rear, open the driver's door wide before crouching down by the front of the car and reaching up; rubbing my right hand along the inside of the arch until I find what I'm looking for.

The miniature black object now in the palm of my hand is easily recognisable as a military-grade tracking device. My first idea is to attach the bloody thing to the poor sod's car next to me and have them follow them instead. Then I smile as a better plan starts to formulate in my head.

They are thoroughly aware I'm going to Southampton, and I can't conceal that. So will keep the tracker, then once on the other side, lose any tail I might have before hiding the small device and pick it up again upon my return. This way, they wouldn't have any knowledge of where I went on the mainland. Yes, they would detect me returning to the Isle of Wight, but I have plans for the little black tracker to solve several issues at once.

Once I board the Red Falcon Ferry, I follow my fellow passengers up the steep staircase into the half-filled lounge. To my surprise, for a weekday at the beginning of September, the boat appears to be crammed with families who'd enjoyed the end of season holiday bargains now returning home. Some kids are still half asleep, some still wearing their pyjamas due to their parents grabbing the cheaper morning crossing.

The loud rumbling in my gut reminds me that I missed breakfast, thanks to the early start. So head for the ship's restaurant and a Full English until I saw the queue. The line stretches halfway around the boat and is at least thirty people deep. Fuck me, everyone must have the same idea. Probably best to give that a miss and grab something later at the pub.

Disappointed, I leave the eatery to find a seat near the window when the phone started to vibrate several times in my trouser pocket to indicate I received an email; will check who it's from once I plonk my arse down.

It isn't long before I am sitting at the rear of the passenger lounge with my back to the bulkhead. My mobile is on the rectangle table in front of me and vibrates yet again. Better pick it up and find out who it is from. Ensure the screen is pointing away from any nosey bastard who might want to read my messages and navigate to the emails.

The first is from some idiot wanting to sell me life insurance. If they had done some homework and understood my line of work, they wouldn't have bothered. The next one seems to come from Derek, but it appears to be wrong. First, the email address ends with 'EU.' It should end with 'DE' for Germany — he'd kept the same email address from when he lived there.

Second, the body of the message criticises me, and the boys fully understand that as part of my PTSD, I can't stand being belittled in any shape, particularly when they try to hide the fact by putting 'lol' at the end. The last person who tried this ended up in hospital.

After deleting them both, scan the room. The two people who placed the device on my car must be on here somewhere. Of course, if they are professionals at their craft, they would appreciate there is no point watching my every move on the ferry as I can't go

16

anywhere. However, they will be close enough to overhear any calls I make.

Their problem is I'm better at my job than them and soon locate one of them in the reflection of the blank screen of the TV attached to the bulkhead to my front; sitting in the first row of cream colour PVC aircraft type seats five metres away; the question is, where is the other arsehole?

Stare out of the window, watching the lush green scenery that lines most of Southampton water for the rest of the journey until the voice in the ceiling invites everyone to return to their vehicles. This is my opportunity to find out the make and colour of my new friend's car.

If I remain seated and wait until he goes past, he will undoubtedly know something has gone wrong. Instead, I make sure that I am the first person down the green staircase after the attendant opens the barrier. I slip through the open door to the upper level. My plan is working. Even though I'm parked on the lower deck, they will also be located here to avoid losing me as I drive off the ship.

A couple of minutes later, my two targets pass the doorway, and I allow other passengers to go by before stepping back on the stairs to follow them to the transport deck. Once at the bottom and past the heavy iron sliding door, I stand to one side and scrutinise the area. The two men make their way to the back and the waiting white BMW. My own car is nearer to the vessel's front, so I will be able to put some distance between us once I exit the terminal.

Turn right along Town Quay. I'm in luck. The traffic lights are on amber and about to change to red, giving me time to make a left onto the high street but hold up the people in the BMW. Unless they plan on breaking the law.

Once through, take the second right into Gloucester Square, followed by another immediate right between two tall cream-coloured blocks of flats and park behind a thick, dense evergreen bush that gives plenty of cover from the entrance and road.

Wait for a short time in case they somehow discover which way I went. Their tracker wouldn't do them any good. I'd spent a few moments while waiting to disembark from the vehicle ferry fiddling with the device and managed to switch it off. Will turn it back on just before I start my drive back to the island.

With my training in anti-surveillance kicking in, I clamber out and walk across to the building on the other side. Enter the white framed glass doorway. Then stand back a small distance inside so I can't be seen and gaze in the direction of my Red Suzuki for any unwanted attention.

Wait no more than 10 minutes before deciding it is safe for me to continue on my journey. First, I must hide the tracker somewhere, it may be switched off, but with technology, they might still be able to track it with more reliable equipment. For want of a better place, I bury it in the ground under the bush near where I'm parked.

It would be conceivable the people tailing me could be driving around the city trying to find me, so my best bet would be to move out of Southampton ASAP and head for Totton.

Time is moving fast, and after spending the next four pleasant hours visiting my hardworking daughters, I need to head back into town and the meeting with Simon and George at the boozer at the top end of Above Bar Street.

After living in and around Southampton for many years, there are not many back streets I don't know that allowed me to travel around, keeping me off the principal routes. Not that I'm expecting the idiots to still be looking for me, but why take the chance.

Luckily, plenty of parking spaces are still available on Park Walk near East Park, close to our meeting place.

When I suspect someone has been following me, I climb out of the car and step away, stopping in a darkened doorway, turning back to face my vehicle, and stand off. Wait for a few minutes to ensure nobody tampers with the car and guarantee I'm not being followed. Enter the park and wander along the grey concrete footpath as it meanders through the perfectly manicured green lawns until I come to the junction. At this point, I make an immediate left and make my way to the intersection where the path ends and joins the street.

Due to the bloody hypervigilance, no way I'm walking in a straight line to the pub. Instead, I cross the highway, then onto West Marlands Road. Then I turn left again past the Guildhall to the end before turning right to the high street. The public house is now on my right.

Not wanting to use the exact location as our meeting with Mark, Simon deliberately chose the boozer thirty metres further down the road. In my book, it nearly always pays to change locations to keep people guessing.

Some unrecognisable music is playing softly over the speaker system when I enter. To my immediate right, there are two grey leather sofas up against the window and divided by a long knee-high glass table occupied by a group of four smartly dressed young ladies. More than likely on their lunch break from some type of posh office.

The teak wooden bar stretches the entire length of the back wall. At the far end stands the barman cleaning glasses. So I wait for him to finish. But after standing on my own looking stupid and with the opinion I'm being ignored, shout out, "Excuse me, any chance of being served?"

"Sorry, sir, I didn't notice you waiting. What can I fetch for you?" he replies, walking to my end of the bar.

Refrain from calling him a lying bastard as he had glanced over at me several times, and ask for, "John Smiths, please," instead.

With my beer held firmly in my right hand, I walk around the downstairs lobby, darting between the many occupied tables, mainly to discover who else is sitting down here. This is something the fucking PTSD always got me doing, plus checking to see if George and Simon have arrived before me. Our standard safety precautions would have us using the seating upstairs, especially if, like this boozer, a fire exit or other way leads down in case of any trouble. Not finding them here, I head back to the entrance, turn right and walk up the worn wooden staircase to the next level.

Only take two steps on the upper floor when the sound of Georges's voice comes from over near the window.

"Look out, Simon, the psycho has arrived."

"Please to see you as well, you fat ugly bastard," I say, sitting myself down next to Simon and scanning for danger. Unlike the lower level, this part doesn't have a bar available, you have to go down to fetch any drinks. Instead, multiple black covered wooden tables and chairs fill the area, some occupied by nondescript people going about their own business and talking loudly. Perfect for us, as anything we talk about will be drowned in background noise.

I wait until Simon takes a massive gulp of beer and places the glass on the wooden table. "So, what have you been up to?"

"Besides being harassed by the police after the previous job...."

"Don't worry about that. Got a plan formulating in my head to take the heat off us once I return to the island," I interrupt.

"As I was saying," Simon proceeds, "Not much, really. Contacted by a man from Kerala but now residing in Southampton, he should be joining us in about half-hour."

"One question before you go and fetch the beers, where the fuck is Kerala?" George asks before gulping down the last of his drink and putting the empty glass in front of Simon.

"I can answer that—it is in southern India, and I have friends who originate from that part of the country," finishing my own beer, not wanting to miss out on another one.

"Those beers will not fetch themselves, Simon, so off you go. You can tell us about your new friend when you come back," George retorts, coughing slightly to indicate a dry mouth.

"That's an easy one—I know nothing about the man apart from a description of what he looks like," says Simon, collecting the empties and heading downstairs.

While Simon is off purchasing the drinks, I move closer to the window and scrutinise the area outside. Want to see if anyone is sitting on the opposite side of the road observing the entrance to the pub. Couldn't spot any, but that doesn't mean nobody is watching the place.

"What about you, George, any issues with the coppers?"

"Same as you, mate, been dragged in a few times but gave them a lot of bullshit. So what method do you have to take the heat off?"

"Remember those numpties who jumped me before the last mission? Well, on the way over this morning, I suspect the police placed a tracker on my car...."

"For fuck sake," George gasps.

"Well, the plan is to plant the device on them and have the cops follow them to Dennis' place. Just need to think up a reason for them to go down to the woods." With that, Simon returns with three pints of refreshing cold beers.

"Any of you two idiots order a couple of goons?" placing the glasses down.

"No, why?" I say with a puzzled appearance.

"While being a well-behaved manservant and fidgeting at the long bar, peer over to my right and detect two men with short-cropped hair who looked odd; bearing in mind it's warm in here they are both wearing heavy black jackets. On a closer examination, spot the curled up wires from a radio hanging down beneath their coats."

"Not my friendly coppers. Lost mine after leaving the ferry, plus when I came in, four women were sitting by the glass window," I say, turning to George.

"Don't fucking stare at me... they're nowt to do with me."

At that moment, a slim man in his late fifties wearing a pair of blue jeans and a light brown open jacket that fell loosely about his body steps off the stairs and peers around the room.

Simon pokes me hard in the ribs with his elbow, "From the description given to me by my contact, Pete, that's our man—his name is Nasir."

We are all too professional to just walk straight over to him; someone could be following him, perhaps the two suspects witnessed downstairs. Instead, we scrutinise the person as he sits at a table at the far end of the room and sips nervously on his drink as he studies everyone in turn. After a few minutes, and we are sure nobody followed him up, Simon walks over to meet him.

To not stand out too much, Simon takes a seat next to him, "Hi, Nasir, are you from Duhfa?" To make sure we are speaking to the right person, Duhfa is an agreed-upon code word.

"Yes, I'm Nasir from Duhfa. Are you Mr Simon?" the man spoke with a broad Indian accent.

"That's me," shaking the man's hand. "The others are over by the window, come and join us," pointing over to us.

Simon introduces us all. I take out my small green notebook and pen to make any required notes. Not the type of person for unnecessary pleasantries, I got straight to the subject of why we are here.

"Welcome, to stop any crossed wires, you are aware of the work we carry out?" Nasir nods. "In that case, can you give us an outline of who you are, the problem and what you would like us to do about it?"

"Sure, you know my name, and I'm the community leader for the Indian population living in Southampton, based in St Mary's. Last week, a couple approached me regarding a relative who works in the gas and oil industry via the Golden Camel, run by a man called John Nair—here is a photo of him. It's an employment agency. He's been there for 14 months, working as an administrator on a workover hoist. All was going well with regular contact with his family back in Kerala until he moved to an island off the coast of Oman called Mano. He has, according to his friends he worked with, gone missing...."

The task he wants from us is now apparent, so I interrupt him, "No need to continue, Nasir. As I take it, you would like us to go over to Mano and find... What is his name?

"Yes, please, the man's name is Joby," Nasir says while producing a large brown folder from his bag. "This is a picture of him and a new passport."

Take the photo and proceed, "Thanks for the photograph. How long has it been since he went missing, and what can you tell us more about this group called the Golden Camel?"

"He disappeared about three weeks ago while on Mano. The Golden Camel is a front for an Indian organised crime syndicate that recruits desperate people to work in the oil and gas industry. They take back money for employment from their wages, which can be as high as 80%. This arrangement lasts for two years. Anyone who takes engagement with them is physically trapped with no escape. With the ultimate price being paid for non-compliance and retaliation on family members."

"I have a question. Why do people go to them if they have to pay back so much of their earnings?" asks George, looking a little confused.

"Three main reasons. Have you ever been desperate with no money or hope and a family to feed? Plus, the remaining cash left after deductions is still better than having no income," replies Nasir.

"You said there are three reasons. What's the third?" Simon interjects.

"Some people borrow from them and find it challenging to repay due to the high-interest rates, so the Golden Camel, in exchange for any owed amount, takes one man from the family of working age until the debt is paid off."

"Thank you for that info, Nasir. This leads us to the problematic question of money — we do not come cheap. Our minimum fee starts at £250,000, but this also includes our operating costs. Do you have this amount?"

"As you are probably aware, Mr Steve, the Indian community is not poor and is tight-knit and cares for our own, so the money is not an issue. But for safety reasons, I'll pay you £100,000 upfront, the rest on your return. When can you start?"

"Tell you what, Nasir, if you go downstairs and get a round of drinks, I'll have your answer by the time you return."

With that, we wait until he disappears down the stairs before I turn to Simon and George. "What do you think, gents? Can we do this and when?"

"Shouldn't be a problem if this folder contains more information such as places, dates, etc." George drags the file over to him.

"I'm in, a few weeks on a sandy beach — what could be better."

"It's a fucking desert, Simon, not a beach, you moron," I say, laughing.

"Yeah, whatever, it has sand," Simon retorts.

At that moment, Nasir appears carrying a tray of drinks which he places down on the black veneer covered table.

After grabbing my own glass and swallowing several mouthfuls, "We have good news, my friend. We are taking your job and can start in one week, this gives us time to make all our preparations and book flights to Oman." I glance at the others for confirmation — they both nod to confirm.

With that, a beaming smile stretches across Nasir's face. "Thank you so much, gents — the family will be so happy. I can get the money to you in a couple of days, is that acceptable?"

"Not a problem. We trust you, and if you don't, we do not travel, and come after you for any expenses already paid out. I'm sure you know our reputation, or you wouldn't be here." With that, Nasir says his goodbyes and leaves.

The boys and I stay for a while longer, hoping the two men downstairs get bored and wander off. The last thing I need right now is to be dragged back to another police station for even more boring questioning.

"OK, gents, here is the plan in case the two numpties are still below and intend to follow us. If they do, at least we can find out who the fuck they are. Are you two finished with your drinks?"

"Ready when you are," says George, finishing his beer and putting the empty glass down. With that, Simon raises the thumb of his right hand, with his left hand he gulps what remains of his own drink.

There are three of us and only two of them, so we should depart separately, with Simon going first, then George five minutes later. I will leave last, each taking a different route to the RV point near the Bar Gate.

"I know this city very well, gents, so here is my plan. If Simon crosses the road at the front of the pub into the city park, then turn right and travel to where the path comes to a road, cross over here and continue through the park to the far end, then make another right. Travel on the opposite side — you will then see York Walk on your left. Go to the end, where you will find some derelict structures. Conceal yourself and wait for us.

"As for you, George, exit the boozer and make a left, followed by another past where we jumped the bloke before the last mission. Then continue keeping the buildings on your left-hand side along Portland Terrace until you come to West Quay. Turn into Bargate Street, follow this road til you come to York Walk. Locate Simon. I will take the direct route straight down the High Street, as with any luck, the two people would have followed you, but there could be someone waiting outside. Questions?"

"I have a point of interest rather than a question," says Simon, now supporting a stupid grin.

"Go on, let's hear it—bound to be some sarcastic comment," replies George.

"It's for you, mate. You're not on parade, so don't walk as slow as a guardsman or me and Steve will have to get a B&B while we wait for your sorry arse to arrive."

"Not going to dignify that with an answer, you fucking Donkey Walloper."

So far, the plan is working as by the time I reach the entrance, our possible tails in the two men have left the bar, with any luck tailing both George and Simon. Before exiting, I pause just inside the lounge for several minutes to see if anybody follows me down the stairs. The coast appears clear, so I step out onto the street.

The area is packed with hundreds of people darting in and out of the rows of shops lining both sides of the road. It shouldn't be hard to lose anyone if I am followed. Others are walking in groups in the direction of the pedestrian precinct at the far end.

All the anti-surveillance techniques I have been trained to use now come into play again. Take advantage of the people who are standing at the bus stop by taking a position just behind them. Ensure a few bodies are between me and the glass and glance back the way I came, doing my best to spot anything that might be out of the ordinary and stick out to the trained eye. One person did.

About 50 metres back down towards where I left a couple of minutes earlier, a man about five foot eight with longish hair and dressed similarly to the others has now come to a halt and is looking in a German kebab shop. Why would you do this? I knew the place, and there were no menus etc. in the window.

Of course, he could be just an ordinary character going about his business, but I will find out. With the bus stop behind me, turn down the next road on my right, Ogle Road, just before it bends round to the left and the precinct starts.

One final glance behind to see if the man is coming my way. Shit, the man is walking in my direction but keeping the same distance between us. Time to lose this idiot. Take a long deep breath and sprint as fast as these old legs can carry me down the road towards the T-junction. When I reach a point close to the end, my heart is pounding, gasping for air, and arthritis in my knees causes agonising pain.

I turn and glance over my shoulder. Fuck, my assailant is running my way. Quick, think. With my breath becoming more intense and rapid, I run down the central road and dart down Regent Street, a small alley-like street on my left.

About halfway up is another alleyway leading to a few staff parking spaces behind Barclays bank, in which three BT vans are lined up against the wall. Take cover behind the last one just as the person chasing me walks at some considerable speed past the alley in the direction of the high street.

I wait five more minutes to ensure the whole area is clear before heading back down Regent Street to the bottom. Turn onto Ogle Road, then another left on Portland Terrace and mingle with the other bored-looking shoppers before hurrying to the entrance of West Quay.

Once more, I use the people standing at a bus stop outside the shopping centre, blend in, and check out my surroundings. Once I'm positive nobody is frantically looking for someone, I turn and head to the meeting point with Simon and George.

Half expecting at least two men from the boozer to be standing at either end of York Walk, decide to avoid this road and approach from the rear. So I take the longer route down East Street, trying my best to move quickly without attracting any attention from other shoppers. At last, I reach the small side street on my left that leads around the back of the building's works.

Stand off for a few minutes. Need to make sure there isn't anybody in the area, before I climb onto a small red brick wall that ran the length of the wooden boarding that encircled the site, there to prevent anyone from gaining access. The place looks clear, so I heave myself up and over, landing in a big shitty mess of twisted body parts on the ground.

On the opposite side of the open ground, about 200 metres away, is the derelict buildings where George and Simon should be. So for the second time in less than an hour, I'm sprinting as fast as my legs can take me over the uneven sand-filled terrain, hopefully staying out of view of any nosy bastards.

Made it. Now all I need to do is get back over the fence. This time there is no conveniently placed wall or any other objects to give me a boost up. Only one thing for it. Walk back 10 metres, turn and run hard at it. Before leaping into the air, landing with my right leg on the cross beam, my hands grasping the top. Then, without pausing, I pull both legs over until they are dangling down the other side.

Unlike the other side, I can not simply jump down, making a vast crashing sound as I land. For all I know, something could have gone tits up, and it wouldn't be George or Simon waiting for me inside.

My feet are only a metre or so from the floor as I hang momentarily from my fingers, listening for any movement. There aren't any, so I let go gently, landing in a crouched position.

Immediately to my front is a doorway leading into the grey building. To the right of that is a couple of holes where windows used to be. They will be my way in. If something has gone wrong, someone could be watching the exit.

I'm in luck. The second window leads to a smaller room, and there is a wall on the opposite side that should cover me as I enter. Once more, I clamber inside and pause to listen for voices or movement. A short distance away, I can hear the faint sounds of people talking. Not coherent at first, but then the distinctive, familiar voice of Simon broke through.

Both of them are standing on either side of a small opening in the damaged wall about 15 metres away. Not wanting to startle them and get the shit kicked out of myself as I close in, I call out, "You numpties are dead."

"About time you put in an appearance. One of the two idiots who tailed us is over there," George points to the building on the other side near the road.

"Where is the other one?" I say in a muffled voice.

"The one that tagged along behind me is at the top of the stairs at the far end," Simon indicates towards a set of stone steps. "What about you, any problems?"

"Some bloke pursued me out of the pub but managed to lose him on the way. The question is, who are they? Think we should go and ask them nicely, or not, their choice. Any suggestions, gents?"

"Well, if George goes the way you came in and makes his way around to the other end of York Walk and attracts our friend's attention, then once he disappears out of our view, we can sprint across and trap him in the alleyway."

"Good idea, Simon, but why am I the one scrambling over the high fence when you could step over, you lanky git?" George replies, half excepting some sarcastic reply.

"Stop complaining, you fat bastard. The exercise will do you good, so off you pop, George," replies Simon, chuckling to himself.

Once George leaves, focus returns to both men to our front and watch for any movement in our direction. The man near the staircase has disappeared around the top corner, while the person we are going to chat with is leaning against the side of a red brick-clad building playing with his mobile phone.

Six minutes later, my telephone vibrates. A simple message on the screen reads, 'ready'. I turn to Simon, "The moment he moves, we go," confirmation came in the form of a raised thumb from Simon.

We don't have long to wait. The man soon vanishes out of view, and we both sprint after him. As we round the corner, George is standing at the far end, coaxing him to come closer, with bent arms, hands facing up while opening and closing, shouting, "Come on then, arsehole."

By the time we reach the target, he's halfway down York Walk, rapidly closing the gap on George. With Simon a few feet behind me to prevent the fucker from doubling back, I raise my left arm, sling it around his neck and try to wrestle him to the ground. In a massive barrage of flailing arms and feet, he tries in vain to get himself free.

With one last-ditched effort to escape, he runs backwards, slamming my back into the wall. With air being swiftly expelled from deep inside my lungs, I squeeze tighter with my left arm while my right arm reaches around the back of his head and grasps his head, holding him in a vice-like grip.

Still struggling, we drag him back to the ramshackle building. Then, at last, his arms stop lashing out as he realises his life may be fading away, and he becomes compliant. With that, George lands a powerful punch to his stomach. The man tries to bend forward as the pain travels throughout his limp body but can't as I still hold him in a tight headlock.

"Whilst I've got hold of him, Simon, check him for any ID. Let's find out who these arseholes are."

Once Simon removes the man's black coat, he checks all the pockets, then searches the rest of the body inch by inch but finds nothing. "We may have some sort of professional here," Simon says, searching the guy's trousers. "Found something," he pulls out a piece of folded white paper and hands it to George.

Feeling the man trying to wiggle free, I tighten my grip. "What does it say?"

"Not much, just the time and place of our meeting in the boozer. Suggest we ask him directly," with that, George lands two more hard punches to his guts.

"Feel that idiot behind you. Well, he's got a nasty habit of cutting the throat of people who do not answer our questions. Recommend you think before remaining quiet," Simon says, standing inches from his face.

"OK," our new friend stutters.

"I'll start with an easy one to loosen your vocal cords. What's your name?"

"My name is Cameron," came the reply through clenched teeth.

Simon continues, "Now the big questions, so take a pause before answering. Your life may depend on it. Who do you work for, and why are you following us?"

The man receives a blow to the side of his head, as George believes he pauses too long, before attempting to respond to Simon's questions. "Don't fucking look at him... look at me," Simon breathes heavily into his face.

"OK, I'll tell you what you want once you release me," he responds in a faint pain-riddled voice.

"Nice try, fucker, now answer the question," I say, confirming my grip around his neck.

"I'm working for the fucking Red Cross, and we are following you bastards because I fancy the fat one over there."

The moment Simon steps back, "Well, fancy that, you queer fucker," George hits him several more times.

I release my grip and watch as the man slides to the floor and curls up in a protective ball while crying out in excruciating pain. "Don't think we will get any sense out of this idiot," I say, kicking him for no reason.

After a short discussion with Simon and George, we decide this is the bloke's lucky day, and he will live, for now. "Right, arsehole, stay on the ground and listen very carefully. If you or anyone else comes anywhere near us again, our pet sniper," I point at George, "will put a bullet in your head from 600 metres away. Groan to say you understand." The man lets out a loud agonising grunt.

With that, we make a tactical withdrawal back through the building and over the boarding at the rear. We need to get out of the area fast. We cover the terrain as quickly as possible, half running, half walking, and head for Park Walk, where I left my car. Once there, stand off for a few minutes in silence to ensure nobody is watching the vehicle, waiting for us to return. There aren't.

After opening the car door, I turn to George and Simon, "Not sure what that shit is all about, but we all know that will not be the last of them. Whoever the fuck they are, they must be professional as he didn't carry any identification.

"Best you two come over to my place tomorrow. As always, gents, make sure you are not followed onto the ferry. Suggest one of you takes the Red Jet. I'll pick you both up the other side near the chain ferry, East Cowes side."

"Sounds like we have a plan to me. We will try to get more info from Nasir," says Simon, now looking for confirmation from George.

"Yea, sure, fine by me as we need to discuss our latest job."

"In that case, I will meet you at 11:00 tomorrow. I will also check in with Derek to see if he wants to join us in our new venture," clambering into my car and driving off towards the ferry.

Chapter Three – Framed

After yesterday's events, I'm taking no chances today as there is an excellent chance the same people could be monitoring my lodge. To this end, once I manage to drag my sorry arse out of my pit, all lights remain off, and the curtains closed, leaving the whole place in semi-darkness. This will prevent any nosy bastard from observing my movements.

One of my PTSD and army training conditions has me always putting things away and in a set order, such as the cutlery, which is always from left to right, knife, fork and spoon, so fumbling in the darkness isn't an issue.

Once breakfast is finished, and everything is put away in its proper place. My attention turns to picking the boys up at 11:00. But getting to the port will not be as straightforward as it typically is because of the need to deploy several anti-surveillance measures along the route.

The first task is to leave home without being seen. Make my way to the place where I abandoned the car last night due to being followed yesterday. Decided it would be safer to find an alternative position on the resort. Therefore making it harder for anyone watching my home to follow, as I should be gone by the time they made their way to where I'm parked.

Through the tiny gap that separates the lounge curtains, I scan the gravel car park opposite. The whole area seems clear, but after finding no ID on the man yesterday, we could potentially be dealing with a professional organisation. They could be somewhere close by but out of my line of sight.

Right — time to leave. Before closing the front door, snap a small brown leaf off the nearby bush and insert it between the door and the frame. Remove a roll of clear plastic tape, which earlier I cut down to form narrow strips.

Then make my way around the lodge, methodically placing a strip from each window to the metal sides in a place it would be hard to see by anyone attempting to break in while I'm away.

Once everything is in place and the lodge is secure, I retreat to the treeline about 50 metres away. As before, I stand and wait for a few mins and examine the area to ensure no fucker is paying attention to the property. Phase one completed. Now to fetch the car.

A quick check in the usual places on the vehicle for any signs of tampering, particularly areas favoured by people who might want to place some type of tracker. Especially in each wheel arch!

Checks complete, press the keyfob, open the driver's door and scramble inside. A single turn of the key has the Suzuki Swift bursting into life. With my right foot pressing down on the accelerator pedal, I inch away and head for the exit.

At the first roundabout I make a complete circle, intending to confuse anyone who could possibly be following me, before returning to my original course. Having driven this route many times, in my head, I already knew points where I could shake off anybody tailing me. A glance in my mirror confirms that the same grey transit van is still behind me as it has been since I left Lake. Time to change the situation.

On the other side of the tiny village of Arreton is a collection of local museums, and a hotel called Arreton Barns. So make a right turn into the complex, drive up the slight incline, enter the half-filled car park, spin around, and face the way back I just came. After waiting a few minutes and no sign of the transit, I continued towards the ferry.

The rest of the route goes without a hitch, but I still need to be safe, so rather than park near the ferry that linked East and West Cowes, park up close to a local newsagent a ten-minute walk away.

Bearing in mind all the precautions taken so far this morning, there can't be any way I am being followed, but the fucking hypervigilance is going into hyperdrive. So instead of taking the direct route, I take the anti-surveillance one. On passing the supermarket, I turn down York Avenue, succeeded by two more lefts before heading up Link Road with a packed Red Funnel vehicle park on my right. Now find myself walking past GKN Aerospace down the street leading to the ramp from which the new chain ferry operated.

To the ramp's left is a small blue and white wooden painted ticket office on which the prices for individual vehicle types are displayed. The only door is entirely open, indicating it is being staffed.

On the other side, behind the railing that protects people from falling down into the sea, a cast iron and teak wooden bench is occupied by two older people, in their late sixties from their appearance. A viewing platform surrounded by black metal railings is to their right. As this place is unoccupied, I make my way over to wait for George and Simon.

While I scan the area looking for potential threats, I glance down at Mickey. The time is now 11:00, and the boys should be here any moment. Five more minutes pass before I catch sight of George on the far bank walking down to board the vessel.

Observe, out of nothing more than interest, as the heavy front chains become tight as it starts to pull them through the mechanisms onboard, propelling itself gradually across the river.

"Morning, George, good trip?"

"Yeah, morning, Steve, everything went as planned. Don't think any of the idiots from yesterday followed me here. Simon not here?"

"No, not yet, mate."

With that, a voice from behind us shouts out, "Morning, numpties, sorry I'm late... no hold that, I'm not, just made some extra turns once I got off the ferry." It is Simon.

"Typical, the recce troop gets fucking lost," George announces as Simon arrives.

"Do one, George, took the long, confusing way to ensure I'm not being followed," replies Simon leaning on the railings next to me.

"What about you, Steve, any issue?" George enquires.

"Nope, everything is normal. The coppers didn't even harass me," I say, indicating we should move back to my car by pretending to turn a key and pointing in the vehicle's direction.

For once, no complaining from Simon because he has to walk to the vehicle. He probably understood my reasoning for not parking closer. When we arrive, more cars are parked in the once-free spaces around my vehicle, including the same grey transit I saw earlier with two people, a man and a woman, still sitting in the front.

We stand off for a few minutes before deciding we couldn't stay here all day. If the van follows us, I will lose it en route to our next destination. Once out of the car park, I drive about 20mph up the hill, glancing in the rearview mirror. The van didn't follow, so once around the tight bend, I accelerate away.

"Put together any plans yet, Steve?" George says, leaning between the gap in the two front seats.

"A few, but first we have other business. Remember the tracker I found yesterday, and who can forget the unwanted attention from the local constabulary about the mission in America Woods? Then the thugs that jumped me? Well, I have an idea to solve them all in one go," I respond while peering at George in the mirror.

"Tell us more, or is this a guessing game?" Simon interrupts.

"Don't worry, it will all become apparent, but first, who's up for a few cold ones down the boozer?" Both Simon and George nod in agreement.

When we arrive at the pub, the place is bustling, this being a Saturday afternoon. The bar area is crammed with men and women chatting away while sipping on various drinks. To our right, the brown leather sofas are occupied. Luckily the table we sat at the last time we were all here is still free.

The tables to the left on the raised wooden platform are packed with revellers. Most importantly, the four youngsters who'd tried in vain to give me a beating a while back are sitting at a table towards the back of the room, perfect.

"Grab our normal table, gents; I'll go and fetch the beers."

When I finally manage to barge my way to the waist-high bar to be served, a different barman is on duty. Our usual barperson, Gary, must be on a day off. Take out a tenner from my wallet, make my own impression of a demented bird with a broken arm, and wave the money up and down, trying to attract Ralph's attention. Overheard someone call him that.

At last, "What can I fetch you?"

"One John Smith's and two Stellas, please, Ralph," I say, now pushing the two people on either side apart a few more inches, so I am facing the bar.

Beers paid for, I head to where George and Simon are sitting. "Here you go, boys, get that down your necks."

Take several big gulps of my beer before indicating that the others should lean in to listen to what I am about to say without other people overhearing. As they do, I reach into my jacket pocket and pull out the tiny black tracking thing our friends left in my car's wheel arch.

"OK, gents, here's the plan. The four young men who tried to beat the crap out of me are sitting on the other side of the room, and this will be planted on them," I held out the device. "All I need you two to do is follow along, ready?" Both take a swig from their beers and begin to rise up out of the wooden chairs.

"Come on, fat boy, let's see those acting skills," Simon said, walking over to the targets.

Overtake him and arrive first to see the group fidget uneasily in their seats and start to stand. The person I picked out last time who instigated their failed attempt is now sitting to my left—I take a seat next to him.

Place my left hand on his now tense shoulder, "Don't worry, gents, we are not here to cause trouble. I'm here to sort out any misunderstandings. We may have started on the wrong foot on our last encounter, so here to make friends. Can I buy you all a beer?" I say, picking up the empty glass belonging to the man on my immediate left, ensuring I only touch the bottom half.

To ease the tension and play along, Simon introduces us all, "I'm Simon, that ugly arsehole is George, and fat git you already know is Steve."

A few long minutes pass before they all relax and accept my offer of free drinks. Now for the next part of the plan. On the way to the bar, stop off and locate one of the man's slightly greasy unmistakable visible fingerprints on the top edge of the empty beer glass.

Take out a fingerprint collecting strip of clear plastic, liberated from some kids play detective kit a while back and brought it with me for this purpose. And press it hard against the glass, lifting the print before putting it away in a tiny PVC see-through box, ensuring nothing touches the fingerprint.

When I return with the beers, I hear George telling them that they looked like an intelligent bunch of blokes who could carry out any task if given the proper motivation. As either George or Simon didn't yet know my plans, he is definitely bullshitting them to build their trust for anything I have planned.

"Here you go, gents, let's forget the past," as I pass around the drinks.

For the next 15 minutes, we talk about a load of rubbish, putting them at ease. Once I have their confidence, I mention we may have some work they might be interested in. It is a simple find and retrieve task. Facial expressions on all their faces indicate we have them hooked. Time to make them all say yes.

"It would appear we have made the right choice. We have a quick job for you that could lead to bigger things, and I'll give you two grand. Before I tell you what it is, are you up for it?" I say before taking another swig of beer.

A quiet eager "yes" came from them all as they nodded in agreement.

"OK, the task is straightforward. While we," I point to Simon and George, "were in America Woods the other week, close to the property in the centre, we lost something valuable to me. A Browning 9mm pistol I liberated from an army barracks near Okehampton back in the early '80s. We don't have time to try and find it ourselves, as me and the boys are off on a booze and birds

Covert-Ops: The Golden Camel

fortnight away from tomorrow, if you understand my drift. So can you do this today for us?"

The apparent group leader, who we've now discovered his name is Rhys, takes it in turns to stare at each of his mates before saying, "Sure, we can do that for you, but do you have the money with you? I don't want you to stitch us up."

Got the idiots. "Of course, want us all to be friends and work together," I lied. With that, I take out a small green cloth bag from my jacket pocket, then, using the others as a shield, count out £2,000. Place the remainder back in the bag and push the two grand towards him.

I emphasise, "It must be done this afternoon. Suggest you leave it to around dinner time to ensure there are not too many people walking their dogs and therefore less chance of you being spotted."

"Yeah, no problem. We will meet you back here at 19:00 tonight with your lost item," says Rhys, shaking my hand.

What he fails to notice, I reactivate the tracker and slip this into his artificial black leather jacket pocket.

As the youths stand up out of their chairs and leave, Simon taps me on the shoulder, "OK, let George and me in on what's going on?"

"Don't know if you saw me or not slip the device into Rhys' coat. What you didn't notice, when returning the empties to the bar, I took a copy of his fingerprint. Now whoever is trying to follow us will be following our four friends. If it is the cops, they should find them going back to a scene of a shootout.

"My plan is to transfer the print to one of our 9mm pistols just in case our friends have more sense than what we are giving them and wear gloves. Then drop the incriminating evidence near Dennis' place, where even the newest rookie recruit would find it, especially after I call them as a concerned citizen and tell them where to look."

"Very smart, often said you aren't always a fucking numpty," George responds with a huge stupid grin.

"Yep, now if it is the police tailing us due to them suspecting us for the shootings, we have now closed this off, so no more trips to the station. And I suggested dinner time to give us time to reach my place, convey fingerprint, drop it off and call the coppers. So drink up...we have work to do."

Back at my home, I take a seat at the dining table, remove the plastic strip with Rhys' fingerprint, and lay it down in front of me while George retrieves one of the pistols from the underground storage box.

This needs to be placed in the right place. Easy for the police person to find with a bit of effort. While drinking, our friend grabbed the glass with his right hand, so I took the impression from the top right side. This has to be his index forefinger.

Therefore, there is only one logical place to place the fingerprint on the weapon, which is on the body just above the pistol grip, a place his finger would have rested before placing it on the trigger.

"Here you go, one 9mm."

"Cheers, George, lay it on the dining table on its left side."

Now all I need to do now is plant the incriminating evidence. Find the correct location where I believe Rhys' finger might reach and press the plastic tape down firmly, and with a small yellow cloth, rub very gently. With as much care as I can muster, I peel back the synthetic strip leaving the print in place.

After putting a pencil on either side of the newly added fingerprint to prevent contact, wrap the whole area with clingfilm to ensure nothing is smudged en route to Dennis' property. Put the pistol in a black bag to keep it out of view until we drop it off.

"That is all done, gents, any suggestions where we leave the 9mm to easily be found?" I say after taking a sip of the coffee Simon had just made.

"How about just in front of the gate? If need be, you can make such a commotion that even a partially deaf police person could detect the disturbance."

"Not sure why I'm even going to ask this... but why am I the one making the ruckus, Simon?"

"That's an easy one—George and I will be hidden deeper among trees undercover, so only you will be carted off if we have a quick moving copper."

Turn and glance over to George sitting on the sofa, who is busy chuckling to himself, "Cheers, boys, at least I know who my mates are."

"Stop complaining, fat boy, and by the way, did you contact Derek yesterday?" George asks.

"Yep, he should be here in a couple of days, and move your lazy arses —we need to go for a walk," I reply.

"On my way, your majesty," declares Simon, heading for the door.

Still unsure who the people following us are, George leaves first and sprints over the trees that run along the back of the lodge, closely followed by Simon. Once they are both there, scanning the area, I pick up the Browning 9mm and leave. Pluck a fresh leaf from the sizeable evergreen bush opposite the door, put it in place between the rim and frame, and lock the glass front door.

Instead of going the same way, I take an alternative path around the lodge's back, noting how the grass stood and what direction it is leaning, if any. Paying particular attention to the ground beneath the entry points, make a mental note in my mind, so I would recognise any disturbance and possible intruders when we return later. The last thing I want is a smack over the head with some type of weapon.

Check complete. Join the others and head to the Red Squirrel Trail. Before we depart, it is agreed that even though this is the long route, we would avoid going past the farmhouse and any nosy bastards who may recognise us from the attack on Dennis' house. Bearing in mind that some of Chad's men bunked here.

As we're trying to blend in as a group of people hiking through the woods, everyone has to fight hard not to do what our instinct tells us to do and spread out. We would only do this once we reach the area close to the front gate of Dennis' place.

It isn't long before we arrive at the path where the scorched ground from the vehicle fire can still be clearly seen. From here on in, we need to travel as if we are on a mission and not be detected. To this end, I take cover in the deep undergrowth by the side of the road. No point in telling Simon and George to follow my lead as they would already be doing this as a matter of professionalism.

After checking for any signs of movement and not finding any, I sprint across and find sufficient shelter. Moments later, I'm joined by Simon. Once he is in position observing the property, George sprints across to join us.

About to move, when Simon places his hand on my shoulder. I turn to face him, then in a faint voice, "What's wrong?"

Simon points down the road, "A couple of people dressed in black overalls are walking down the track in our direction. They must be searching for something, by the way they are ambling along and thrashing out at the undergrowth with some type of long stick."

"Well spotted, mate. Better make a move before they come closer to the location for the drop-off." With that, I lead deeper into the woods.

Due to the two persons close by, we need to change the approach. We would travel faster than planned. Not a problem for us as we gained a lot of experience moving fast through dense undergrowth while making minimal sounds over the years, unlike most of the population who will make more racket trying not to make noise than if they just walked normally.

Shortly after, we reach the start location from the last mission. From here, I've been kindly volunteered by the other two nutters to scramble down to the road and place the 9mm pistol where it can be found.

Move close to Simon and George, "OK, gents, I'll make my way down to a point about four metres away from the track but still using the cover provided by the thick undergrowth and straight across from the entrance and drop the evidence into place. If things become fucked up, I will meet you back at my place, or you two fuckers could come down and give me some help dealing with the situation."

"Did you comprehend the same as me, Simon — if Steve gets into trouble, laugh for a couple of minutes, then return to his place and treat ourselves to a few cold ones."

"Sure did, George."

"Won't be long, you pair of twats."

I remove the pistol from the black bag, take off the clingfilm, and leave. Where possible, make the most of the available camouflage as I creep forward one metre at a time. About to make the drop when a noise from across the way attracts my attention. Fuck, an armed policeman is now strolling in my direction.

Through the tiny gap in the foliage of the ferns which have instinctively taken cover under, I lay motionless and watch as the man comes to a halt about five metres from my location. He scrutinises the treeline to his front like he is looking for something or someone before peering down the road.

Seconds later, the gushing sound of fast-moving water. The bastard is having a fuking piss, which is landing too close to my feet for my liking. If that twat starts waving the flowing stream of piss around, and I get wet, I don't give a flying fuck about the task at hand. He is going to have the proverbial crap beaten out of him.

After what seems the world record attempt for the longest piss, he leaves and goes back to the other side and disappears behind the wall. Right, time to put the weapon where it can be found, but not too easily. Spot the perfect place, half under a small clump of green ferns with the barrel sticking out. Didn't want it to appear like I had planted it under the bush, even though that is precisely what I've just done.

When I rejoin the others, they both support huge stupid grins, "OK, let's have it."

"Nothing, mate, just wondering what the weather is like down by the road, perhaps a little rain?" George blurts out, trying his best to hold back a mouth full of laughter.

"Hilarious, children," I say, glancing down at Mickey on my wrist.

It is time for the next part of the frame-up plan to be implemented. Once we leave America Woods behind and are walking down the Red Squirrel Trail heading for my place, I remove my mobile and spare PAYG SIM card from my jacket pocket.

Swap over the cards and dial the cops. A stern-sounding policewoman answers, "Shanklin Police, what is your emergency?"

Failing badly to disguise my voice by doing an Irish accent, I reply, "Yes, this is Mick... Me and my pals were walking through America Woods earlier when the dog uncovered a pistol."

"Can you describe where you discovered it, please?" comes the voice on the other end.

"Yeah, no problem, it is near the entrance to the posh property located in the woodlands, not far from the road. Left it where I found it, in case you wanted to take fingerprints etc.... is that the right thing to do?"

"Yes, sir, exactly right. Anything else you can tell us?"

"No... hold on a moment. There is something else... but not sure if it's connected. At lunchtime, the lads and I were down the local boozer for some bevvies and overheard a group of four youngsters saying they have lost something in America Woods and need to find it quickly this afternoon."

The policewoman came back over the line, "Thank you, Mick, you've been helpful. If we require to contact you — is this the best number?"

"Yeah, that's right, just being a good citizen." I knew her switchboard would be displaying my number — that is why I changed the SIM cards. With the call over, take the card out of the phone and snap it into several pieces. As we walk back, I toss the three bits at irregular intervals into the undergrowth.

We reach the edge of Parkdean Resort several minutes later, close to the Barn House bar. "Tell you what, gents, the time is getting on, and I can't be fucked to do any planning tonight, so does anyone fancy a few cold ones instead?"

Before I asked the question, I knew this is a stupid thing to ask, and of course, the boys would find that a more suitable option.

"Excellent idea, Steve, far better than watching your ugly mug twisting and turning like a chewed toffee as your brain tries to think," says George, heading for the entrance.

"What about you, Simon?"

"They say there isn't such thing as a ridiculous question... well, that is one, count me in."

"Beer o'clock it is," I proclaim.

Rather than enter through the principal double glass and wooden doors, we divert via the outside seating area, comprised of ten weather-matured wood bench-type tables surrounded on two sides by a five-foot-high brick wall. Along the front, down a couple of stone steps, is the bigger of the two heated swimming pools in the resort, while on the right is the complex and bar.

As all are occupied, we make our way inside past the smokers and vapers that stood near the doorway, blowing out clouds of toxic smoke and hazardous thick white water vapour indiscriminately into the air.

The wooden bar, with several slushy drinks machines on one end and several beer taps located behind plastic screens, is off to the left of the door. There is a multitude of spirit bottles hanging from the teak backdrop at the back. Several people sit at the tables close to the vast windows enjoying the sun that penetrates the glass as we enter. More bodies jostling for position to have their drinks served next. Ahead of us is a small dining area raised up a level and accessed by wood stairs.

On one wall is a 60 inch flatscreen television displaying the BBC news with the volume so faint you could only just hear it over the ambient noise if you are sitting immediately below the screen. As this is one of the only tables available, we plonk our arses down here.

Take out my phone and scroll to the Parkdean app, "OK boys, what are you having... the usual?"

"Yes, please," comes the instantaneous reply from George and Simon.

As I knew we all drank like fish gulping for life-giving water after we'd been on a walk, take the liberty of ordering two rounds of drinks. Within minutes, one of the bar persons came over with a tray full of glasses of cool, refreshing beers.

"Cheers, Al Presidenty," I have known him for four years now, and I think his real name is Rob; there is always excellent banter going back and forth between us.

"You're welcome, Steve. You lot eating tonight?"

"Possibly. Are you on microwave duties?" I answer, looking at the other two. With that, Rob left and entered the kitchen.

About a half-hour later, and beers going down far too easy, Simon says in a low voice, "Take a look at the fucking TV."

Across the bottom of the TV screen is a red banner stating 'Breaking News'. To the right of this, a message reads 'Four young men arrested over the shooting in America Woods'. As he is the closest, George reaches up and turns the volume up just enough that we can understand what is being said.

A reporter standing near the entrance of Dennis' place is on the screen, telling viewers that the local police have made a significant step forward on the case thanks to an anonymous telephone call earlier today. This led to them finding a Browning 9mm pistol, which led to four men who, on questioning, admitted they were searching the woods for a lost weapon someone had dropped. The men are now in police custody, helping them with their enquiries.

"Well, appears like another plan came together," I say, raising my beer. "Hopefully, that should keep the police busy for a while and off our backs."

"I'll drink to that," Simon also raises his own beer glass, followed by George doing the same.

On a high, the rest of the evening is spent drinking and generally forgetting about the next mission — this can wait until tomorrow.

Chapter Four – Pre-Planning

Wake up this morning with a mouth like a camel's flip-flop and a rock band playing loudly in my head. Reach out with my left hand and fumble around on the bedside cabinet until I feel the cold metal of my mobile phone. Drag it in front of my blurry eyes. Fuck, the time is 08:00 — better drag this messed up body out of my pit. What makes it worse is that I don't even remember leaving the clubhouse last night.

My half-poisoned senses are brought back from the brink with the aroma of bacon sizzling and freshly brewed coffee. As I enter the kitchen, I'm greeted by Simon standing next to the oven cooking a Full English breakfast.

"Morning, you lazy fucker. How's the head?"

"Think it went to a rock concert, but getting better, thanks. How come you're up so early?"

"Couldn't sleep, and my stomach thought my throat has been slit due to the lack of food intake. So decided to make brekkie," says Simon, passing a mug of steaming hot coffee.

"Cheers, mate, need this," I grab the cup and take several large sips. "Any sightings of George yet?"

"Yeah, he was up earlier but went back to bed. I'll wake him in a few minutes when breakfast is ready."

"Scratch that, Simon... I detect movement coming from his bedroom."

A short time later, a quilt-wrapped figure of a body emerges in the doorway, looking far worse than I did, and I felt rough.

"Morning George, plonk your arse down. I'll pour you a brew and bring it over," states Simon, pointing to the sofa.

"Thanks, Simon. Morning, Steve, if I look like you, then I'm fucked for the day," says George, taking the hot brew from Simon.

"Not going to argue with that statement, George."

With my senses starting to regain some normality, Simon shouts, "Breakfast is ready, the best cure for a hangover."

With that, stagger over to the table to be confronted with a plate full of crispy bacon, four slightly burnt sausages, cooked beans and two fried eggs dripping in cooking oil. After fighting back the tiny mouthful of regurgitated substance, which, for some reason unknown to man, has made its way from the gut on the sight of food, so grab my diggers and dive in.

As always, Simon is correct—again, I eat as much as possible to try to return back to some sort of normality.

"Any chance of another brew, Simon?" I ask, looking down into an empty mug.

"Sure, what about you, George? Want another tea before my helpful side fucks off?"

"Yes, please, mate."

While Simon makes the brews, I grab a handful of white paper from the printer and a black pen and name each sheet.

- deployment
- fact-finding
- trip to Mano from Oman
- weapons
- recce extraction
- withdrawal
- collection of the rest of the money

We will have a lot more to plan for, but this should be enough to get us started for now, at least.

Take a swig of coffee while the cheap biro pen hovers over the blank page. Come on, idiot, think, you are supposed to be the planner. "If you're ready, gents, let's go over what we know, and then we can start on the planning.

"So far, we know our contact is Nasir, and he is the one financing the operation, which reminds me, when we finish here, Simon, can you check your bank account to find out if Nasir transferred the requested gelt? No point in continuing if he didn't."

"Give me a moment — I'll do it now," Simon picks up his mobile phone from the laminated kitchen worktop and scrolls to his banking app. A couple of flicks of the screen later, he glances up. "Yep, all funds transferred as promised."

"Appears the mission is a go then, gents," I say, pressing the pen down onto the paper, willing it to start writing.

Like all our missions, the first point to discuss is how we get to our deployment destination. "This is how I perceive it at the moment. Due to the fact I lived in Oman a few years back, I will, as always, travel ahead of the rest of you and try to re-establish some of my old contacts. You two idiots can fly on separate planes and meet at Muscat airport if I can arrange flights to land simultaneously. What's your input, gents?"

"Did you say Derek is flying to the UK in a couple of days... wouldn't it be better for him to join us at the destination?"

"Great point, George," I say, looking in Simons's direction. "I'll call Derek later today and tell him to re-arrange any plans he might have made."

"Makes sense to me," says Simon.

"Will work on the flight's details this morning, once we finish with the preliminary planning," I reply, after putting down the mug of caffeine which is slowly doing its job and bringing me back to life.

"When it comes to fact-finding, we need to find out more information on the Golden Camel. This can be done once everyone is on location. Talking of which, I will hire a vehicle and collect you from the airport and take you to the hotel.

"From what I remember, Muscat has some dodgy areas where we should find out what we need on the organisation as the population is mainly Indian...."

"What's the area called, out of interest?" Simon interrupts.

"If my memory serves me, the suburb is named Ruwi. Made up of shops and cafés run by Indians and owned by the locals. There are plenty of dubious back alleys and small production facilities where the workers would sell their grandparents for the right price."

"You should fit in well, Simon — it's full of numpties," comes the sarcastic comment from George.

"Do one, idiot," comes the response from Simon.

"OK, gents, let's move on to getting to the island of Mano. There is a place me and my mate, Eddie used to go to at weekends called Jebel Sifah. It is an excellent place, more laid back than the rest of Oman, and even has a bar/restaurant where you could sit outside and admire the small harbour. The place also has a hotel where we can stay for the night. More importantly, for us, the harbour always contains posh yachts flying the Union Jack moored up that may at a price take us over to Mano."

"Hope it's bigger than when we travelled across from St Halb back to St Bethanie, nearly emptied the stomach overboard. Reminded me why I joined the army, not the fucking navy."

"Sure it will be, George, and hopefully, the sea will be calm," I say.

"Glad to hear it... if it's not, I'm putting the blame squarely on you, Steve."

"No problem with that. Right, weapons. As we are going international, we can't take any firepower or explosive equipment, so we will need to purchase stuff when we arrive. From what I remember, it has plenty of western-style shops plus a few local ones we can pick up the things from. Best give Katie and Cody a call, Simon, to find out if they also have contacts in Ruwi for the rifles and close range pistols."

"Would appear like I'm making all the calls, but will do this today," comes the reply from Simon.

Pause and take another swig of coffee before continuing, "Any questions on what we've covered so far? I know it's only a basic outline, and we will fill in more details later."

"Yep, got one. We know Derek is the communication guy, and he will sort out some comms once we are all on location, but how will we contact you once you've left?" asks George.

"Good question, and something I've been considering since we met with Nasir. Will ensure my flight is on a Monday, probably with British Airways, as they fly out to Muscat daily in the morning. The rest of you will travel on Wednesday, leaving Tuesday free. We are still unsure who the people following us are, they could be professionals, so phone calls will be out.

"Not sure if you know, but over the last few months, there has been an increase in the number of webinars of late. The issue here is that people type away via the chatbox that has nowt to do with the subject at hand. If we all go on YouTube at 18:00 on Tuesday and join Autocrit Live, I will leave any messages in the chat."

"That coffee must be doing its job, Steve, if you can come up with that plan," Simon grins.

"I try," I reply, finishing off the remainder of the brew in my mug. "Whose turn is it to make the brews?"

"Yours!" comes the instantaneous response from Simon and George.

Knowing I am outnumbered, there is no point in complaining about it, so head towards the kitchen, grab the black plastic kettle, identify the fill line and pour in the cold water. Within a few minutes, the sounds of bubbling water coming to the boil could be detected just before the switch at the bottom flicks up, turning it off.

Without looking back, I shout, "We all having one?" From behind me, I heard two grunts of 'yes'. Still not feeling a hundred per cent, pour two cups of liquid caffeine and one tea.

This proves my head is still not on my shoulders correctly, as a shiny new coffee machine is positioned next to the kettle. Well, fuck it—George's teabag is only getting several swirls in the mug rather than letting it infuse with the boiling water.

Return with two drinks and place them on the dining table before returning for my own. Take two sips of my drink before I continue with the planning. "Just a couple more parts to cover for now. Next on the list is the recce of the position. We can't really do this part until we are on the ground. The same goes for extracting Joby's alive or dead body. So let's move on to the withdrawal from Mano and home."

"Roger that," comes Simon's reply, sipping on his cuppa.

"When I book everyone's flights, I will make them open-ended, so we can be flexible on the return date. With any luck, the boat owner who takes us will be willing to pick us up and drop us off on Mano. Before I go on to the final part, any more questions?"

"Not from me, mate, too early. I'm still getting my head around the basic plan, and this hangover doesn't help," says George, holding his head with both hands while leaning forward over the table.

"What about you, Simon."

"Not at the moment, Steve."

"In that case, time to move onto the most crucial stage, retrieving the rest of the money. Once back on English soil, we will contact Nasir and arrange a meeting. If he even thinks of stitching us up, all the necessary steps will be required to send a message."

As the boys didn't have any questions, we each move on to our individual assignments. For me, this meant finding flights leaving from London and Berlin that arrived in Muscat at an identical time or close to it on the same day.

With the mug of brewed coffee in hand, walk over and fire up the old computer. For ease and the fact that I can't be bothered to search several airline sights, I navigate straight to the Skyscanner website.

It isn't long before I find two airlines, British and Qatar Airways, that not only do both take off at 05:55 but also land at Muscat airport at about 12:10. This will be perfect for George and Simon. Now to see if I have any luck with any departures from St Bethanie for Derek. Can't find any direct routes, so he will need to travel via New York and then on to Oman. But at least I found connecting flights.

Might as well book them now to ensure they don't do a vanishing act on me, so look up from the computer screen and shout out, "Simon, transfer some of the dosh to my bank account, so I can reserve these."

"Sure, on one condition...."

"OK, what?" I enquire, waiting for some stupid answer.

"You don't sit me next to fat boy over there, don't fancy playing a game of battle of the armrests," he points towards George.

"Can do better than that — I'm sending you both Business Class and on different airlines. I will give you more details once I've booked all the flights."

Booking is easy as I already have everyone's passport, DOB etc., in a folder locked in my safe in case anything ever went wrong on a mission. Made sure I note everything on separate pieces of paper, ready to give to the boys. Once I'm finished, I plonk my backside down at the table and call Simon and George over.

Split the notes up and push them in front of each person, "On them is your own individual flight details. Both departures are on Wednesday and leave at 05:55, which means you will have to be at London Heathrow at 04:00. I will book an airport hotel for the night before. Like me, Simon, you will be flying with BA; as for you, George, you're going with Qatar Airways. As they land at approximately the same time, 12:10, you should be able to meet up after security.

"Remember you have to apply for an Oman visa online. If you do it today, we are covered. If anyone is denied, we will have to make alternative arrangements. Better phone Derek to let him know his new flights."

Pick up the mobile and dial, no answer. Not a problem; it gives me time to book everyone a hotel at the airport, including one in New York. Right, hotels booked, time to try again and call Derek. Second time lucky, after a few rings, he answers the phone.

"Hi, Steve, something up?" came the voice on the other end of the line.

"Morning, afternoon, or whatever the time is over on St Halb. Been a slight change in the mission plan. Rather than come over to the UK, I need you to fly to Oman. Sorry no direct flights, so you need to travel via JFK. Do you have a pen and paper to write down the details?"

"One second... OK, fire away."

"You needed to make your own way to John F Kennedy Airport by 21:00 on Tuesday, as your flight with Eithad leaves at 23:45, and you land at 12:40 on Wednesday. Once you are past security, we will all be waiting for you at Caffe Nero, located at Arrivals level one. Any questions?"

"Nope, see you all when I arrive."

"OK, take care," I reply before disconnecting the call.

Simon is on the sofa chatting on his phone, and from what I just overheard, 'Hi, is that Katie from Perth?' Along with the continuing conversation, he must be talking to Katie regarding any possible contacts in Oman about the supply of weapons. Turn to view George sitting at the table, going through his notes.

Time seems to be going fast this morning, and it is now lunchtime. Though the caffeine and Full English are doing their job in clearing the hangover, I need the hair of the doggy.

"When you're finished, gents, does anyone fancy a couple of cold ones down the boozer? I, for one, need something to remove this splitting headache."

"Sounds like some sort of a plan to me," says George, putting down his notepad.

"You coming as well, Simon?"

While holding the phone to his left ear, he raises the index finger of his right hand as if to say, one second. Then as he staggers from the sofa, "Count me in."

Unlike the last time we were here, the place is empty apart from two men who, from their appearance are in their late sixties, sitting at a table off to my left. Turn towards the fire, blazing away in the grate, reflecting light off the brown leather sofas located directly in front.

Nobody is serving behind the bar when we walk in, so I tap gently on the wooden top to attract someone's attention. A few seconds later, Gary emerges from the back room.

"Sorry, Steve, just changing a barrel. What can I fetch you, your usual?"

"Yes, please,"

"Take a seat. I'll bring them over."

"Cheers, we will be on the sofas."

Slump into the sofa with my back to the door, sinking deep into the soft foam. Stretch both arms out along the back and take a long slow breath filling my lungs with air. On the other couch, Simon and George also relax. Even though all of us would be thinking about the upcoming mission, this wouldn't be discussed here, just in case any nosy bastard we haven't seen is listening. It isn't long before Gary appears with the welcomed beers.

"Here you go, get these down you. By the looks of it, you had an exciting night yesterday. Something that might cheer you up - remember those idiots who jumped you a while back. Did you know they have been arrested for the shooting in America Woods? You three wouldn't know anything about this?" says Gary with a suspicious grin.

"Not us, mate...we are good boys," I reply, between swigs of the life-giving nectar.

The first beer eases its way down the throat, fighting the body's reflexes as it protests it couldn't take any more. However, the second and third go down easy as excellent conversation flowed. More importantly, the doggy's hair is working, and I could sense the body returning to normal.

Suddenly, I receive a sharp kick from under the small table that divides the two sofas. I raise both hands, palms up and say, "What?" before looking up to witness George nodding towards the door.

George leans forward, "The four people we framed have just walked in and gone over to the table near the back door. Don't think they saw us. The police must have allowed them out of the nick while investigating them more. Best we slip out of the front. Last thing we need before a mission is a ruckus with them idiots. We can beat the crap out of them when we return."

"Yep, agree, let's get the fuck out of here," climbing out of my seat.

As we exit the front entrance, I glance back over my shoulder. Fuck, Rhys is walking this way. Make sure the door closed after me and then push George and Simon down the small side alley that leads to the rear of the brick building. Once behind the corner, bend down and peer back in the direction of the main door. Our man is smoking his head off, sitting on one of the wooden benches close to the entrance. This can only mean one thing, he didn't spot us leaving.

A long five minutes pass as we watch before Rhys has enough of developing cancer and goes back inside the pub. To be entirely sure, we wait another two minutes before heading at some speed to the road, taking two right turns until we are lost in the crowd of people walking down Shanklin high street.

When we arrive back at my place, still unsure who has been following us, we stand off for a few minutes to watch for signs of movement in the lodge's vicinity. Once this is confirmed, I walk around the back with Simon, checking the ground for any indications of a disturbance, while George takes the front. The area is clear.

Once inside, my telltales are still in place. The black doormat, which moves every time someone stands on it, is still hard against the door frame. And the strips of Sellotape remain fastened to the interior of the window.

Chapter Five - Travel

Still have several hours before I have to depart on the journey from the Isle of Wight to London Heathrow for my flight to Muscat, so I spent the time checking out Mano.

From what we already know, the mission is close to Oman, so I'm making the educated guess that the island will consist of a dry desert. We need to know possible landing sights, the location of any small towns or villages, and road conditions. With that, I walk over to the computer in the lounge, switch it on, and navigate to Google Maps, a good starting place.

Soon found the island of Mano about 20 miles from the coast between Muscat and Jebel Sifah. The first task is to locate a suitable landing point away from the busy port and people, but not too secluded that people who take us over don't start thinking we are up to no good, even though we are.

Found one on the far side of the small island, away from what seems like a compact industrial area. Now to find an alternative alighting point, in case the other is unavailable for some reason on the day. Spot another more dangerous location. From what I can determine from the digital map, the primary landing stage for landing equipment and people is just a bit further along the coastline.

Print off several copies of Mano's aerial view and mark the drop-off points on each before moving on to the central area.

Zoom in as far as I could with the computer mouse. From the looks of it, this place only has one black tarmac road leading from the port, which continues through the camp to the other end of the built-up area before turning into a gravel or dirt track. Can't tell from the map, but if it's anything like Oman, it will be compacted sand.

As you enter Duhfa, find the place's name on Google Maps. A row of what appears like shops is on your left with an open flat area, where three vehicles have been parked facing the business premises. On the same side is a fuel station, while on the opposite side, further down, is the first of the motels. Guess these are for the workers. More roads loop off the tarmac highway, winding their way through fenced-off areas containing numerous buildings.

Off to the far left, the ground slopes up steeply, forming a mountain range of sorts. This might be a good area for us to base ourselves in while carrying out any recces. The other side of Duhfa is flat all the way to the coast. In my experience, this is where most of the drilling will be taking place.

Another two more motels are on the right of the road, with the last being on the far edge of the built-up area as it turns to sand. Different businesses ranging from desert trading to several automobile repair shops are on the left.

Once more, print four copies, one for each of us to familiarise ourselves with the whole island; we need to know the destination inside out before we arrive.

With the information collated, I'm ready to brief Simon and George. Will have to inform Derek once in Muscat.

"Can you give me five minutes, gents, so we can go over some info I found on the target?" while separating the papers into four separate neat piles.

They both finish what they are doing and join me at the computer. With my index finger on the screen, I point to the first of the two landing points identified earlier.

"This is the best place to land without being discovered, as it is on the far side away from civilisation. If for any reason, such as bad weather making it impossible to alight here, our backup location is here," I move my finger to the other touchdown spot.

"Remember, this is from a map, and we could be faced with a climb from the shoreline to the top, so we will have to take the appropriate equipment just in case. If you do not have any questions on the landings, let's proceed to the main target area."

Both shake their heads as they know the way to discover the actual lay of the land can only be done once on the mission and gathering information from the local people.

"As for the only built-up part," I change the view to cover Duhfa, "appears like it is chiefly an industrial zone with the living accommodation all located to the right on this road here," I drag my index finger along the screen, following the contours of the roadway.

"Is that sand dunes here?" Simon enquires, pointing to the printout of the area.

"From what I can detect, they are more than that—would suggest they are more like a small elevated range. Perfect for us to base ourselves when we are on Mano.

"Plus, to help us out, I found a company website called Splash Maps, which provides wearable, washable, all-weather maps. Have ordered four of their Toobs which should be perfect for protecting us from any sand storms, with the added benefit of a printed map in case our recce troop get us lost. They should arrive tomorrow so bring them with you."

"Do one, Grunt," barks Simon, who's now crossed the room.

"You have any questions, George?"

"Not yet, mate."

"In that case: study the printed maps, and get familiar with the layout. One last thing, make sure you pack your kit for a hot desert climate."

"Really, Steve, I was about to stuff my parka and warm clothing into my bag, you fucking numpty," says George, launching a pillow at me.

Take my own advice and empty the contents of my Bergen onto the floor before re-packing with items I will need on the mission in a suitcase. Fortunately, this is not our first operation in this environment, so I already have plenty of clothing suitable for this type of deployment, including a desert camouflage jacket and trousers.

Not knowing what communication equipment is available once on target, we will take the radios Derek modified for the OPs on our last outings. With luck, as we are travelling separately, they will not raise suspicion by any nosy Customs persons either here or when we land.

Next, pick up all the clear plastic containers that house the tripwire mechanisms and break them into their individual components before placing all parts back in separate boxes along with a few pairs of smelly socks. With any luck, this should prevent any customs officer from investigating the package too closely. I will re-assemble it all once in Muscat. All my personal items I always take with me to make my life easier go in next. One last thing is to place the Bergen in the case, and I'm done for now.

After the last job, Derek had left all his equipment at my place instead of carting it back to St Halb, which made sense. He will no doubt need some of it. To ensure nothing looks conspicuous in one bag, each of us will take bits of his kit in our baggage.

Look over towards the other two, who have just finished packing everything back into their Bergens for now. They will need to purchase suitcases sometime before they leave.

"Anyone else for a brew?" I say, turning on the kettle to boil water for George's tea while pressing the red cup symbol on the coffee machine.

Over the sound of fresh coffee beans being ground, I hear, "Thought you would never ask."

"I'll take that as a yes then, Simon."

"Sorry, my mistake. Can I please have a mug of your freshly brewed coffee, sir?"

"Fuck off, you sarcastic bastard, and yes, you may. What about you, George?"

"It would be rude not to."

A few minutes later, three brews made, I carry the white mugs of steaming liquid over to the dining table and plonk my arse down. Promptly joined by the other two.

Take a couple of sips from the mug, "I will be leaving soon for the airport. If you can give me a lift to catch the Wightlink catamaran from Ryde, you can use my car for the next few days."

"Any reason you're taking a different route to the mainland and not using Red Funnel?" says George in between swigs of tea.

"Besides-you having a habit of throwing people overboard, we still don't know if we are still being followed. But the chief purpose is the ferry lands not far from the bus station where I can catch a coach to Heathrow."

"Fair enough," comes the reply.

"When you've finished your drinks, we better make a move if my connections are to work without me sitting around for hours."

The short drive to Ryde Pierhead went without a hitch, and Simon is soon proceeding at 10mph along the wooden pier towards the collection of buildings. At the end is a small car park surrounded by black metal railings about four feet high on two sides that prevent people from reversing too far and ending up in the ocean.

Once the vehicle comes to a halt, I clamber out, turn and put my head back through the open door, "OK, I'm off. Remember, any messages will be shared on the AutoCrit live chat at 18:00 on Tuesday. Plus, make sure you place the usual markers in place on my lodge before you leave on Wednesday."

"No problem, boss man, catch you in Muscat. Don't forget to pick us all up from the airport," says Simon, revving the engine as if to say, 'OK, fuck off, we know what we are doing'.

Of course, he is right—they are both professionals at what we do. So close the door and amble across to the doorway of the largest buildings. Take several steps inside so that anyone watching me will think nothing of my actions and believe I'm going in to catch a ferry. Instead, I turn around, walk back and watch to see if any vehicles I spotted on the way to the terminal are not following Simon and George back down the pier.

When I am satisfied nobody followed my car, I spin around on the spot and go back into the spacious hallway. On the left, as you enter, is the Wightlink booking office. Through the window, I can perceive several people queuing to be served by the youngish-looking woman behind the counter that stretched back to the far wall.

In the centre of the hall is a set of wooden benches occupied by a young couple, who should go and find a room as the display of affection is slightly awkward for passersby. Off to my right is what I'm hoping for - a ticket machine.

Working on the principle that the fewer people who see my ugly mug the better, I would purchase my boarding pass from here. A few taps of the screen later, I have my coupon to board the high-speed catamaran and head for the queue. Some intelligent marketing person from either Wightlink or Costa has designed the layout that forces you to go through the café to reach the ferry.

While you stand waiting, the sight of the beautiful array of prepared sandwiches, and cakes, along with the aroma of ground coffee wafting through the air, attracts your attention. It works on me, and I'm soon stood in line with an Americano with milk and stuffing my face with a blueberry muffin that I didn't realise I needed.

Didn't have long to wait before the rumbling sound of a moving barrier got everyone fumbling for their tickets. Take mine out and hand it over. There's no point in keeping it as they know everyone's paid past this spot, and it isn't checked in Portsmouth.

After walking down the wooden boards of the covered gangway, I enter the craft via a glass door into the passenger lounge. Due to my hypervigilance, and the fact that I can't stand anyone sitting behind me, I scan the room, trying to find a seat with a bulkhead behind it and spot one on the other side.

Unlike the car ferry, the vessel is devoid of any shops or drink machines on board. Just rows of seats laid out in three blocks in front of the baggage area, in the middle of the ship with another set of chairs beyond that.

With my mind now starting to return to mission mode, I observe every person on board for a few seconds, looking for potential threats that might come my way. For the moment, everyone I can see from my position seems to be minding their own business. Of course, there are still the people sitting at the back half — I better also check them out. Plus, I need a piss anyway, and the toilets are at the back.

Like everything I do, I require some sort of plan. The easiest way would be to pretend to stretch my legs by walking up and down each aisle. Need to make sure that I face the people sitting at the rear of the ferry when I walk towards the back. In practice, this is more simple than in theory.

Stroll down the side I'm on to the back before crossing over to the opposite lane. Then amble along the whole length to the front, at the top and back down. At the bag storage area, cross over to the other side and head for the bogs down the far side.

Task complete and no signs of anything out of the ordinary. With the pressure on my bladder reminding me of the other reason for doing this, I open up the pace and enter the gent's washroom.

Let out a sigh of relief while aiming for the yellow sanitising block at the bottom of the urinal. Just finish when I feel an arm grasp tightly around my neck, squeezing hard, making me gasp for air. Instinct and training automatically kicks in, and I drop to my knees in a bid to release the person's grip. It worked. In one movement, I roll to my right and stand up to face the assailant.

In front of me is a six-foot muscle-bound man in his thirties, wearing black jeans and a blue bomber jacket, holding a six-inch knife that glistened under the artificial lights of the toilets. No time to think, I launch myself forward, knocking him into an open cubicle. The force of the impact made him drop the weapon to the deck.

If I'm to get control of the situation and this idiot, I need to get him in a headlock, then somehow restrain the person. Moments later, I receive two punches in quick succession, striking me on the side of my head, forcing me to flinch and loosen the grip I have on him.

Before I know it, I'm pinned up against the back wall, his right forearm pressing hard across my throat. Both my arms are trapped between his body and mine, unable to move. Time to think quickly, only one option open as I raise the left knee rapidly, hitting him squarely in the bollocks. As the man doubles over in agonising pain, I seize my chance.

With one swift movement, I shift positions, grab the still doubled-over figure and run it headfirst hard into the wall. Then in slow motion, the man's body gradually slides down the tiles to the floor, where it lays motionless, blood oozing from the open wound and fractured skull.

Shit, who is this man and why the fuck is he attacking me on a ferry? People must have heard the commotion and will be here soon to investigate. Better act quick. A search of the jacket pockets uncovers a white envelope with a blue strip down the middle. Inside are several photos of the boys and me, plus one that made me pause.

I've seen this one before. It is of Chad and his Navy SEAL buddies. In the front row, the one on the right is the man lying on the ground soaked in his own blood. Maybe these are the people who have been tailing us all along.

Whoever this man is, I can't leave him here. With a plan formulating in my mind, I start to act. I glance outside the toilets. Everyone is oblivious to what's just occurred and are still going about the business of gazing out the window. Next, grab a handful of bog paper — I will need this shortly.

Wash some of the blood off my attacker's face and pick him up, wrapping his left arm around my shoulder in the pretence we are good buddies. Then make my way to the rear of the ferry, stopping beneath the CCTV camera that the bridge use to watch for idiots fucking about at the back. Lean the dead man against the bulkhead, holding him with a knee while I cover the camera with toilet paper.

For the next part of my plan, I have to move fast before anyone can investigate why their monitor went black. After a check, no other passengers are in the vicinity; take the body and slip it overboard. A glance down at my hands confirms they are covered in thick crimson blood. Close by is the disabled washroom. The perfect place to clean up before returning to my seat and join the rest of the bored-looking people staring out of the glass windows.

This route is a lot shorter than the Red Funnel, so I soon find myself mingling with other people walking up the ramp towards the train station. The bus depot is via the station office located further along platform one. A locomotive pulling several carriages pulls in, blocking any view from the other side. To ensure I didn't stick out like a spare prick at a wedding, stay in amidst the crowd, and luck is on my side for once.

Once out of the building, I stand to the left of the door; want to make sure I've lost any people tailing me. Wait for 10 minutes to be safe, then head to the National Express coach, which, to my reckoning, is due to arrive in the next 20 minutes, give or take. There is no need to go to the office and interact with people as I used the app to buy the ticket.

In front of the terminal, local buses are parked in bays, with customers getting on and off via double see-through doors that only open once a bus has arrived. Inside are many shops and counters selling boarding passes, and outlets plying their trade to passengers with time to waste. Banks of brown plastic seats line the area closest to the floor-to-ceiling glass windows, broken up by the numerous parking bays. The one I want is on the far right.

A few holidaymakers are also waiting for the coach, with one hand grasping their suitcase. You can see from their white knuckles that they fear that some undesirable thief will go out of their way to make off with their bags.

Nothing out of the ordinary happens apart from the hustle and bustle of people going about their daily lives and the voice in the ceiling announcing departure information and other unnecessary crap. Plus, the loud ticking of the enormous clock hanging on the wall behind me.

Dead on time, the coach pulls in, and like magic, the doors open to allow us to stand by the side as the driver opens the luggage compartment. Because of the PTSD, I need to get to the back of the bus. This is not the first stop on the driver's route. With any luck, nobody will be sitting in the rear two seats. For the second time today, luckily, the back row is vacant.

Like the ferry, especially after being unexpectedly attacked, I scrutinise everyone just getting on, plus those seated in the fabric-covered seats. If I encounter any problems, I'm sitting near the emergency exit. The thought of jumping from a moving vehicle reminds me of training for Northern Ireland, where our MT platoon sergeant decided it would be a good idea for us all to leap from a yellow transit van fully kitted out with our 40kg packs at 30 miles per hour.

The journey to London Heathrow terminal five will take around one and half hours, so sit back in the leather seat and try to relax by watching the world go past the window.

When we arrive, the usual hustle and activities are in full swing, with minibuses, buses and other traffic picking up and dropping off passengers at their designated stops.

My coach pulls into its stop on the left of two lanes that travel through the tunnel. Not wanting to get involved in the scramble to collect the bags from the driver, stand back and wait until everyone's claimed their assortment of suitcases. All are individually marked, hoping they will jump out on them at the conveyor belt at their final destinations. Eventually, every person departs on their merry way, leaving one case standing alone by the edge of the road, mine.

Book myself into the Moxy Hotel for the night along with a one way on the Hopper shuttle service. This place is perfect as it is away from the airport. More importantly, a free local bus runs 24/7 to all terminals leaving from outside the entrance.

If anyone's been following my paper trail, it will end here, as tickets are not required. You just get on and off where you like. Therefore, any nosy bastards will think I'm still at the hotel, until the checkout time of 12:00, that is.

Once you enter through the rotating doors, the place opens up into an open plan space with a generously-sized bar in the middle of the room, which also acts as a reception desk.

Off to the left are an array of coffee tables complete with dark leather chairs. Closer to the rectangle wooden beverage serving area is a bank of computers on a high teak-looking counter. I guess this is the business centre. More tables and seats are at the far end, and a giant TV screen shows some idiots playing football. The breakfast section is off to the right. I've booked brekkie here in the pretence of staying longer than I plan.

After scanning the lobby and all the people inside, I approach reception. A young Indian man greeted me, "Good afternoon, sir — how can I be of assistance?"

Like always, my eyes are drawn to the name badge. If someone can make an effort to wear one, I will use their name. Otherwise, it is simply 'mate'. "Hi, Gijo, I have a reservation under Barker."

"One minute," my friendly receptionist taps away on his computer, "here is your room key, the room number is 2111, and the lifts are over on your right, have a pleasant stay."

"Thanks, I will... what time does the bar start serving drinks?"

"It is open now... would you like a drink?"

Having a mouth like a camel's flip-flop, "Yeah, why not, IPA, please."

With the case in one hand and the beer in the other, make my way to the leather seats close to the television. Not that I like football, but it's something to stare blankly at while drinking.

Must have sat here slowly sipping away on the brown nectar of ale for around 30 minutes before deciding it is time to check out the room. The room is what you would expect and need for a one night stay. A double bed occupies the middle of the room, with wooden cabinets on either side.

A bright ray of sunlight floods in via the vast window that overlooks the bedrooms across the courtyard. To provide more space, a wooded floating board about one metre by 50cm protrudes from the wall under which a red square felt-covered box acts as the seat, half under the desk and partially out.

Not knowing if I would have time in the morning, decide it would be best to shower now. Thankfully, the brain is working, and I realise that if I can see across to the rooms facing mine, they can view what I'm up to here. So before getting my kit off, I close the blackout curtains, leaving the place in darkness. At this point, the intellect went on a coffee break, and I forgot to turn the lights on. So when I walk back towards the bathroom, I end up going arse over tit over the red box this numpty hadn't put away correctly.

They say sometimes accidents happen for a reason, and in this case, it gives me a brilliant idea. Place the stool a few feet from the door, giving any attackers a couple of feet inside before tripping over the damn thing and alerting me from any light sleep. Working on the theory, if I can fall over this, so can someone else trying to break in to take me out.

Chapter Six – Trip to Muscat

Even at 04:15, the double-decker bus is full of people half-asleep, wishing they are somewhere else. All make the most of the free commute service and head to the airport. Not that I am any different. Stand with one hand on the stainless steel handrail and am prevented from falling by the ever-increasing number of bodies packed in as the driver went for some sort of record.

At last we arrive at terminal five, stopping near the tunnel entrance that passed under the complex. With my PTSD now ready to explode due to the close proximity of people on the bus, I can't jump off fast enough. So before heading for the lifts to the departure lounge, I take a moment to compose myself and complete several repetitions of my breathing exercises.

Don't fancy playing sardines in the lift with a group of workers, so wait a few minutes for them to disperse before pressing the button to take me to departures.

The time is only 04:45, so the terminal is light on people, and there are more staff than travellers, perfect. A scan of the overhead notice board indicates the place to drop my bags for my flight is down the hall, beyond the rows of self check-in kiosks.

There is no rush as the baggage drop doesn't open until 05:00, so with my case in tow, I stroll past the precisely positioned blue cloth strips stretched between metal uprights to form lanes for people to act like sheep as they make their way to speak to BA staff at the manual check-in desks.

At the far end is the only coffee shop on this side of security. Might as well grab a brew while I wait for the bag drop to open. After being served a cappuccino by a young lady whose grasp of English is poor at best, find a table on the opposite side of the red banner displaying the name of the joint.

From this advantage point, I have a perfect view of the entire area. While I sip from the white china cup, I observe everybody who, in my opinion, is or could be acting suspiciously. Not taking any chances after being attacked on the ferry.

The question is, are all the people that have been following us connected? Sure, the man on the catamaran with the photo of Chad is one of his mates. But what about the men we jumped in Southampton? They didn't have American accents; maybe these are the police still trying to find info on the last job, but we set the youths up for that. Then, of course, the two Middle Eastern-looking men who planted the tracker on my car. Whoever they are, I'm taking no chances.

A glance down at the timepiece on my wrist confirms time for baggage drop is about to begin. So I finish what is left of the brew and head over to dispose of my suitcase. Even though I checked in online and am in possession of a boarding pass, the smartly dressed but bored-looking woman trying her best to keep a false smile on her face wanted to view my passport and other travel documents.

With a forced smile of my own, I comply with her demands, not wanting to cause a ruckus and maybe not be allowed through. Soon in the procession of yet another boarding pass, and this time a thick card one, and heading for security.

Learned a long time ago rather than do the humiliating security tango at the conveyer belt, put everything into your hand luggage before you enter. Not being arsed to remove my phone from the case, I place the printed ticket on the scanner to open the electronic gate, allowing me to pass through to join another line.

A few minutes later, I'm removing the grey tray from under the rollers and placing my hand baggage inside and thanks to some idiot shoe bomber who was going to teach us all some type of lesson by blowing himself up, my boots.

Do not know why but every time I go through security, I am subjected to an extra check with a handheld scanner. Plus, my bags take a longer route via the security staff, ready to investigate what's in my bag. Suppose the team is only doing all this to keep us safe from other idiots who want to try and teach us a lesson. Despite any inconvenience, I always make a point of thanking them.

Due to flying business class, head straight for the BA lounge to make the utmost of the free food and drinks. It is still early, so the place is not yet packed with families with young kids running around, all making the most of the complimentary pass given to them by their travel agent trying to close the booking.

Time for brekkie, several long hot plates are filled with eggs cooked in multiple ways, an assortment of dead pig items and crusty bread. Another with that continual breakfast crap while the counters along the wall are full of cereals complete with small cartons of milk. Grab a small plate from the stack and load it with lukewarm bacon, sausages and four wheat rolls. The next task is to obtain yet another hot beverage from the lines of self-serve machines.

With my flight not departing for another three hours, plenty of time to sit back, eat and drink while watching the comings and goings of people, grabbing as much as they could so they didn't have to pay for food on the aircraft.

To make it hard for anyone who might still be observing me, move to another part of the lounge every 10 minutes, making sure I'm out of sight of the previous location. If I now spot the same person occupying a seat near me, this would be a good indicator I'm still under surveillance. Did this for around one and a half hours before deciding to change locations. Time to wander around the many shops and restaurants within the terminal.

A glance at one of the numerous display boards scattered throughout departures; the digital text alongside the flight details shows the plane will be departing from A10 instead of showing a time. From past experience, any traveller leaving from these gates will be driven to the waiting aircraft by shuttle bus rather than the normal gangway, which typically transfers passengers from the terminus to the plane. At least I didn't have to travel to another of the three terminals that form terminal five.

By the time I arrive at the gate, several people hoping to be the first to get on board are hovering near the desks' entrance. Other passengers are sitting on the fronts of their seats, eager for boarding to start.

With the knowledge that I'm going to plonk on my fat arse for the next six and half hours or more, plus, not travelling cattle class I would have priority, so I stand at the back, leaning against the wall and wait for the voice in the ceiling to call me to board the aircraft.

Not long before I'm sat in the enclosed capsule of the BA business lay-flat seat with the TV screen neatly packed away, ready for takeoff. Even manage to reserve the last one of the row. This means I can get in and out without stepping over some inconsiderate idiot in the one next to me, all sprawled out blocking the exit.

The flight is over six hours, so there is plenty of time to study the map of Mano that I printed off earlier. Want to make sure I instinctively knew every part of the island without referring to any charts or diagrams. Muscat isn't an issue as it wouldn't have changed that much since I worked there. Run through each possible route from our landing point to the main camp, where, with any luck, Joby might be held. After staring at the map for several minutes, close my eyes and tried to visualise the whole island in my mind.

My deep concentration is interrupted by the gentle voice of a female air steward, "Would you like a glass of champagne and a wet towel?"

Eyes fully open, "Yes, please." Not sure about the purpose of the cloth, but take one anyway.

"There you go... let me know once we take off if you would like anything else." While she passes me the drink, I make a note of her name.

"Thanks, Mia, I will."

Study the plans for about an hour, only stopping once I'm sure I am familiar with every inch of the place before turning my focus to running through every scenario of our mission.

After several action films, two meals served by the helpful Mia and a short nap, the long trip is almost over. Time to put our seats back to the upright position, fold away tables and fasten our seatbelts for landing. Sure, the only reason for seatbelts is so they can identify your mangled corpse in the wreckage in the case of a crash from the seat you're hopefully still strapped to.

Customs and immigration should be straightforward as we all successfully applied for and received the Oman visa before I left the UK. I am correct. The queue isn't that long, and I am soon standing in front of a young man, dressed in a white dishdasha with a plain massar tied skilfully around his head. Handing over my passport, feeling as I always do, guilty of some crime, drug smuggling or attempting to enter the country illegally, which isn't the predicament at the moment. Maybe later, but not now.

The next step, collect my bag from the baggage hall. When I arrive, the suitcase is already enjoying a ride on the carousel, disappearing back through the black rubber curtain to make its way around again. Something that's become a habit due to the hypervigilance and our standard operating procedure on a mission, stand back and watch it go around once more to confirm nobody is paying any attention to my suitcase.

On the following pass, I reach out, grab the handle, drag the bag off the conveyor belt, and head for customs. This is the same as I remember it. You load your case onto the x-ray machine while a couple of bored-looking Omani customs officers pretend to be interested in what's in your baggage. Then you take it off the other side and depart to the main arrivals lobby. In the past, mates of mine have taken cases full of dead pig through without them even raising an eyelid, bearing in mind that Oman is a Muslim country and doesn't eat pork.

This is what I am hoping for. Some of the stuff in my case if put together could be used to make IEDs. If they've been switched on, I could now be escorted to an Omani jail, and they still have the death penalty here for terrorism.

After immigration and other checks, I exit into the arrivals hall crammed 20 people deep with an assortment of Omanis and Indians with the odd spot of white-faced westerners.

All are here to meet incoming passengers. Some to start a new life in Oman and the Middle East, while others, mainly from India, have been brought here under a false hope of a better life, only to be shattered when they arrive at their accommodation. A forty-foot metal container lined on both sides with iron beds stacked three high. The lucky ones will share a four-man room on an oil rig site in the heart of a desert.

Once I have managed to push my way through the ocean of people, I head towards Caffe Nero. Might as well check the place out while waiting for the next incoming international flight that's arrived from any location other than Europe.

The coffee shop is easily recognisable by the blue sign above the open span of the doorway. A couple of brown wooden tables line the front; behind them, the glass cabinet full of an assortment of cakes and biscuits identified in Arabic and English. Beyond the counter, an Indian man and woman work frantically at the shiny stainless steel coffee machine, concocting one of the vast arrays of beverages on sale.

Before entering to grab a brew, I stand a few feet away. Take out my phone in the pretence I'm trying to locate something. Then scan the café and surrounding area on the lookout for anything that seems out of the ordinary. And, of course, any personage that could be following me and standing out like a spare prick at a wedding.

All appears normal, so enter and order an Americano with milk from the young man whose name tag read Premjith. Rather than pay with the limited amount of Omani Rial, I paid with my multi-currency card.

With a drink in one hand and my case in the other, I cross over to the small enclosed area of tables and chairs reserved for Caffe Nero customers.

Locate a spot in front of a set of escalators that covers me from the back, with easy access to an escape route if needed and overlooking the coffee shop. This will be the perfect place to watch the others arrive on Wednesday, plus I can observe anyone coming asking questions about my movements. Then if Premjith points in my direction, I would have the advantage of distance to give me the all-important head start on losing them in the airport.

At last, the arrival terminal is starting to become busy again, so finish what is left of my coffee and walk over to the arrivals board. A flight from Cairo just landed. Time for me to make a move and find a cab. To err on the cautious side, I go via departures. There will be someone offering a ride from an unlicensed taxi firm. Usually, I wouldn't go anywhere near these people in any other part of the world. But here, it's normal for a person to supplement his wages by becoming a cabby for the day.

As suspected, the moment I step out of the automatic doors of the terminal, a man dressed in a brown dishdasha approaches me, "You want a taxi?"

Learned the hard way when I worked here. If you didn't set a price before you leave, you're in for a nasty surprise when you get there. I always remember the teachings of an old Omani taxi driver who I called Mr Eight, mainly because he has eight kids and two wives: barter the cost before getting into any cab. As customary in Oman, I shake the man's hand, "Yes, please, how much to the Muscat Holiday Hotel?"

After a short 20 minute drive, we arrive at the hotel. Pay the driver and enter via the unimposing main door into a spacious open-plan room. Immediately to the front is a long staircase leading to the next floor. The reception is off to my left, running along the far wall. As I approach the long ebony counter, the young lady wearing a plain black jacket with the hotel's logo printed on the top breast pocket welcomed me with a huge smile, "Good afternoon, sir. Do you have a reservation?"

"Yes, in the name of Barker, here for three nights." My first reaction is drawn to the array of clocks on the wall telling times in different cities worldwide, to confirm it is still the afternoon and not early evening. Booked an extra night just in case we need to alter our plans, plus it creates a false trail for people to follow if they try tracking us down after the mission.

While the receptionist named Cali-Jane tries to find my booking on the computer, I scan the area. Halfway down the back, a door opens to an office where I watch an Omani man working at a workstation. Behind me, at the other end of the room, is another counter with an older looking man sitting on a wooden chair beside it, flicking through a magazine.

To make some small talk, "What's the desk over there for?" pointing to it with my outreached right arm.

"That is a local car hire firm," she replies, handing me a small piece of folded cardboard with the plastic room key inside, "you are on the second floor, room number 2142, have a nice stay."

Take the passkey from her and reply, "Thank you, I will. There are some places I want to visit, so I will require a car," turn and head for the man on the other side of the room.

He stands as I approach, "I need a 4x4 car for a couple of weeks, if you have one available," I say, pointing at a photo of one on the display boards for some stupid reason, as it is obvious the man speaks English.

"When for?" he replies half-heartedly, as to say, 'I'm only here because I'm being made to and don't really care what you want'.

"Today... if possible, mate," he isn't wearing a name tag.

"That's not a problem... got one here ready to go."

"How much?" I enquire.

"Three hundred Rials plus a deposit of 100."

"Sounds good to me. I'll take it." Fortunately, I had loaded my multi-currency card with a few thousand pounds before I left the UK, so hand it over for the man to swipe.

"That's all done. Leave your bag behind the counter. It will be safe there. Follow me to the car park and your vehicle."

At the parking lot located at the back of the hotel is a line of vehicles parked in bays reserved for Manu car hire. On the far end is a white Toyota Land Cruiser complete with roll bars already for a wilderness adventure.

"This one is for you — I'll be inside once you have checked it over. Come in and put your signature on the remaining paperwork," handing me the keys.

Like nearly every vehicle in this country, it comes with several dents due to being one of the worst countries in the world for the standard of driving. Records show there are more deaths on the roads in Oman than anywhere else in the world.

Apart from that, the Toyota is in good nick and will do what we need it for. Take a few photos of the complete car, ensure they are date stamped, put my signature in the relevant places on the damage sheet, and head back indoors to sign the rest.

Our friend is sitting back in his chair. "There you go, all ready to go." He smiles and takes the sheet of paper.

The lift stops on the second floor, and the doors slide open. A green notice opposite indicates my room is off down the corridor to my right. Stroll along with my bag being dragged behind, checking each door as I pass for the correct number, 2142. At last, on my left is my room.

On entering, the bathroom is across from a built-in wardrobe. Further, into the room, a substantial double bed is against the wall. Under the window is a cream desk on which sits a teak tray complete with a coffee percolator. On the other end is a wooden box containing hotel literature. Leaning on the table is a steel cross-frame structure designed to hold your suitcases rather than dumping them on the clean white quilt spread over the bed.

It's been a long day, and a whiff of my armpits confirms I stink. Better head for the shower before heading down one level to the main bar. This is one of the reasons I chose this particular hotel. Years back, a friend of mine, Eddie, and I regularly frequented the place. One of the misconceptions about Muslims is that they don't drink. Trust me when I say a lot do, and there are many bars in the city if you know where to look.

If memory serves me right, the hidden bar is on the first floor, down a flight of stairs next to the restaurant. There is a second one in this hotel: a sports tavern with a pool table and dartboards. The quieter one will do me for tonight.

The teak counter of the bar is directly in front as I enter, curving away towards the back of the room. There are three wooden rectangle tables about knee height and chairs lined up along the wall to my right. Beyond that, another three-steps lead up to a square glass cordoned-off area in the corner, generous enough to hold four cancer addicts to puff away on their tobacco. A few more bench-type seating arrangement is also up here.

This area must be popular with smokers, as they didn't have far to go to the smoking room. In fact, one of the tables is being occupied by two Indian-looking gents sipping away on glasses of amber-looking beer. Two Chinese people sit around another table just below the raised area at the back.

While waiting to be served, the noise of someone behind me entering the room attracts my attention. Turn my head to the right in time to witness an Omani gentleman who I would estimate to be in his sixties enter the room, walk over and sit at one of the wooden tables he had reserved with half a glass of beer.

My focus returns to obtaining my own drink when a woman I recognise appears from the back office. Not seen her since my last visit four years ago.

"Hi, Rachel, how are you?" I'm not very good at remembering names, but she wears a name badge like most good employees.

A gentle voice with an Indian accent came back at me, "Hello, my dear, I have not seen you here for a while. Didn't you used to come here with an older man?"

"You have a good memory, and we did. But Eddie is not with me this time. He's back in England. Can I have a pint of Stella, please, Rachel?"

"Sure, coming right up."

As she pours my beer, "Have you been home lately?" I ask politely.

"Yes, went home six months ago, but now I have to work every day for the next year and a half before I get time off to go home again," she says, grimacing and chuckling to herself.

She hands me my Stella, "Nothing changed then... you lot are still treated like slaves."

"Afraid so."

Pick up the glass, and scan the room, more out of habit than anything else. I'm not sure if it is my anxiety, but the two Indians at the back of the room seem to be pointing at me and whispering something. Decide I'm overacting and turn around to face the rows of bottled spirits lining the countertop behind the bar and continue drinking.

Several more minutes pass, with me minding my own business and thinking of the upcoming mission and the plan for tomorrow. Then, out of the corner of my eye, I catch the same pair still, watching me in the mirror's reflection.

Try my best to suppress the emotion that yet another set of people are following me. After all, they were in here first, I suppose. But something isn't right.

Brought back to the real world when a female voice calls out, "Would you like a refill?" Turn to observe Rachel holding the beer tap with one hand while the other grasps an empty drinking glass under the pump.

"Sorry, miles away, yes, please," I say, finishing the dregs in the bottom of my pint.

Several minutes later, the opportunity arises to discover why the two men keep looking at me. As I look at them, the man on the right stands up and leaves the room. Probably going downstairs to the restroom. Take a gulp of beer. Turn, put the drink down on the counter and follow the man out the door.

When I reached the first step of the flight of stairs leading to reception, the target turns left after stepping off the staircase. Perfect, the bogs are that way. When I enter the lobby, the only other person is a young lady standing behind the desk looking down at a computer screen. The fewer people around, the better for what I have got in mind. Especially if I don't get a suitable response from the man in the toilets.

The door opens onto a small tiled walled entrance stretching back no more than a couple of feet. Past this are three porcelain urinals mounted on the right-hand wall. To the left are two compartments for the actual bogs. One is western-style, while the other is a local toilet, which means it's a hole in the floor.

On the other side of the Arabic cubicle door are the sounds of a man shitting. An Omani friend of mine, Jacoob, once explained how these work. If I'm correct, the man will be squatting down with his pants around his ankles.

This would usually be perfect for an attack as there isn't much you can do with your jeans wrapped around your feet. But if this is innocent and not just my imagination playing havoc, the last thing I want is some man's dick dangling in my face.

Decide to pause until I recognise the undeniable sound of a zip being pulled up before a crash through the door. Move into position in front of the door and wait. Finally, the noise I've been waiting for. With one movement, I smash the door open with my left shoulder, grab the target by the throat with my right hand and pin him against the back wall.

I can detect the fear in the man's eyes as they look back at me, wondering what the fuck is happening. Squeeze tighter as I slide my hand up higher, forcing him to stand on the balls of his feet. As he gasps for air like it is his last, I look down at the sound of gushing water. Looks like he forgot to take a piss as this is now running out the bottom of his trouser leg.

"OK, my friend, one question. Get it wrong, I'm going to beat the shit out of you. Give the correct answer, and I will let you go. Nod if you understand." The man nodded the best he could several times.

To make sure he understands I am not fucking about, land a punch to his left side. He cries out in pain, and his body tries to curl up to protect itself.

"Shut your fucking mouth unless you want another smack. Why are you and your mate talking and pointing at me, and are you following me?" The man shakes his head, and fear of what might come his way builds up within.

"Sorry, I can't hear a head shake. Try that again," I move my face so close I feel my nose touch his.

Through a trembling, scared voice, "No, my colleague thinks he used to work with you in MB a few years back. Please don't...."

I stop him short, "Never worked there, now fuck off home. Don't even think about reporting this minor incident. We both know the Royal Oman Police will take the word of a westerner over that of an Indian every time."

A quick glance in the mirror confirms none of his splattered blood is on me, and he managed to keep his piss to himself. So after straightening my clothes, I head back to the bar as there is no way I'm letting this little fucker stop me from having my beer.

When I re-enter, Rachel has placed another beer ready for me. "Thanks for the beer," I say, pointing to the glass.

"Thought you may want another—besides, you can't leave... you haven't paid your bill," she replies through a slight smile.

After several swigs of Stella, I turn to look at the back of the room towards the lone Indian now fidgeting in his seat. Probably thinks his mate bailed on him. Eventually, curiosity gets the better of him, and he leaves.

Stay for a couple more drinks before settling up and heading for my room. Tomorrow will be a long day.

Chapter Seven – Muscat Day One

This morning's first task is to remove the tripwire I placed in front of the door last night. After the incident with the man from the bar, I couldn't afford to take chances.

Once the wire is concealed away from the eyes of any nosy cleaners, I make my way downstairs to the main restaurant for breakfast. As I enter, I'm welcomed by a young Indian lady in her mid-twenties, dressed in a black skirt and matching jacket covering a plain white blouse.

"Good morning, sir. Can I have your room number, please?"

"Yeah, morning, it's 2142," I reply, heading over to an empty table near the back of the room.

Take a seat with my back close to the wall, then scan the area looking for anyone or anything that appears not quite right, that might potentially be a threat. Over to my right are a couple of men wearing traditional dishdashas, plus a third man wearing a red polo shirt and blue jeans, sitting at a round table covered in a white tablecloth, chatting away in English.

About to stand up and walk over to the buffet bar to grab some brekkie when another Indian appears, this time a young man carrying two silver thermos flasks.

"Morning, sir, would you like coffee or tea?" says the man now standing over me, ready to pour the beverage of my choice.

As usual, I have woken up with a mouth like a camel's flip-flop. So I reply, "Coffee, please, and can you leave the flask?"

"No problem," he pours me one cup and places the remainder down in the centre of the table.

At the buffet area, a glance down the line of shiny metal containers full of an array of different types of food on display reminds you that you are in Oman. As Omani and Indian food is very similar, there is yellowy-green dahl and crepes on offer along with pita bread with olive oil. Gone are the pork sausages and bacon, replaced with turkey versions of both.

Returned to my table with a plate loaded with breakfast stuff, in time to witness one of the two men from the main bar last night walk in and sit at a table near the door. With both hands around my coffee, I take a sip, while observing the man closely out of the corner of my eye, in such a way as not to make it too obvious.

Kick out the first idea the hypervigilance put to the front of my mind, that he is still following or watching my every move. Besides, I can't sit here all day. There is a lot of stuff to be done before messaging the boys via AutoCrit chat at 18:00.

The only thing to do to confirm I'm not being followed is to leave the restaurant and step into the room next door. Then wait to see what happens. Right, plan sorted, drink the rest of the brew, stand up and walk out, passing close to my new man of interest. Luckily the door to the bar is open, so go inside, turn around and peer through the gap between the two large frosted glass swinging doors. A few seconds pass before I detect a female voice from behind me.

"Can I help you? The bar's closed."

I immediately froze. Shit, the thought of someone being in here didn't enter my head. Quick, think, idiot. "Sorry made a wrong turn and was about to leave when I spotted someone passing on the other side. Was waiting for them to pass rather than hit them with the door," I lie, turning to face the voice. It is Rachel.

"You must be having a bad morning, Steve—you are familiar with the layout of the hotel. But OK, enjoy your day," she says, continuing to clean the tables.

A glance down at the timepiece on my wrist confirms the time is 09:00. Need to call Tony, a man I used to work with here in Oman, to arrange a meeting for this afternoon. If anyone knew how to cross over to Mano, he would. I always like to have more than one plan in case something gets fucked up, for example, if nobody is willing to take us from Jebel Sifah.

I locate the mobile back in my room and scroll through until I find his number and dial it. The phone rings several times before a female voice answers, "Hello, who's calling?"

"Hi, Jenny," I recognise her voice, "is Tony there? It is Steve… we used to work together."

"Hi Steve, long time no speak, how are you?"

"Not too bad—over here on holiday, wanted to find out if he wants to meet up," for the second time today, I extend the truth.

"That sounds nice… I'll go and fetch him for you."

A few moments pass before Tony comes across the airwaves, "Steve, great to hear from you. How are you keeping, you old git?"

"All good here, mate. Fancy catching up later, about 14:00?

"Sure, where?" comes the response from Tony.

"I'm staying at the Muscat Holiday Hotel… we can meet there."

"OK, Steve, see you then."

The phone goes dead, so I put it into my trouser pocket before picking up a black leather shoulder bag and heading out of the room towards the car park at the back of the property and the vehicle I hired yesterday.

The Land Cruiser is where I left it, reversed up hard against the brick wall. This prevented any nosy bastard from opening the back door. One of the better habits I picked up in the Army. Another is always walking around your vehicle to check for flat tyres and other issues that would make your ride inoperable. Plus, in my line of work, ensure it hasn't been tampered with.

Before approaching, I stand off and scan the area for people acting oddly. I give it a couple of minutes, then start my checks on the rear right-hand side, looking for telltale signs that someone had interfered with my car. The tiny clear cellophane strips I put in place yesterday are still there, bridging the window and doorframes. After checking the wheel arches, I lay flat on the concrete and peer underneath.

Tucked up near the prop shaft at the front is a small black plastic box with a few brightly coloured wires hanging out. Now, this could simply be an innocent device put there by the hiring company in case some lowlife decides to steal their vehicle or something more sinister. I'm not taking any chances either way, and I don't want anyone to discover my movements while in Muscat.

With the aid of my multitool, the container came away with ease. The question now is what to do with it. I could simply stash the device behind the fence, making it appear like I didn't move the vehicle, but this will seem odd. Only one thing for it. I search the parking lot for a saloon car with a yellow number plate to identify it is owned by a local. Once I'm sure nobody is looking, bend down, reach under the vehicle, and re-attach the box. Now, any nosy bastards will be following an ordinary innocent person.

Time to set off to Ruwi, which is only a short 15 minute drive away from the hotel, and I must remember they drive on the wrong side of the road in this part of the world.

After joining highway one, I drove past the opera house and where I used to live, Hattat House. Then, just after the Apollo Hospital, I take the slip road down to the roundabout and take the first exit onto Al Jami Street before turning left into 2996 Way and head for a car park I used before on my last visit, halfway down the street.

This place hasn't changed much since I was here a few years back. An array of shops, from the local ones suppling items to cater to the Indian population to make them feel at home, to modern electronic premises, plus what I'm looking for: small, dirty-looking cafés that you wouldn't usually touch with a 20-foot pole.

Further down the street, I come across a few manufacturing shops and then pass men sitting on tiny wooden stools hammering at metal pots. I would take an educated guess that these people are working under the control of someone connected with Golden Camel in some shape or form. It won't surprise me if the organisation does not own the businesses. But if we are to find out more about this criminal organisation, these places will be our best bet.

If you didn't grasp where you are, you would think you are walking down a street in the centre of Mumbai, as the place is filled with Indians. Some dressed in what looked like pyjamas, while other men are sporting a traditional dhoti - a single piece of cloth tucked around their waist, covering the entire leg, plus a western-style shirt. Alongside them is a multitude of women clothed in a variety of different coloured saris. The Muslim ones are draped in black burkas with their heads covered in various states, depending on their husbands' beliefs.

Sparsely dotted around are a few local Omanis going about their daily lives, expecting the Indians to remember their place in this country and do everything they are asked under the constant threat of being deported.

Finally, I come to a junction in the street to my left. On the other side is something I couldn't have planned better if I wanted to.

Located right on the corner is a local café with two large tinted windows to deflect the hot summer rays of sunlight in an attempt to keep the interior cool. Two square plastic tables, about two and a half feet high covered with flowery PVC tablecloths are located outside on the pavement. Two older gents drinking what resembles a tea-like liquid from a couple of glasses occupy two red plastic chairs on either side.

Situated next door is a shop with a vast assortment of metal pots and pans hanging from iron hooks on both sides of the doorway. Perched on a small wooden stool is a middle-aged man, wearing a white dhoti and a cotton vest, turning a sheet of aluminium into a circular cooking container. With any luck, I will find some of the information I need from here.

As I enter the café, everyone stops what they are doing, and all eyes are now fixed on me. With a tingling sensation running through my entire body, I sense my every step is being analysed. Suddenly I'm overcome with the usual fear of entering a strange place for the first time, but my military training prepared me for this sort of situation.

Inside, the same arrangement of tables as the ones outside. The only difference is the array of plastic sauce bottles with the thick remains of their contents dripping down the sides, and plastic water jugs are located on each one. The walls are painted a warm orange colour on which hung several old dirty, tattered paintings.

So with the feeling that all eyes are still on me, I approach the older-looking man dressed similarly to the others and standing behind the wooden counter decorated on the top with the identical PVC covering as the tables.

Close to the counter, two men are seated, drinking a beverage of some type and playing a game involving marbles and a printed cloth board. Like the others in the room, their eyes hadn't left me since I came in.

As I reach the end, the man standing in the kitchen's doorway in broken English with an Indian accent asks, "Hello, what can I get you, sir?"

"A coffee would be fine with a bit of milk." Remembering from when I used to live here that they tended to throw in lots of condensed milk in the drink, I indicate a small amount with my thumb and index finger.

"No problem, take a seat—I'll bring it over... would you like some food as well?"

"Thanks, a few dosas will be good," I say, as I take a pew near the people playing the weird-looking game. In any other part of the world, this would appear strange. But not here, as Indians—in my experience—always came too close and had no concept of personal space. Sit with my back leaning against the wall to prevent anyone from surprising me.

Like on any mission, the first element is to listen to what's going on around you. With any luck, you might pick up the odd word you understand, and with a chance, they might be conversing in English as it's one of the principal languages in India. Then, of course, always have your head moving to scrutinise everything going on.

This must be my lucky day as the two gents are talking in English. While I wait for my brew and nosh, I watch them closely to give the impression I give a flying fuck about the game they're playing to come up with a reason to strike up a conversation.

Finally, the man furthest from me lifts his head and peers in my direction, "Would you like to play?" he waves his hand over the board.

"No thanks, it looks like a challenging game—what's it called?" I ask like an excited schoolboy.

"Navakankari. So what brings you to Ruwi? We don't see that many westerners down here. Are you on holiday?

Excellent, my way in, "Yes, here for a short break and find a friend of mine." Done this too many times to jump straight in with the objective of finding out more about the Golden Camel.

Allowed the conversation to flow on everything from cricket to the weather for the next 20 minutes. Even bought my two new friends several cups of tea. Then once I have gained their trust, I make my next move.

I take a gander at Mickey strapped to my wrist. I don't care what the time is. This is all part of the act about to unfold. I turn to face the two gents, "Sorry, gentlemen, I'm going to have to leave to meet my friend in five minutes. We're meeting a company called Golden Camel at the Hyatt hotel. He wants to see if he can find some employment with them. You any idea where that is?"

It would seem I just invited the devil himself into the room as the place goes as quiet as a graveyard in the middle of a dark mist-filled night. The only sound is the clock on the wall as the big hand ticks away the seconds. In my head, the brain is speaking, perfect — I have hit the right chord, just what I am aiming for. For several minutes, the only voice that could be heard in the café is me announcing, "What's the matter, gents? Is there something I missed or should know about?"

Eventually, Sajith, one of the two men I've been chatting to, breaks the eerie silence. "Do yourself a favour, my dear, stay far away from this organisation. They are not friendly people."

With a pretend shock expression on my face, I ask, "Why is that? They sent some fantastic information across, and their website appears OK."

For the next five minutes, Sajith continued to explain facts about the Golden Camel and what an evil organisation they are. Stuff I already knew. Then at the end, he says something that I was hoping for the entire time.

"Did you see the man outside? You should go and chat with him—he is employed by them. Been here three years... he is a medical doctor back home."

"Thanks for the advice, gents. I'll talk to him now before I go and meet my friend. Would hate for him to be mixed up in anything dangerous or illegal."

With that, I finish the remainder of my lukewarm coffee and head outdoors. The man I saw earlier in front of the hardware store is still tapping away on the aluminium pot. Took up a seat on the concrete step next to him before attracting his attention.

"Good morning, sir," taking for granted the fact that as he is a doctor, he would be able to understand me. The quiet voice of someone that has almost given up on life came back.

"Morning," continuing to pound away.

"The boys inside said you would be able to give me some information on the Golden Camel."

The heavy wooden hammer pauses and freezes in mid-air for the first time since seeing him, coming to a stop halfway between his shoulder and the metal on the stand in front of him. He stays motionless for the next few seconds, not saying a word. With a slow, calculated movement, he swivels on the stool and faces me. I must have struck a sensitive point.

In a slow, laboured voice, "What do you want to know?"

Pick my words very precisely and clarify that a friend of mine is thinking of taking up employment with them and would like some more info on the company and where they are based in Oman. Once more, he glances up and me and starts to explain.

"I was a junior doctor working in Kochi in Kerala when I was approached by a smartly dressed business-looking man who offered me a senior consultant position running my own clinic here in Muscat. Being an educated man, I did some research on their website, and all looked legit."

"We did the same — please tell me more."

"Well, it all went to plan until I arrived at the international airport in Muscat. Then instead of the driver taking me to the promised accommodation, I was driven to a rundown hotel in Ruwi with darkened windows and the yellow paint peeling off the walls. Of course, I complained but was told it was only temporary as my new four-bedroom house was being renovated."

I tried to show empathy for his situation the best way I knew. The problem is that due to my PTSD, this emotion eludes me. To help clarify I understood, I place my right hand on his slim, boney shoulder.

He continues, "After seven long days of staying there, a man arrived and brought me to work here in this metal shop. I was locked up in the store's backroom for the first week to ensure I comprehended what was happening. Not wanting to stay here, I did attempt to escape once. Made it all the way to the airport, where my family back home wired me money to purchase an aeroplane ticket."

"What happened... why are you still here?" I interrupt with a puzzled appearance.

"About to head for the plane when I received a phone call. It is another man from the Golden Camel, he is at my home in Kochi. In the background, I can detect the voices of my two young daughters crying hysterically. My heart began to sink when agonising sounds of my wife being beaten up came over the telephone."

"That must have been heartbreaking, knowing there is nothing you could do about it," I watch as tiny droplets of water appear in his eyes and rolled down his swollen face.

Once more, in a faint voice, fighting back the tears, "I was informed that if I try anything else, my whole family will receive more than a beating and would be killed one person at a time until I comply with all their demands."

"So sorry to learn your story, don't worry, sir. They will get what's coming to them one day."

Wish I could explain to him what I had planned to give him some hope in life. But the fewer people who are aware of our plans and what is about to happen, the better. Would hate to be in that situation myself, listening to the sounds of Lucy being attacked over the airways. A broad smile began to stretch across my face when I realised that if anyone was being assaulted, it would be her doing the beating.

"One more question before I leave you to continue hitting the pots, do you have the address of where their office is?"

"No, nobody does. But if you come here about 17:00 tomorrow, a couple of the hired thugs will be here to take 80% of my wages before the boss man," he points to an Omani figure now standing in the doorway, "pays me."

"Thank you, my good friend — I may be back tomorrow!"

With that, I glance down at my wristwatch. The time is 13:30. Need to make my way back to the hotel to meet up with Tony, as planned, at 14:00.

When I reach the reception, Tony is already there sitting on one of the small green-backed wooden chairs, talking to someone on his mobile. As I approach, he puts the phone away and stands up, "Good to see you, buddy. What brings you back to Oman?"

"Let's go up to the bar, it should be open, and I'll tell you all about it over a cold beer or two," I say, leading up the stairs.

The only person inside is Rachel, standing behind the counter attending to the pumps. "What can I get you two gents?"

"Two ice-cold Stellas, please, and can you bring them over? We will be sitting up at the back."

With our backs to the wall and where nobody could overhear our conversation, I start to inform Tony why I'm here. I pause for a few seconds while Rachel places the drinks in front of us before saying, "Besides wanting to catch up with you, do you still have contact with anyone who is employed at the quarry?"

Without any hesitation, Tony replies, "Yes, a man called Darwood who works there. Why?"

"Simple, I need some explosives. Do you think Darwood would be able to retrieve something for me, or will me and the boys have to do some self-service shopping?" He knows what I mean by this.

"Put it this way, I wouldn't trust the man as far as I can throw him, so best you go on a shopping trip."

"One more business thing before we close shop. Do you know how the boys and I can cross over to the island of Mano unofficially?"

"It must be your lucky week. A new HSE manager, named Carl, just started with the company and owns a large boat moored up at Al Mouj marina near the airport. He might take you as he is ex-RAF. Shall I ask him for you?"

"Yes, please, mate, we want to go in about four days," which is not entirely true, but the only people who need to know the details are Simon, George, Derek, and myself. In our line of work, as I always say, it's always best to be in possession of more than one plan just in case, and this may be an option for crossing to Mano and, more importantly, back again.

We spend the next few hours mulling over hilarious events that happened while working together in the desert. And what meeting wouldn't include remembering old colleagues, some no longer with us? Goes without saying that far too many beers were consumed. So much so that Tony needs to make the difficult call to his wife to come and pick him up from the hotel as he's drunk too much and can't drive.

Not that it matters in Oman, as the typical punishment for drunk driving is a night in the cells before being sent on your merry way. Mind you, that was some years ago, and things might have changed since then.

When Jenny arrives to pick up her drunken husband, the time is 17:15, which only gives me 45 minutes to reach my room and sort out the codes ready for the AutoCrit deep dive live.

Halfway down the corridor leading to the central staircase, Tony turns, "I'll give Carl a call tonight and let you know what he says."

"Cheers, Tony, speak to you later," I say, walking towards the lift.

Still working on the motto of trusting nobody. No matter where you are in the world. The moment you let your guard down, some idiot will ruin your day. With that in mind, I stop short of my room. Take up a position with my back leaning against the wall, pretending to check my phone and wait for a few minutes. OK, no one is coming out, so approach the door with caution to examine the strip of paper I had jammed between the door and the frame earlier is still there.

Fuck, it's gone. Plus, I'm sure I overhear someone inside. My first thought is to charge straight in and attack anyone within but fight this urge. Instead, delicately place an ear to the door. Some person is definitely moving around in the room.

Pause and listen to the distinctive sounds of people making contact with different objects to give me a clue of where they are in my room. Next, take out my multi-tool knife blade and hold the handle so tight in my right hand you can see the whites of my knuckles. Ready to fling the room door wide open with the left.

As the adrenaline starts to pump through my veins, making its way around the body, my heart rate quickens, nearly doubling as it mimics physical exertion. Need to get this under control. So breath in deeply for the count of seven, hold for five before slowly exhaling. Repeated this three times.

You can't fucking stay here all day, I think to myself. With one last deep inhale of air, swing the door open and rush in, knife at the ready, sprinting hard towards whoever is standing near the window. Totally focused on the task at hand, the figure appears as a silhouette framed by the windowpane and highlighted by the bright rays of sunlight beaming through the glass panes.

A second later, I hit the target with so much force that they are instantly knocked off their feet, staggering back a few feet before landing on the purple carpet. Suddenly a female voice cries out in pure fear as the person beneath me struggles with arms flailing wildly, trying to set themselves free. Now returning from the daze of an attack, I peer down to see the face of a young woman staring back at me, tears streaming down her face.

Confused, I stand up gradually, my eyes settled on the shapely body still lying on the floor. My mind now coming back to reality. I recognise the woman I just attacked. Shit, it's the maid. As I reach out with my arm, I realise I am still holding the knife. Still fixed on her, I fold the blade away with a slow, deliberate movement and place the weapon back in my trouser pocket.

As I go to pick her up, she is still yelling out, so I raise my index finger to my mouth in a vain attempt to have her shut the fuck up.

"I'm very sorry. Didn't mean to hurt you... thought you were someone else who's been following me around since I landed in Oman. Are you OK?"

The woman, who has now stopped screaming but is still shaking, moves her head backwards and forwards in an effort to nod. Then in a trembling voice, "Yes, but I need to fetch the manager to call the police."

"No, please don't do that. I said I was sorry, and it was a case of mistaken identity. Tell you what, if you keep quiet about this, I'll give you 200 Omani Rial."

This is a safe bet as, from my experience, most Indians working in this country only receive about 50 OMR per month for a seven day week.

The young lady thought for a few moments before replying, "OK, I'll take your money this time, but stay away from me until you depart the hotel."

Once she left the room, I glance at the time, fuck I'd only got 10 minutes until I need to be online. Who says men can't multitask, as I take the laptop from my case and fire it up while studying the codes ready to send to the others.

We developed the systems during the lull in missions, and is a simple one if you have the answers in front of you, and based on a clock face. It didn't take me long to put together the times for the events so far on the mission. The first code I will convey is 02:05, which the boys should read as 02:00 – followed by 00:05 - boat. They should build up the picture that I was tailed onto the catamaran as it left Ryde.

Dead on 18:00, Daniel and Mark launch this week's deep dive live; a look into the books by Tom Clancy. As expected, the chatbox fills up rapidly, with everyone saying hello from different parts of the world. Several people give the time where they are located to show they are either up late or early to join the webinar. Once the chat slows down, I enter my first message, 'Hi folks, the time is now 02:05 here, or if you are on the other side of the pond, 03:00', meaning the situation has been dealt with. It isn't long before Simon enters 20:00.

Run my finger all the list of codes stopping at 20:00. It reads, 'are you OK?' Allow a couple more messages to be entered, then enter 01:00 to indicate all OK. Wait another few minutes before entering my final time code for today, 12:01, so they can be sure that the pickup and the airport are confirmed by car. Once more, Simon types in a message, 19:50. Great, the flights are on time. Wondering if Derek is online when he enters 01:00 & 19:50.

Perfect, everyone is OK, plus everything is running to plan so far. Out of interest, continue to view the whole AutoCrit webinar. Couldn't help wondering what AutoCrit would do if they knew a group of mercenaries are using their platform to communicate. You never know, one day I might decide to write my own book on our adventures and have posters plastered all over a shopping centre by Positive Media.

By the time it is all over, and I turn the computer off, it is 19:15. Not sure if it is the jetlag catching up with me or the amount of alcohol consumed this afternoon, or maybe a bit of both, but this boy is tired. Once I've placed the tripwire across the door, let's face it, my maid will not be back soon, and checked all the windows are secure, I climb under the crisp white quilt for an early night.

Must have been laying there for about an hour listening to people walking up and down the corridor. Some drunken ones even bounce off the walls. All while the mind mulls over something I missed today.

Damn it, I was supposed to call the one person in the world who brings me back down and is always there when my PTSD is playing havoc in my head. The only person who reminds me I am human and am in the procession of some feelings. I should have called Lucy.

Chapter Eight – Muscat Day Two

Just because I don't have much to do before picking the boys up from the international airport later today, doesn't mean I can take it too easy. Instead of running around like the proverbial chicken minus its head, I need some sort of plan that ran in some kind of order.

After a few minutes, I have the day's hierarchy formulating somewhere deep in the brain matter. The first task will be to eat breakfast, and rather than go to the restaurant in the hotel, I will dine out. When I say not dining in, I mean McDonald's. There is one not far from here.

Next, still need play equipment such as cheap mobile phones, light-sensitive switches, matches, cotton wool, etc. The final part of my plan is to arrive at the airport at least an hour before Simon and George reach the meeting point and stake out Caffe Nero.

Time is getting on, so I better move my arse. Something that I got used to while on this type of mission is always taking everything with you or ensuring it is packed away, just in case. A scan of the room confirms nothing is left out that might indicate our plans. After removing the tripwire from the doorway and collecting the multi-tool from under my pillow, I head towards the Land Cruiser parked in the hotel's car park.

Before leaving the building, I check the area outside to confirm that no arsehole is loitering anywhere near my motor vehicle. The only other person in the vicinity is a local dressed in a white dishdasha heading for the car where I planted the tracking device yesterday. I chuckle to myself, knowing that someone is stalking his every move. Once the man departs, I stroll over to my own transport and, as I always do, complete a walk around to check for any tampering.

Not long before I'm turning off highway one and down the slip road to the burger joint and fuel station. This is only a small store, mainly catering for the passing motorist via the drive-thru, so there is limited parking with only five spaces to the store's right. Find a space and enter through the double glass doors at the far end.

On my right is a room consisting of soft foam objects covered in various coloured PVC and some worn-out toys making up the kids' indoor playground. Rows of metal tables are to the left, with formica tops fastened to the tiled floor. Several people are busy preparing food or waiting on customers from behind the counter to my front at the other end of the store.

Off to the right of the serving area, two Omani gentlemen sit at a table closest to the glass door leading to the petrol station. Knowing how some Omanis are so full of themselves, they've probably left their vehicles parked at the pumps.

One of the things I love about McDonald's is that it doesn't matter where you go in the world, apart from a few regional variations, the menu is always the same. So, when I'm ready to be served, I know what I want.

"Good morning, sir... what can I fetch you," came the gentle female voice of a young Indian woman standing in front of me.

"Yeah, can I get a Chicken Sausage McMuffin and a white coffee, please," I reply as I pause, waiting to tap my card on the payment terminal.

Once the young lady passes me the brown plastic tray with my brekkie on, I head for an empty table close to the door I came in just in case I need to make a fast exit. As I'm sitting drinking the steaming coffee from the thick red paper cup with the words, 'caution hot' stamped on it in big white letters. - thank fuck for that - didn't fancy a cold one, I sense someone watching me.

Surely nobody else would be following me, made a point of covering all my possible tracks, and the idiot from the bar hasn't got the balls to keep tailing me. But why am I feeling uneasy?

Without turning my head, I peer into the reflective brown wall straight opposite me. About three tables down to the left is an Omani-looking gent wearing a light blue t-shirt. Whoever it is, they are not ruining my brew. Shift my body in the seat until I'm at an angle facing the menu board. Then out of the corner of my eye, I gain a better glimpse at the man glancing in my direction but trying his best not to make it too obvious.

Drink the remainder of the coffee, place the cup on the tray, reach into my trouser pocket, take out my multi-tool, and unfold the blade underneath the table. Slip it up the sleeve of my sweat-top handle first so that if I need to use the knife, it would slide out in the correct orientation.

I could have left by the same door I came in, but I wanted to resolve this. With any luck, the person will follow me to the car park. Stand up naturally to not arouse any suspicion from the other people sitting, minding their own business. Then saunter past the man who's been up to now observing me, to leave by the exit closest to the counter. As I push the door open with my left hand, I study the shape of the figure behind me in the glass. Good, I'm being followed.

On reaching my vehicle, I walk down the side. Cross over and head down a dirt track between a block of flats and the light brown brick wall that runs along the front of the parked cars. Halfway down, the building dips in slightly for about 10 metres before coming back out. Perfect, I will hide there, then glance around to see if I'm still being pursued.

The gap is now on my immediate right, so make a rapid dive into the recess. Not wanting to risk being in his line of sight by putting my head around at head height, I jump to the floor. With my whole body lying flat on the dusty ground, I peer around the edge of the wall. He is still coming my way.

While I search for a place to dump a person's body, I run the plan through my head just in case it comes to that. I stand up, remove the multi-tool, and hold the handle firmly. Take numerous deep breaths to control the rapidly increasing heart rate as the adrenaline flows through the body. Once he's taken a few steps past my location, I will grab him from behind and drag him back into the dark corner.

As I wait, several scenarios run through my mind: if this man is innocent, why is he coming after me? Whatever the case, I can't take any chances. We are too close to the mission.

Moments later, he takes his final steps, and I fling my left arm around his throat while dragging him around the corner. He shouts out something in Arabic, which I don't understand. Only one way to shut this fucker up.

I raise the blade and slide it into the right side of his bulging, throbbing neck with one movement before pulling it sharply forward, slicing and tearing the windpipe clean out. His lifeblood soon spurts in long thick streams, reaching a metre through the air before dropping and staining the light grey sand that covers the ground.

The gurgling sounds muffled by my hand slows as his limp body slips from my grasp, landing in a shitty mass of body parts on the deck. At least he dies in a halal way by gradually falling asleep.

Once more, my eyes dart about the place, desperately seeking a place to hide him out of view — I can't afford to leave it here to be discovered. A little further along is a drainage ditch passing under a raised area between the wall and the building. That should be sufficient to conceal the body.

Before I drag this twat over there, I better search him. Somehow he knew where I was going, and as I had only made my mind up this morning on going to McDonald's, he must have followed me from the hotel.

The only thing interesting the man retains in his possession is an envelope with that fucking blue strip down the middle containing a bit of paper with the words, 'Muscat Holiday Hotel' and my photo.

This cannot be linked back to Hadley on St Halb or even Dennis, for that matter. But I do remember Stuart telling us there was a connection between them.

No matter what the link is, I don't have time to fuck about worrying who is following me. Need to move this body out of view from any nosy fuckers who might call the police. With the man's feet tucked under my arms, I drag the still limp body across to the drain and feed it painstakingly down the pipe headfirst, ensuring no part could be seen by someone staring out of the windows above. Luckily there is sufficient room to allow the water to keep running underneath him.

This means it should be a couple of days before anyone investigates any blockages. By then, we will be long gone. My attention now turns to the blood-soaked dirt where I dispatched the man and the lines of red sticky blood leading to here. As I go back over my steps, I use my feet to shovel the loose sand over the remaining evidence.

As I leave, I turn and glance over my shoulder at the man I'd just killed and feel sorry for any family without a husband or father, but he knew the risks of this line of work, so the feeling soon left. Besides, I have some shopping to do.

About to head for the car when I peer down at my hands. The cheeky fucker covered me in his blood. Frantically, I check myself over. Yep, it's on my top as well. Only one thing for it, I remove the green sweatshirt and turn it inside out. Will change the top when I get back to the car. I'll wash my hands in the stream after it passes back under another path leading back to the store and my vehicle.

OK, now the next part of this morning's task, buy the stuff I need to make things go bang. When requiring this type of equipment, I will always use different locations. My best bet for the phones will be Ruwi — the Indians don't ask too many questions as they are not interested in why you want it. A westerner purchased from them, so they must be trustworthy. I will buy the rest of the stuff from the LuLu hypermarket near Muscat Grand Mall.

If I remember correctly, I passed a shop-come-market stall selling everything from imitation leather wallets to mobile phones close to the place I parked up yesterday, so I'll head there. Now back in the Land Cruiser heading down highway one towards Ruwi, which I reach in under 10 minutes.

Park the car, cross the road, and head up the busy street bustling with people darting in and out of various shops toward the café I used previously. In the distance is the place I am searching for. And after this morning's little episode, I am not taking any chances. So I stop short and stand off, making use of a closed shop doorway to glance the way I just came and on the target area.

Wait for around five minutes before approaching the brightly covered stall, leaning against the cream painted wall just below the enormous glass window and to the right of the door leading into an electronics store.

At first, I couldn't spot any telephones in the vast array of goods, neatly lined up in rows on the massive wooden stand stretching out from the side of the building. Been there less than a minute before the local stallholder tries to sell me some dodgy-looking leather handbags.

"You want a handbag for wife or girlfriend or both perhaps? Good price for you," as he rams one under my nose.

"No thanks, I'm after some handys." I remember this is what they call mobile phones in this part of the world.

"You wait there while I fetch some for you from inside." With that, he enters the store and comes back a few minutes later with a hand full of cardboard boxes. "How many you want?"

"That depends on the price, my friend," I say, ready to barter as is the custom here.

"OK, for today only and just for you, 15 Omani Rials each," he replies with a big stupid grin now stretched across his face.

"Tell you what. Ten, and I'll take all five."

"No, that's too low. Are you trying to rob me? I must support my family, 12, my last offer."

"In that case, forget it," knowing there is no way he will let the sale slip out of his sweaty hands. I pretend to depart when a hand comes to rest on my shoulder.

"Deal, you still want five or maybe seven?" he says, in an attempt to squeeze me for a couple more.

"Good enough, I will take the six," I hand over 60 Rials while he puts the phones in a blue and white striped plastic bag. Nothing else I need here, so I might as well head for LuLu's for the rest of the stuff. Time must be now getting on, and I need to be at the airport ready to meet the others when they land. I glance down at Mickey on my wrist, confirming there are only two hours left before picking up the boys. Should be sufficient time.

The place is packed with people from India and Pakistan, partly because the enterprise is owned by an Indian company. Plus, like most companies in Oman, they are required by law to have an Omani backer, who basically sits on their arse and does nothing. The other reason is a matter of cost, as LuLu's Hypermarket is the cheapest.

Off to the left as you enter is a small area of various food outlets, from local delicacies to KFC. More importantly, for me, this is where the ATMs are located. I will need some gelt for later, so I push through the noisy crowd chatting away in different languages. Stop at the cash point closest to the window, and insert my debit card. After a quick check, nobody is standing too close, I enter my pin and withdrawal 100 Omani Rial.

Luckily for me, been here many times as I used to live in the Muscat Grand Mall just across the road, so I know where I'm going - if they haven't moved things around, that is. Leave the hustle of the food department and head upstairs via the long travelator situated to the right of the entrance.

Didn't take too long before I had everything I needed to make homemade detonators: cotton wool, plastic straws, wire and a box of matches, and I soon found myself walking towards the tills and the way out.

Throw the stuff in the boot of the car and check the time – one hour before the first of the three flights bringing the boys lands. The journey isn't long from here to the airport, especially if you drive like a local, don't care about traffic laws, and even less about the speed limit.

Inside the terminal, head for the meeting point at Caffe Nero. Several international flights must have just landed, as arrivals is now packed with people dragging various types and colours of suitcases as they make their way to the main exit and their waiting family and friends. The unlucky ones heading to a stormy meeting with a representative of the Golden Camel.

Once I reach the seating area of the café, I stand off and scan the place for any unwanted attention while pretending to hear an announcement in the ceiling over the loud noise of a busy terminal. A quick check of the arrivals board confirms that both flights are on time, so there is nothing to do but wait, perhaps with an Americano with milk.

To prove these poor fuckers never receive a day off, Premjith is still behind the counter, making brews from the stainless steel machine steaming and hissing away along the back wall.

Grab my usual beverage, pay with the cash I got earlier from the ATM, and turn and head for a table close to the escalator. I made sure I am facing the customs exit to spot the boys coming out, not that they would head straight here. They are too professional for that.

Due to the fact I trust nobody apart from a tiny few people I got to know over a long time and the hypervigilance kicking in, I scrutinise each person close by in turn. Before long, my attention is focused on an Indian gentleman sitting opposite.

Observe in pure amazement as he unwraps a square bundle fastened with a thin blue nylon rope. Takes out a white t-shirt before reassembling the package into a neat box-shaped parcel.

With both hands holding the mug of coffee tightly and raising it to my lips, I glance up to catch sight of Simon heading in my direction. About 50 metres behind him is George walking behind a group of holidaymakers. I monitor them over the rim of my brew as they exit the terminal.

A couple of minutes later, they re-enter via a different door and push past the waiting crowds standing near the doorway. From my vantage point, I witness Simon entering an open-fronted shop selling an array of bottled perfumes of all sizes and prices, only to re-emerge within moments. Meanwhile, George headed straight for Caffe Nero and is purchasing a drink at the counter, knowing him probably a cup of bland white tea.

After scanning the area, he sits at the table next to me, waits a few seconds, and then joins me. Another few minutes pass before we are joined by Simon.

"Glad you could make it, gents — how were the flights?"

"Same as usual, boring," comes the reply from George.

"Mine wasn't. I spent most of the time sipping bubbly and watching movies," says Simon, after taking a sip of his hot steaming coffee.

While we wait for Derek to arrive, I catch the boys up on my activities since I landed in Oman, particularly the man who followed me from McDonald's.

Take a swig of the cold brown liquid floating around at the base of the mug before looking up. "Did you buy yourself any perfume from the shop you went in, Simon?"

"Thought you might have been watching, and no. Why, did you want some to cover up your stench? "

"Not for me, but George could do with some," I reply through a big stupid smirk.

"Don't fucking bring me into this, you pair of idiots," George says, placing his cup of tea down on the rectangle-shaped table.

About to go over to the counter to replenish my brew when Simon elbows me in the ribs. "Over there, Derek is heading this way."

By the time I return with the drinks, Derek has plonked his arse down with the others. "Glad you could make it. Any issue we ought to know about?" I ask, putting the brews down.

"Nein, alles lief nach plan..." comes the response from Derek.

"Now try that again in English, you fucking numpty," George interrupts.

"Sorry, force of habit—nope, all went as arranged", says Derek in a language we all understand.

Once everyone is ready, I lead them to the waiting Land Cruiser. Once inside the vehicle, I rotate in the driver's seat and explain that a short detour to Ruwi is required before going to the hotel.

"Now, nobody is trying to overhear anything we say. Yesterday I visited a small café. Next door was an old man making metal pots with whom I struck up a conversation. He is one of the unlucky bastards working under the Golden Camel. They will be around at 17:00 to take their share of his money. We will need to stake the joint then follow them to see where they are going; hopefully to their base here in Oman."

"Before you drive us to this place called Ruwi, wherever that might be, one question. Is there a plan to find out what is in the Golden Camel's office, if that is where it turns out to be?"

"Yep, got that covered, Simon—Lucy arrives on the 19:00 flight," I reply through a giant smile that develops on my face at the thought of her joining us on a mission.

The drive into Ruwi takes longer than the last couple of times, probably because it is coming up to rush hour, and the roads are blocked with slow-moving vehicles. Plus, I need a different place to dump the car this time, as using the same car park on three separate occasions could be setting an unwanted pattern.

Lucky for us, on my reccon of the place the other day, I spotted a small parking space down one of the many side streets that led off An Noor Street. Not too far from our objective, and it is still free. In case we need to bug out, I spin the Land Cruiser around and point back down the alleyway towards the small street crossing the front.

"OK, here is the plan. About 100 metres from the target, we need to separate. If you go into the café, Derek, buy a drink and sit on one of the outside tables."

"No, problem—what does the man look like?"

"He should be sat on a small wooden stool at the front of the store. If he isn't there, I will go inside and flush him out."

"Roger that," Derek raises a thumb.

"If, for some reason, the members of the Golden Camel enter and leave through the back of the property, George, can you take the street running along the back?"

"OK, hand over one of those new untraceable mobiles I know you would have purchased, so I can contact you if they come my way?" George requests, sticking his hand out.

"Here you go, mate," I hand out four of the phones I purchased earlier. "Don't worry about phone numbers. Took the liberty of entering all the contacts into each telephone. As for Simon, can you stay with the vehicle? We may require a swift departure, especially if they go via the rear."

"Sure, once you move your fat arse out of the driver seat."

"I will blend into the crowds bustling around at the end of the street. Any questions, gents?"

"Just one... how do we identify our targets and not follow the wrong people?"

"Cheers, Derek, nearly forgot that vital bit of information. Our worker is right-handed—when he is contacted, he will swap his hammer into his left hand to signal the persons with him are from the Golden Camel."

"Perfect, but to be a dick, what if he is summoned inside the premises to hand over the money, which makes sense as I'm sure the thugs don't want to do business where everyone can witness what is going on, even though most people here already have some idea of it?"

"Got that covered as well, George. He will place his hammer on the stool before going inside if that happens. If there aren't any more questions, let's make a move. There are only 15 minutes before we all need to be in place."

At the end of the street, close to the target, I dart into the doorway of a closed shop whose metal roller shutters are down to prevent any fucker from relieving it of its contents. Watch as Derek enters the café and witness George heading off down the road past the store to make his way to the rear.

A few long minutes pass before Derek reappears and takes a position at the square table closest to the pots and pans store. Now, the time is 16:50, and we are all in our designated places. Only one thing missing: the old man sitting on his stool as planned.

With plan B starting to develop in my mind, I take a massive gulp of air and begin to move when I glance up. At last, the old geezer appears from inside, sits down and starts banging away on a metal sheet. Thank fuck for that.

17:00 comes and disappears quickly with no sign of any money collectors. A peek down at the hands of Mickey on my wrist says 10 minutes have passed. What's happened? Have they changed times, or even worse, days? Stay calm, Steve — these things never stick to a time schedule, comes the voice from deep inside my head.

Turn back in time to catch the old man standing up, placing his tools on top of the wooden painted stool he sat on, and going back into the shop. I take the mobile from my trouser pocket, type in the message box, 'all inside', and press send to all.

From my vantage point, I can see past the assortment of cooking utensils hanging on either side of the door and straight into the store, illuminated with several lightbulbs dangling from the ceiling.

Inside are two men who, from what I can see, are dressed in dark trousers, and bluish-coloured shirts over which they are wearing grey jackets.

Our friend is leaning against some sort of counter, facing the two gang members with one shaking hand stretched out, holding what looked like banknotes. The bigger of the two snatches the money and then starts pointing and shouting something I can't understand, more than likely Hindi.

Whatever it is, it must be something awful as the old man is now on his knees with both hands clasped in front of him, as though he is praying or pleading for something. I bet the arseholes threatened him or his family to keep him compliant.

A few more minutes pass before they disappear into the backroom. As I prepare to move, my phone vibrates in my pocket. It's from George, 'they are coming out the back,' thinking ahead, George must have preprogrammed the message ready, as there is no way he could type the text so fast as he only uses one finger like me.

As I turn to leave the doorway, Simon and the Land Cruiser pull up at the curbside, and the door swings open. Meanwhile, Derek is sprinting across from the other side of the road to join us. Not wasting any time by allowing us to get completely in the vehicle with the doors closed, Simon drives off, stopping on the small street to the right of the café.

"Don't worry, Simon, my feet are still attached to my legs," I state, closing the door.

"Stop moaning, you fat bastard," comes the voice from behind the wheel.

To my left, George walks coolly towards us, to not draw attention to himself. The moment he passes a black BMW, he points to it with the index finger of his right hand, which he keeps by his side. Inside are the two men I witnessed terrorising the old geezer in the store.

While we wait for them to drive off, the person in the passenger seat puts a mobile phone to his right ear. With any luck, this will be the boss telling them to return to the office and not go and beat the crap out of some other poor sod.

Seconds later, the car drives off and turns left, heading for highway one in the airport's direction. Slowly easing away, Simon follows, allowing another vehicle to manoeuvre between us and the target vehicle. As we all keep our eyes on the objective, Simon uses all his skills as a recce troop commander and his undercover driving training, to ensure he stays close enough not to lose them. But also keeping a short distance apart so they wouldn't become suspicious that someone is tailing them.

Unlike most people in this country, the BMW sticks to a constant speed, as we drive through Al Wutayyah and continues until we reach the Oman Avenues Mall, next to the LuLu's hypermarket I used earlier.

Just in case Simon didn't notice, I call out, "Simon, he's taking the slip road off to Al Grubrah."

"OK, got him," comes the reply from Simon.

Eventually, they pull into one of the parking spaces that line the front of the light brown stone-clad Muscat Grand Mall and enter via the small entrance on the left-hand edge of the shopping centre. Without coming to a complete stop, everyone except Simon jumps out and heads for the same entry point.

On both sides, up a small flight of stairs are two banks of single lifts with the up arrow illuminated.

"Shit, we've lost them... there is no way of knowing which floor they are going to," George shouts with a pissed off tone to his voice.

"Not yet, mate — I think I know where they may be heading," as I press the other lift button.

"Yeah, and how the fuck would you know that?"

"That's an easy one, George. I used to live in one of the flats above us."

With that, we are joined by Simon, and I press the number three to take us to the third floor.

Once out of the lift, we turn right through double glass doors and step onto a vast roof garden. In the distance, about halfway along one of the painted paths that meandered through raised flower beds blooming with an oasis of green bushes and tended flowers, are the people we are following.

We watch as they pass close to the waterfall, where water gently cascades down a glass wall, as they head for the top left-hand corner. From memory, this is where all the businesses are located. The Golden Camel must be operating from one of these offices.

We can't afford to lose these people once they go into the building, so Derek sprints around the outside to reach the door before them once I point out where they are heading.

A minute or so later, the idiots enter via the door that Derek kindly holds open. "As-salamu alaykum," says Derek in his best attempt at the local language, as this is the customary greeting in this part of the world whether you're Arabic or not.

"Wa alaikum salaam," comes the automatic response.

Once inside, we follow the target down a twisting corridor where bright rows of fluorescence strips of light are housed in a stainless steel case embedded in the ceiling, helping you see down an otherwise dark passage. As we round a corner on our right, we are confronted with a glass-fronted room that houses a reception type set-up.

The men we are tailing are standing in front of a black, highly decorated wooden counter about four feet high. Behind that is a young woman indicating that they should enter the back office with her left arm. From here, we lose them, for now.

"At some point, we will need to get in there and find out more information on the Golden Camel. Any ideas, anyone?" Simon states the obvious.

"Yep, as I said, this is where Lucy comes in. She can go inside tomorrow and do a recce." Talking of which, we are close to the airport, we better go and collect her. This is one woman you don't want to fuck about or be late for."

Chapter Nine – Golden Camel Office

"Are you three numpties coming inside with me to meet Lucy?"

"No thanks, we'll wait here for you. Would hate for Lucy to realise she needs a real man and come over to me," says George, half laughing as he spoke.

"OK, will be back ASAP."

The airport must be seeing its second busy period, even more packed than when I picked the boys up earlier. My plan is to wait for Lucy in Caffe Nero. However, all the tables are taken. So headed for the same spot as all the other morons, standing or leaning on the four foot high metal railing outside the customs hall.

One of the conditions of my PTSD is that I can't stand people coming too close to me and decide against barging my way through the crowd of eagerly waiting people. Instead, I stand towards the back and watch as they all jostle for prime position at the barrier. All yelling out in different languages and volumes at passengers emerging from behind the screen. All with the terrified look of 'what and where do I go next' etched on their faces.

After a small break in the number of people coming out comes Lucy, the new love of my life. As she exits the cordoned-off area, I walk over, swing my arms around her and plant a short passionate kiss on her soft, warm lips before grabbing the suitcase she was dragging behind her.

"Hi, honey, how was your flight?"

"Excellent, first time I've flown first class — thanks for arranging that. How's you, getting everything sorted?"

"I'm fine, thanks, almost there. Will tell you more back at the hotel. You never know who could be listening." I say, still supporting a massive stupid grin splattered all over my face like an excited schoolboy.

Back at the Land Cruiser, the boys jump out and hug Lucy while I throw her case in the boot. While I drive to the Muscat Holiday Hotel, I take the time to catch up on how her mum is doing; I told them earlier why she was staying at her mum's and not my place.

Back at the hotel, the first job is to get Simon, George, and Derek booked into their rooms and add Lucy to my booking. As we approach the reception area, a familiar voice can be heard behind the desk.

"Hello, Steve, are these friends of yours?" Told her to call me Steve and not Mr Barker at the first meeting when I checked in.

"Yes, Cali-Jane, they all have bookings," I hand over their passports as forms of ID. "Apart from this young lady," I point to Lucy, "she needs to be added to my room."

"That's not a problem, Steve." She taps away on the computer for a few minutes, then glances up over her thick-rimmed glasses. "Here are your documents back and your room keys. You three gents are in rooms 3142, 3147 and 3149 on the floor above Steve's room.

"Thank fuck we're not next to you, didn't fancy listening to you two banging away all night," says Simon, grabbing his bag.

Turn to face Lucy, and for a woman that would kill you without even a hello, she has a rosy, barely noticeable embarrassed glow to her cheeks.

"Tell you what, gents, go and sort your rooms out and we will meet you in the bar closest to the restaurant in about 30 minutes," I say, picking up Lucy's bag.

When we enter, the rest are sitting at the long table to the right of the door, throwing down their first beers. Rachel is behind the counter, pouring another beer from the pump.

"Your usual, Steve?"

Before I could answer, George shouts across the room, "You have a usual? Now we know what you've really been doing since you arrived. Fuck all, just sat here drinking."

"Slap him for me, Derek. The lady said, 'my usual', as we go back a long way, as I used to drink here with a friend of mine, Eddie, when I lived in the flat above Muscat Grand Mall."

Turn back to face Rachel, "Yes, please and a Southern Comfort with one lump of ice."

After grabbing the drinks, we join the others at the table. Then spend the next couple of hours drinking and relaxing before the mission gets fully underway tomorrow with a visit to the Golden Camel office. Plus, we still need to relieve the quarry of some of its plastic explosives. Even though I am always running plans through my head, we can leave the complicated stuff until the morning. Tonight is time to relax and take the rare opportunity to enjoy ourselves.

It must be about midnight when we all fail the leak test, and our output is greater than the input, so we call it a night.

"Will see you at breakfast at about 08:00," slightly slurring my words.

"OK, you two, don't make too much noise," comes the reply from Derek.

Back in my room, we fall flat onto the soft double bed and sink into the white quilt. The gentle breeze of her warm breath could be felt on my cheek, so I pull her close, wrap my arms around her, and pull her tight against me. Stay this way for about 10 minutes, enjoying the moment which had eluded us since she went to her mum's several weeks back.

In a soft sensual voice, she whispers in my ear, "I need a shower — you can wash my back if you like."

Feeling the pressure building between my legs, I press it against her. She gives a quiet sigh, "Shower first," then smiles, stands up, and turns on romantic music on her mobile phone. Then to tease me even more as she walks to the bathroom, she grasps the bottom of her jumper before pulling it tantalisingly over her head, revealing her naked back. In the doorway, one inch at a time, her jeans and knickers fall seductively down her shapely legs to the tiled floor.

With one final act of her enjoying teasing me to the maximum, Lucy spreads her feet a little and bends over, exposing her womanhood to the full. It's no good — I can't contain the throbbing in my pants any longer, so I quickly undress and lay nude on the bed with my manhood standing to attention, anticipating what's to come.

The sound of running water cascading over her well-formed body with visions of a foam-wrapped figure became too much to handle, so I open the shower door and climb in with her. Without saying a word, I spin her and hold my body sexually against hers, my manhood now pressed hard against her pelvis. Lucy smiles seductively before planting a romantic kiss on my lips.

"That feels good. Can you wash my back?" turning and handing me the soap.

Place a small amount of gel on my hands before I reach around and rub it softly into her belly. With slow movements, I make my way up until I'm caressing her ample, firm breasts, working the foam in as I pinch gently on her nipples. She lets out a faint moan of pleasure.

With the smell of lavender and the sensation of water flowing over my still throbbing cock I reach down with my left hand sliding it deliberately between her thighs. Then with tiny circular movements, I rub the side of her inner thigh. As I move from one leg to the other, I pause momentarily and give a gentle squeeze. Once more, sighs of pleasure flow from Lucy's mouth.

Still dripping wet, I carry her naked body to the quilt-covered bed and lay her flat. Seductively biting her bottom lip, she whispers, "Take me now."

With a smile, I grab her legs, parting them carefully before resting them on my arms and gradually sliding inside her. She gives out a loud, "Oh yes."

While making slow thrusting movements, I respond with, "That does feel good."

Before I realise it, she pulls me out, lays me on my back, then straddles me before reinserting my cock and rocks backwards and forward. As she does, I reach up and caress her breasts with both hands. With warm fluid dripping down over my thighs, I orgasm.

Lucy bends down, laying flat on my chest before we roll over on our sides, still embracing our entangled naked bodies. We smile at each other and drift off to sleep.

My eyes open the following day with a bright light penetrating the gap in the curtains and the sound of water flowing from the shower. As my feet land on the blue carpet, I turn to face the washroom to see Lucy standing with an enormous white towel wrapped around her and defying gravity. A glance at my watch on the bedside table indicates the time is 07:00. I better move my fat arse out of bed.

"Morning, " she smiles, "what time do they start breakfast in this joint?"

"About 06:30, I think, but remember we are meeting the others at 08:00," heading to the bathroom.

"True, forgot about that."

By the time I have finished showering and all the other morning rubbish, it is time to head for brekkie. When we arrive at the restaurant, the boys are sitting at the back of the room with several mugs of hot beverages.

"Good morning, you two sleep well?" enquires Simon, through a stupid grin.

"Yes, thank you," replies Lucy, sitting next to him.

"Have you tried the offerings yet?" I ask.

"Nope, we're being gentlemen and waiting for you... well, the young lady at least," comes the reply from George, trying his best to maintain a straight face.

Breakfast is identical to what I had eaten yesterday, but as I always say, food is food. Grab a plate from the warmer, fill it with an assortment of what closely resembles something edible, and go back to the table. The others followed suit, apart from Simon, who is still on kid-sized portions.

"Don't eat all of that in one go, Simon," I joke.

Without even looking up, Simon raises the middle finger of his right hand, "Swivel, fatty! Unlike you lot, I will not suffer from Mohammed's revenge."

Once the waiter finishes swapping over the coffee pot and boiling water for the tea-drinking idiot, and check nobody can hear what I'm about to say, start to outline the plan for this morning.

In a low voice, "Once we've finished here, we need to go back to the Golden Camel's office. Then Lucy can go inside to complete a recce of the place and identify any locations files may be kept. Plus, ask questions on their movements over on Mano."

"I'm sure you are going to tell me you have this covered, but how is she going pull this off? They aren't stupid and not going to give answers to a white westerner," Derek says, after finishing a sausage he rammed in his mouth seconds earlier.

"Yes, got that…"

Lucy interrupts me. "While I was back home, Steve asked me to visit St Mary's in Southampton and find a clothing shop that specialised in Indian and Islamic women's wear. Found one and purchased a burka, the complete letterbox kit. That way, they will not see my face, plus it is against the law for anyone apart from her husband to remove it."

"Knew you would have some sort of plan. One more question for you, Steve, as you lived here. What was that horrible racket just before first light?" Derek enquires.

"That, my friend, is the Fajr where the muezzin calls the Islamic faithful to prayer from the local mosque. Here is an interesting fact for you, unlike the crap we are fed back in the UK, Islam is a peaceful religion that teaches peace and tolerance to its fellow men and women."

"Sorry I asked, only wanted to know what the fucking noise was, not a full sermon," Derek states before swigging back the remains of his brew.

"If there are no more questions, ensure your stuff is ready — we will meet back at the Land Cruiser in 15," getting up from the table.

Once everyone is back and in the vehicle, we drive to Muscat Grand Mall but instead of parking in the same place as yesterday, Simon parks up in LuLu's car park across the road, among the other vehicles, to conceal it in the wide open.

With the boys and me making a semi-circle at the back, Lucy opens the tailgate and slips on the burka before heading towards the roof garden between the tall blocks of flats located on the top of the shopping centre.

Not to raise too much attention to ourselves walking in a group once we reach the lifts, we separate, with myself and Lucy taking one while the boys take the one opposite. Unlike yesterday, several small Indian children are playing in the garden, running around the raised flower beds. From the amount of laughter coming from them, they are having a fantastic time in the hot sun as it shone on the water of the rooftop swimming pool.

Sticking to our plan, we make our way to the bench closest to the waterfall and wait for the others to take their positions. When George sits next to us on the seat, we stand up and head for the Golden Camel offices without saying a word.

To be absolutely sure Lucy isn't walking into the main reception full of people, we both stroll along while checking our surroundings as we go to the office. The plan is that when she is inside, I will wait in the corridor not too far away, ready to give assistance if she needs it. I'm not concerned about sending her in if the shit hits the proverbial fan — she can handle herself. It's them I'm worried about.

Good news, through the office's glass doors, I could see the reception is empty, so I continue down the passageway while Lucy pushes the door and enters the premises. All we can do now is wait until she comes back out, hopefully with some helpful intel.

*****

Lucy is standing in front of the black desk inside. She is greeted by a neatly dressed Indian woman wearing a red and gold sari and an array of metal bangles hanging from both wrists tapping the counter as she types into a computer, before she glances up and says, "As-salamu alaykum."

Thinking quick, Lucy replies, " Wa alaikum salaam."

The woman then says something in what sounds like Hindi. "Sorry, I don't speak Hindi," Lucy replies with her limited Arabic.

Arabic is the vocabulary of the Holy Quran, so something that all Muslims have to have a basic knowledge of. Plus, prayers are all said in the same language.

"I'm new to Islam and only converted several months back. Can we converse in English?"

The Indian woman smiles, "No problem—how can I help?"

"I want to talk to someone from the Golden Camel about repaying an owed debt."

"Not a problem. I'll check to see if anyone is available to meet you. You can wait over there on the green leather sofa along the back wall," comes the response before she disappears into the back office.

Perfect, everything is going to plan so far. To obtain a good view of the office's interior, I sit down on the sofa in a position where I can see through the glass door.

It isn't long before a young gentleman in his early twenties dressed in a white dhoti wrapped tightly around his waist with a bright red shirt covering his upper body comes to the reception area.

"Hi, Lucy, can you come with me, please?" holding the door open.

While taking a deep breath, stand up and walk into the main office complex. Several cubicles are on my right, with people working away on computers positioned on metal desks. To the left are two glass-fronted smaller offices. One is occupied by a local-looking female while an older man sits behind an enormous teak wooden table in the other. Down the far end, I spot a sign for the toilets that will come in handy later, to acquire a perspective of the rest of the place.

The young man opens the door, and the man behind the desk stands up. Steve has told me that this is nothing about politeness and has more to do with local customs.

"Good morning, I'm Masoud. Please come in, take a seat, and tell me what I can do for you."

Pull out a brown wooden chair close to the table and sit down. I now pay more attention to the man sitting in front of me. The first thing that becomes apparent is that this person is not a man to be messed with, as he dismisses the office guy with a flick of his right wrist. Second, he is immaculately dressed in a grey pressed suit with short black hair and is handsome for his age which I would put in his late fifties.

Before I can speak, he asks me a series of quick questions, probably trying to check my story, which is something I would do.

"The receptionist says you have only just converted to Islam—why was that?"

"I married a Muslim who I met in St Marys in Southampton. And all the stuff he told me about his faith made sense, so I changed my religion," I said, lying and thinking on my feet.

"Fascinating—I know people there," Masoud says, looking at me in an attempt to try to catch me out. "Which of the Mosques do you pray in?"

"We both go to the Medina Mosque," as this is the only one I know in the area.

"OK, let us get to business. I'm told you want to pay off someone's debt. What is the name of the person?"

At breakfast, we had all agreed we should use the old man's name from the hardware store, as we know he works under the organisation's control and therefore won't raise too much suspicion and can be found in their records.

"Praveen, he is a relative of my husband," I reply.

Masoud gets up and walks over to the tall filing cabinet, which matches the teak desk, opens the second drawer, flicks through the row of files, and pulls out a green file. At least we know it isn't locked, in case the plan is to come back and remove some of its contents at a later stage.

While he is doing this, I seize the chance and glance down at the paperwork laid out on the desk. One bit jumped out at me. Under my burka, a smile starts to form across my face. With several of his colleagues, he is travelling to Mano in the next couple of days. This is the type of information we wanted; movement of the Golden Camel people, as we need to know the likely strength of resistance we may encounter during the mission. Maybe once we find and rescue Joby, we can simultaneously take out some of the top scumbags.

With the document open, Masoud looks up, "Here we are. It would appear Praveen owes the company 5,000 Omani Rials. How would you like to pay? Cash, or would you like to offer yourself as payment? My men need female attention after a hard day."

My body crawls at the fact he just suggested I become a prostitute for his men. "Will bring you the money tomorrow once I withdraw it from the bank, if that is OK with you?"

"That's fine by us. Let me show you out."

"Thank you, but can I please use the bathroom before I leave?"

"Sure, it's down the end on the left," Masoud points down in the general direction.

As I walk to the ladies' room, several more desks which aren't occupied are on my right, with boxes stacked on top. The back right-hand corner appears like a rest area with soft brown leather seats and coffee pots sitting on a table under the window, with four men relaxing in the chairs, chatting away in what I would guess is Hindi. After a quick count, I calculate at least 12 people in the office.

I rejoin Steve back in the roof garden, walking around a raised decked platform that circumnavigated the pond.

*****

After seeing Lucy head for the exit, I slip out of the back door and head for the tranquil peace and sound of the water cascading over the glass blocks of the fountain. Then out of the corner of my eye, I catch a glimpse of a figure dressed head to foot in a black burka.

"Is that you under there, Lucy?"

Without saying a single word, the garment is slipped over her head. Then as the mass of cloth hits the deck, "Yep, it's me."

"Thank fuck for that—I was starting to become worried and formulating a rescue plan," I call the other three over from their cover positions.

A scan of the rest of the garden confirms the place is empty apart from us, so we make our way over to the lifts by the swimming pool before making our way down to the shopping centre's second floor. Of course, nobody mentions anything about Lucy's visit inside the office in case someone overhears. Will do this later, back in the Land Cruiser.

After noticing the time is 12:00, "Anyone fancy a meal? There is a fantastic restaurant I used too many times when I lived here."

"Sounds like some sort of a plan to me, Steve... where is it?" says George, looking around.

"On the far side, follow me."

A few minutes later, we reach Chili's. The whole front is open, with the extended multicoloured serving area running across the back wall, while along the left, stretching to the back, are thick red leather seats facing each other to form private cubicles. A couple of workers are darting around, pouring soft drinks from a dispenser located towards the middle of the counter, and taking orders from hungry customers.

The joint isn't too packed, so when the waiter comes over to show us our seats, we choose the cubicle at the back of the room close to the extensive window, which overlooks a closed dining area.

From the look of the menu, the food here is far better than at the hotel, with a selection of what I would describe as American looking grub, from burgers to steaks.

"Well, don't know about you, but the 8oz steak with fries sounds good to me. What you lot having?"

"Same for me, Steve," says Lucy, putting down her menu.

"And me," declares George, taking a mouth full of water from the glass our waitress just placed on the decorated tabletop.

With her pen poised to take the order, we all look at Simon. "Think I saw a kid's menu complete with crayons. Can fetch one for you if you like."

"Do one, George. I'll have the fish, please," states Simon at last.

Forty minutes later, with the meal finished, I turn to the others, "Come on, folks, we better make a move and make our way back to the hotel, as we have a shopping trip to make early in the morning."

Soon after, we arrive at the car. Once inside, Lucy briefs us on what happened at the Golden Camel office.

"Inside, I counted 12 people, but there could be more out doing business. However, I found out that one of the top bosses, who goes by the name of Masoud, and several other members of his organisation are making their way to Mano in the next couple of days. Plus, they keep records of people who they have conned into working for them in a filing cabinet inside Masoud's office. It isn't locked if we plan to retrieve some of the files."

"Thanks, honey, that should come in handy, especially as it gives a rough number of people from the Golden Camel there could be on Mano. We can confirm numbers once we are on the island. When you're ready, Simon, take us back to the Muscat Holiday Hotel."

On the way back, I fill everyone in on the plans for getting our hands on the explosives from the quarry early in the morning. Almost back, when my mobile phone starts to ring. The number on the screen is Tony's.

"Hi, Tony, anything wrong?"

"Not much. I've heard back from Carl... he is willing to take you to Mano on his boat if you cannot find another way across. I'll text you his details."

"Cheers, mate. Before you go, do you know what time they start work at the main quarry?"

"About 07:00, I think, but I can't be sure," comes a hesitant reply from Tony.

As the call ends, Simon drives into the hotel's car park. "OK, gents, go have some kip—we will all meet up back here at 04:30, ready to go."

Chapter Ten – Jebel Sifah

By 04:25, we are all at the Land Cruiser and ready for the trip to the mine, which, according to the satnav, is about 30 minutes in the opposite direction to Jebel Sifah. As we drive off, I turn a little in the passenger seat to face so everyone can hear me.

"From what Tony said yesterday, there are two ways into the quarry: the primary entry point to the whole complex, and a back road operated by a single security sentry. The same applies to the front gate. Once inside, a couple of portacabins are being used as offices, also protected by another guard."

"What's the plan of attack?" comes a voice from the rear seat.

"First, Simon will drive around to the rear entrance and drop you and Derek off, George, to deal with any person you find. Remember, these are innocent people, so do your utmost not to kill them. Once this man is dealt with, join us at the offices."

"OK, got that, but not waste him?! I think you've gone fucking soft on us, Steve."

"In my defence, I did say try, George. If it comes to it and you do not have any other choice, feel free to dispose of him."

"That's more like you — welcome back."

"The remainder of us will continue to the front, stopping short where Simon and myself will disembark and tackle the bloke on the main gate. When we've done this, Lucy will drive into the quarry, stop at the primary office, find the security person and pretend she is lost, giving the rest of us time to make our way down the dirt roads and join up with her. Any questions?"

"Just the one for now. Where are the explosives kept?" asks Derek.

"From what I was told, they are in a red container next to the offices. If the guards are anything like the ones I know, this should be unlocked as they are too lazy to keep locking it. If it is locked, the key will be in the office, which will be Lucy's job to retrieve."

Once we drive onto private land, Simon turns off the lights before stopping 200 metres from the rear gate. The doors open, and Derek and George alight and disappear into the darkness without saying anything.

Seconds later, pressing gently on the accelerator pedal in an attempt not to rev the engine too much, causing unwanted noise that could potentially attract someone's attention, Simon spins the vehicle around.

Once more, the vehicle comes to a halt in the pitch-black away from the gate. Before getting out, I whisper into Lucy's ear, "Once you witness the light flicker in the gatehouse, you know the situation has been dealt with, and you can drive into the quarry." She nods to confirm.

The land between the drop off point and the target is open ground, with the occasional large rocks lining the dirt road. The area on the left is identical to this side, with a hard sandy surface covered with a scattering of enormous light brown-coloured sandstones. On my right is the mine with a six-foot-high wire mesh fence set back a few feet from the edge to stop people from falling into the quarry beneath.

Now 50 metres from our target, I crouch down behind a giant boulder and wait for Simon to join me. From our position, we can peer straight through the windows that surround the small wooden illuminated gatehouse.

Get close to Simon, then in a quiet voice, "Appears like only one way in. The door must be on the opposite side. If you take the right side closest to the fence, I will take the other side. Meet up on either side of the door before making entry."

Before I move, I peer across the open mine toward the other security hut. In the distance, I witness the lights briefly go on and off. Excellent, George and Derek have completed their part.

Tap Simon on the shoulder without saying a word and point with the index finger of my right hand towards the target. On this, we both move forward.

Now within 10 metres of the hut. The interior light shines through the glass, illuminating the sandy dirt near the building. But tonight, we don't have the luxury of taking our time. Only one thing for it, proceed at speed, trying not to make a noise and dart across the ground until I'm beneath the window. Turn my head to my left, to notice Simon has done the same.

Pause and try to detect any sound of movement inside. Can't hear any. Need to check the front, so lay flat on my stomach and peer around the edge of the building. About to move when the sound of a door being opened catches my attention. Instantly I withdraw my head back around the corner and listen. A few seconds later, the door is closed again. Then follow the same procedure as before and poke my head back around. On the floor are the glowing embers of a cigarette butt.

On seeing me move, Simon joins me close to the door. Wait and compose myself, then give the signal to burst through the door. Instantaneously we leap to our feet and slam the door open, rush in and knock the guard to the deck before he even has the chance to comprehend what is happening.

While I hold the body mass, trying its best to escape with his arms and legs going in every direction, Simon grabs a leg and removes his boot to reach his sweaty sock. This he stuffs in the man's mouth, holding it in place with several cleaning rags found close by. He screams out with a dull, muffled sound as his hands are forced around his back. They are then fastened with a thick black cable tie; something we all keep on our person as standard equipment on a mission.

A rapid scan of the room locates a small cupboard space to keep cleaning stuff. Perfect, after binding both of his legs with another cable tie, we throw him inside. One last thing to do in case he does manage to get free, grab the telephone and rip out the wires.

Soon found the man's mobile phone. It would appear that he didn't detect our approach because he had been listening to music through a set of white headphones. No way could we afford for him to call for help on this, so I walked outside and tossed it over the fence into the black abyss.

OK, the first part is completed, now reach for the light switch, press the button off, and then back on again. A minute later, Lucy drives past and down the hill.

Turn to Simon, "You ready, mate?"

"Right behind you."

With that, we run down the steep winding incline of the sandy track leading down into the darkness. Finally, the ground flattens out and to our front, about 50 metres away, are the offices and, more importantly, off to one side is the red metal container containing explosives.

My first instinct is to sprint over to the explosives. Derek is already there when I arrive, "It's locked, mate."

"Shit, now we better hope the guard is compliant and hands over the key," I say, making my way to the Land Cruiser parked outside one of the portacabins.

When I reach the vehicle, Simon and George are waiting close by. "You two stay here and keep a lookout while Derek and I go inside and help Lucy with a bit of persuasion."

Enter via the metal door on the rear of the office. Several tables are shoved against the wall at the far end, and blue-backed chairs are scattered around the floor. A man is tied to a separate chair in the centre of the room. Thick red blood is running down from his swollen nose. He lets out an agonising scream as Lucy lands a punch to the side of his head.

"Hi, honey, asking a few questions, I see."

"Yes, this man is about to tell me where the container keys are," she replies, through demented eyes.

"Did you try requesting the info with a smile first?" I enquire.

"Of course, I'm not you. You did say we shouldn't kill any of the guards," Lucy said, inches from the man's face. "But you didn't say I couldn't forcibly negotiate."

"Do you mind if I try to make him talk?"

"Help yourself," she steps back and rubs her right fist into the palm of her left hand.

Stand close to the frightened man and say in a quiet, unthreatening voice, "Look over at that psycho bitch. She would like nothing more than inflicting a lot of pain on you just so you give her the answer she is looking for. So make it easy on yourself - where do you keep the keys? Ask yourself this: is your life worth more than your boss's company? Nod if you understand."

The man nods and, in a trembling submissive, pitched voice, "They're over in the desk drawer by the door as you came in."

"Now, isn't that better?" I ask in a soft, gentle tone.

As I grab the keys, Lucy couldn't help herself and gives the man a final smack just for the fun of it.

While Simon backs the Land Cruiser up to the store, I swing the heavy red metal doors fully open. Inside, the place is packed with boxes of PE4, detonator cords and detonators.

Within minutes the back of the vehicle is loaded with all the equipment we need for the mission. All we need to do now is get the fuck out of here before the police arrive.

First light starts to break through the night sky as we come close to Ruwi on the drive to Jebel Sifah. One of the many benefits of working here and having plenty of time off was that I knew many roads that will keep us off the primary routes. Let's face it, the moment the robbery is discovered, the very capable Royal Omani Police will man roadblocks on all major highways.

No point in telling the others if caught. This might be classed as terrorism, and the penalty for this in Oman is execution. Even though we all accept we may not make it back from a mission alive, the thought of being led to a hangman's noose is something we would like to give a miss.

After turning off the highway that runs through Muscat and into Ruwi, the street goes straight for about 200 metres before cornering to the left. At this point, we take the small dirty back street on the right, winding its way through lines of old dusty houses. Some appear to be still under construction. Outside several rundown homes is everything from worn-out cars that hardly appear roadworthy to motorcycles. You can tell you are in the poor part of Ruwi, where only the Indian population would live.

At the end of the street, it winds up through hairpin bends as it meanders up the side of a steep cliff before flattening out. From here, the route is narrow as it makes its way up and down mountain roads, passing ocean inlets where the shores are lined with traditional fishing boats.

If you are here on holiday and you have the time, you could take in the beautiful scenery of the mountains that come down to meet the winding road, where steeply banked streams carved by oceans criss-cross the unspoilt landscape. But unfortunately, we don't have time for this today, so it is imperative we reach the secluded spot of

Jebel Sifah and hide the mission equipment until we require it tomorrow.

Soon, the black tarmac winds through a small Omani fishing village with the sea on one side and dusty grey houses that have been in use for centuries on the other. Like most hamlets of this type, you rarely catch sight of any villagers. They are in their homes, sheltering from the hot weather outside, even at this time of day.

Skillfully Simon drives around the many animals lining the roadside or sat on the warm tarmac. You may not see anyone but hit one of these damn goats, and before you can drive away, you will be surrounded by people demanding money for the world's most expensive animal.

When we reach a point closer to Jebel Sifah, the road turns to hard-packed grey sand with nothing around apart from some dead bushes. Even the mountains we've been driving through are now in the far distance. With the resort only a few hundred metres away, this would be the perfect place to stash the equipment.

"Pull off here, Simon and take the dirt track to your left, and stop," I instruct, turning in my seat to witness the other three all snuggled up in the back, sleeping like babies. Who can blame them?

As the army always says, you should be asleep if you aren't working or eating. But I'm awake, so reach over and shake Lucy while shouting, "Take cover!" Simultaneously they all go into autopilot, spring out of the vehicle and head for shelter among the dunes.

Out of the Land Cruiser, I stand next to the door, glance over to Simon, who is in hysterics and shouts out, "Morning, people."

"Fucking dickhead," George retorts.

"You will pay for that later," is the first response from Lucy.

146

As for Derek, no verbal communication comes my way. He just starts lobbing rocks in my direction.

"Now I've got everyone's attention, the place we are staying tonight is not far from our present location, but best we do not leave the explosives in the car overnight, in case some nosy bastard such as the police decides to look in the back.

"This could possibly be a good place to temporarily hide the stuff," I turn towards Simon, shouting from on top of a sand dune.

A small area with sandbanks built up to form a basic square shape is on the other side. Reaching into the back of the vehicle, I grab a shovel. While I'm busy digging, the others start to fetch the boxes from the Land Cruiser and place them around the hole. Each makes sure they walk 50 metres away before crossing the dune to avoid leaving footprints leading straight to our equipment.

"Tell you what, Simon, while we do this can you try to reach the arms dealer Katie passed on to you and arrange for them to meet us at that fish restaurant over there," I point with my right arm, "at about 18:00 — tonight."

"On it, boss."

Once the stuff is out of view, we drive the rest of the way to Jebel Sifah Resort and the Sifahwy Boutique Hotel, where we are staying the night.

Conveniently, the car park is straight outside the three-storey whitewashed structure of the hotel, so it is a short walk from where Simon reverses the Land Cruiser into a parking space and the extensive glass doors.

"Not very big, is it?" Lucy announces, looking at the building.

"Wait, you will be impressed," due to the fact I have visited here several times in the past, I know that the place is hiding more floors on the other side.

Managed to book us all into a suite with three separate bedrooms on the way down, so all we need to do is check in. Once you step through the doors, you enter a sizable white marbled floored lobby. Off to the left is the reception desk, where a man in his twenties, wearing a brown dishdasha is standing, welcoming us to his hotel.

"As-salamu alaykum."

As customary, I reply the traditional way, "Wa alaikum salaam."

"Good morning, sir—how can I help?" comes the response.

"Yes, we have a reservation under the name of Barker," I say, while removing my phone from my pocket and scrolling to the room confirmation.

According to the small brass name tag, the man's name is Hammed. He checks the computer on the front desk to his front, "Yes, here it is, a three-bedroom suite overlooking the marina for one night."

"That sounds perfect, " as I reach for my multi-currency card.

"That will be 191 OMR, please, sir," as he places several room keys on the top of the counter along with a hotel guide. "You're in number three, which you can access via the lifts over in the corner." He points to the far end of the lobby.

The suite is divided into three separate bedrooms running off a central lounge area. A wooden framed patio window leading to a small balcony is on one wall and overlooks the pool and the magnificent marina in the distance.

Lucy heads straight for the kingsize double bedroom, not wanting to miss out.

"It would appear like my room is sorted. You lot can sort yourselves out," I say, joining her.

Once everyone is settled in, and after a check of the info stuff laid out on the dresser, "If anyone fancies a couple of cold ones, we can go down the Breeze Lounge & Bar down near the harbour. "

Of course, the answer is yes, not that I expected anything else from Simon, George or Derek.

"I'm going to grab a shower, so I will meet you four gents down at the Breeze Bar in 20," says Lucy, heading for the bathroom.

Love coming here because, unlike the rest of Oman, where all drinking in bars is done inside to not offend the Muslim population, where most people say they don't drink alcohol, here you can drink outside.

Several knee-high glass-topped tables wrapped in a brown basketweave surrounded by soft cushioned chairs in the same style are located on a raised marbled area outside the bar's open doors. Two are occupied by locals, drinking away on glasses of beer.

Sit at one of the free ones and wait for the Indian waiter to come over and take our order. Sure enough, shortly after, a young lady appears as smartly dressed as the man upstairs, wearing a black skirt and a white blouse. This was an easy bet as I knew it would not be an Omani, as they class this type of work beneath them.

"What can I bring you?" she asks in English with an accent.

"Four beers, please," I reply. No point asking for different types here as there is only one.

The first few drinks slide down very nicely as we survey in silence the tranquil way of life unfolding in front of us, with rays of the sun skipping across the water of the harbour. I am in deep meditation when a tender female voice brings me out. It's Lucy.

"That looks refreshing... where's mine?"

"Coming right up," Derek calls over the waitress.

After 30 minutes and several more cold ones, I sit up from the slouched position I'd been in. "As we are not here on holiday and have work to do once we finish this drink, we better wander down and check out the bigger boats. From memory, they are usually down the far end."

The walk along the pier wall takes us past small shops. Some sell tourists gifts, while others sell high-end clothing and bags. On the opposite side, wood and metal gangways lead down to the waterfront, to several smaller watercraft that wouldn't be any good for our purpose. They need to be ocean-going as the trip to Mano is about one hour across open water.

Our luck could be in, as off in the distance are two larger boats moored up together against the grey marina wall. As we get closer, I catch a glimpse of the British Merchant Navy Ensign stretching out from a pole on the stern. Hopefully, they will take us over to Mano in the morning without too many questions.

On the bow is a young man wearing nothing but a pair of blue shorts scrubbing the deck. To make first contact, Lucy yells out, "Hello, sailor." The man stops what he is doing, glances our way and laughs.

From over my shoulder, George shouts, "Are you British then?" pointing at the flag flapping around in the gentle wind blowing in from the sea.

After a short conversation, we discover the man we are talking to is called Paul. It turns out the crew are all from the UK, including the craft owner who is away on business in Muscat for several days.

To keep the dialogue going, "We're here for one night, staying in the hotel. Fancy joining us for a few bevvies at Breeze?" I say, pointing back the way we just came.

"Why not?" replies Paul, calling his two crewmates.

Not long after, we are all back sitting outside the bar, chattering away about anything but the mission or that we may need them to take us to Mano in the morning. If they didn't, I still have Carl and his vessel up my sleeve as a backup.

After three more cold beers, I skillfully turn our conversation to a possible boat trip. The trick is to make it seem like it's their idea. That way, they are more likely to make the voyage. Carefully slip in the point about us only staying at the hotel for one night, then we want to visit more of the coast of Oman before we leave the country in a couple of weeks. And what we want to do the most is a private beach party on a remote island, then camp for two or three nights.

The camping part is because they said their boss is away only for a short time. Therefore, they will need to come straight back and not hang about to observe what we are really up to.

With his drink finished and glass placed in the centre of the table, Paul turns around to his shipmate, "Didn't we pass an island on our way down from Muscat the other day?"

"You're right," declares John, another boat crew member. "Fancy going there for your party? We can take you tomorrow morning, if you like, and pick you up in a few days if we are still here. If not, you can make your own way back, as we saw some workers landing on the island via a ferry that could bring you back to the mainland."

"That sounds perfect, Paul. Tell you what, if I give you 300 OMR, that should pay for your fuel, so your boss doesn't need to know."

To emphasise what I just said, I take out 100 Omani Rial and place them in front of him. "You can have the rest of the gelt when we land. Just a little security as we need to make sure you're still here in the morning and not fucked off with our gelt." He turns to his mates, John and Kev, who nod in agreement.

"It's on then. One thing... it can become a bit rough out at sea. Are you all good at sailing in turbulent water?" asks Paul, picking up the money and putting it away.

"Yeah, all good sailors here — the rougher it is, the more we enjoy it." With that, George gives me one massive dirty look.

Spend the next hour or so chatting away with our new friends before Paul stood up and said, "We've got so much work to do. See you at 07:00 tomorrow morning."

"Love your handiwork, Steve. Couldn't have done better myself," says Simon, leaning back in his chair with a fresh beer.

Following Paul's lead, I peer down at Mickey, who tells me it is 14:15. We have a weapons drop at 18:00, and the kit still needs sorting out. "Drink up, boys and girls. Let's head back to the room and sort out equipment."

My first task is to turn the mobile phones into remote detonators by soldering two small wires to the speaker output circuit. When the phone rings, the current flows to the trigger and bang, ensuring I leave the two cables exposed to connect to the detonator later.

After that is completed, I balance precariously on a wooden chair, reach up and extract the light bulbs from their fixing. Once I've taken several more, I remove the small hobby drill from my Bergen, make a tiny circular hole beneath the metal cap, and fill it with lighter fluid to make three incendiary devices.

While I'm doing this, Derek collects all the individual radio parts from us and is busy reassembling the components to make four working transmitters.

Once he finishes, "Here you go, PRC 350 radios that should reach anywhere on the island. Sorry, we only brought enough for the four. Remember Lucy wasn't with us on the last job. Mind you, this may be sufficient, depending on Steve's plans."

Meanwhile, the others empty their own Bergens onto the floor and are busy repacking only the stuff for the mission, leaving room for the shared gear like explosives, detonators, ammo and ropes. The personal kit we do not need will be left in the Land Cruiser, which will be hidden among the sand dunes.

After everyone is finished packing away all the equipment we will require and double-check nothing makes an unwanted noise when walking or running by jumping up and down and sprinting across the room while the others watch and listen, nothing to do now but get ourselves ready for the meal at the fish restaurant and meet up with Katie's contact.

As the eatery is only about 300 metres from the hotel, there is no point in taking the vehicle. Plus it's a beautiful sunny evening, so we decide to walk. On the way, Simon scans for a spot to hide the Land Cruiser in the morning that he can drive into easy with little noise that would attract attention from any nosy bastard.

Approach the restaurant from the front, as our route takes us along the sandy shoreline and through the dunes. Several tables lined with white and blue squared tablecloths stand on the brown timber veranda beneath a dark wood beamed ceiling. As we get closer, I catch sight of rays of sunlight dancing off the glasses placed on each table.

At the rear of the terrace, a four-foot-high wooded planked wall similar to the outside divides the interior and exterior. Apart from the man standing behind the bar with its rows of stacked bottles of spirits, which occupies the far right corner, nobody else is in here.

"Before you lot grab any old table, I told the weapons guy that we would be sat outdoors at the furthermost table on the right," Simon says, plonking his arse down.

"To be nothing more than an annoying twat, what if that table is taken?" asks Derek through a vast stupid grin spread across his face.

"Sure if you show them your fucking ugly mug, they would move," Simon retaliates.

"Now, now, children, but he does have a point, Derek—you are ugly," I say, pulling out a chair.

We are sitting, checking out the menus when an Indian gentleman, dressed like the ones back at the hotel, comes over, grasping a notebook in his left hand while a black pen held in his right hand hovers over the pad, ready to take our order. It would appear that the group that owns the resort also owns this restaurant.

"What can I fetch you? The catch of the day is the local kanad," he articulates, looking straight at me for some reason.

"Ladies first," I say, partially to be a gentleman and because I didn't have a clue.

Lucy smiled at the man, "The kanad, please."

"Sounds good to me," I reply.

"And me," George says, looking at the waiter, whose name badge reads Md Thaseen.

After several long agonising moments, Simon looks up, "Make mine the chicken."

"Can we get five beers with that?" I shout, as Md starts to walk away.

Glance down at my timepiece, which tells me it is 17:45. Still 15 minutes until the contact should arrive, but here they work on what we referred to as Omani time. Even if we arranged the meeting for 18:00, the person could be half an hour late and still be on time. This should give us plenty of time to eat.

After taking a mouthful of beer, I glance up over the top of the half-filled glass to see Md and another man we hadn't seen heading coming our way with massive circular silver trays filled with plates of food. He places one white china plate with what we ordered in front of each of us before laying the rest loaded to the brim with an assortment from fries to rice and local vegetables.

"Cheers, Md. Can you bring us another round?" I point to the empty glasses.

Just finish eating when the distinctive noise of a vehicle engine drives up and stops to the right of where we're sitting. Moments later, a man who I would guess is in his forties and dressed in flimsy blue cotton trousers with a matching top comes into view. Still not trusting anyone, I hold the sharp fish knife, so it runs up the inside of my right arm.

With an Indian accent, he calls out, "Are any of you Simon?"

"Who wants to know?" Simon replies.

"If that is you, there is a delivery for you in the car," comes the response.

Without saying a word, Simon nods and stands up. Everyone at the table follows suit and joins him. The person leads us to the vehicle concealed behind a sand dune, where a smartly dressed man in a black jacket sits in the passenger seat. As we reach the Jeep, he climbs out and asks, "Who is Simon?"

"We are all together. Did you bring what we wanted?" I ask.

"Yes, they are in the back."

The man in blue opens the rear door to show three green wooden boxes. He lifts the lid off the biggest one, containing four 5.56mm L119A1 assault rifles and 10 30-round magazines. Remove one and hand it to George, our weapons expert, to inspect.

"Everything OK with that, mate?" I say, grabbing another.

"All appears OK — better check them all in case they try to fob us off with only one rifle working."

As George checks the rest, I open the smaller box of the three. Inside are five 9mm Browning pistols complete with mags.

Before I can remove the lid of the last crate, Simon stops me and says, "Nearly forgot, George; I ordered you an old friend, minus the fancy bits."

"Thanks, Simon, I didn't know you cared."

George stops what he is doing and opens the last wooden box. Inside, his beloved sniper rifle, the 7.62mm L96A1. "Thanks again, Simon. Do not worry about the sight and wind indicator — brought the ones from home."

After checking all the equipment, my attention turns to the man wearing the black jacket, as he seems to be the person in charge. "Do you have ammunition to go with these toys?"

He reaches into the far end of the vehicle's rear, uncovers four metal containers, and pulls them toward him. The sleeve on his right hand slides up his arm as he does.

"OK, as you have already transferred the money earlier today, you can take your purchase," he announces, dragging out all the boxes and dumping them on the floor.

Before we could say anything else, they both climb in the Jeep, spin around and drive off into the distance. Can't leave them here, so it is decided to store them in a separate location close to where our explosives are buried. It's best not to keep everything in one place just in case someone stumbles across them. Zeroing the weapons can wait until we are on the beach of Mano.

"Did anyone else spot the tattoo of a camel on the man's right wrist when he reached inside the vehicle?" says Derek picking up one of the boxes.

"Yes, I did, but it hasn't registered until you just mentioned it," says Simon.

A horrible idea flashes through my mind; did we just buy weapons from the people we are here to perhaps eliminate? No, it must be a coincidence, so let it go.

"Due to the fact we need to get our arses up at sparrows fart and be back here before first light in the morning to recover our stuff before heading to meet the boys at the boat for 07:00, suggest we head back to the hotel."

"After one more cold one, Steve," comes the response from George.

As we sip slowly on several more beers, with only us and the two waiters here, I outline the plan for tomorrow, what there is of it.

"Once we land on Mano, our first task will be zeroing the weapons in the shelter of the beach. Once that is done, we can make our way up the cliff. This is where you come in, Derek. As you are the one who's been on mountaineering trips, I'm making you our radio-carrying mountain goat. You will find the best route up, then lead the team up the cliff with the rest of the equipment."

"Don't have a problem with that."

I continue, "Once on top, circumnavigate the industrial area and make our way to the sandy hills on this map." I take off my Splash Maps headscarf with the printed map from around my neck. "Here we will establish an operating base. You're the motor vehicle man, Simon, so at some point, you will need to acquire a vehicle of some sort."

"Got it, five camels coming up," says Simon, laughing at his own joke.

"If that is all you can obtain, then camels it is. As they say, a second-class ride is better than a first-class walk," says Lucy, trying to take the thunder away from Simon's comment.

"For the rest of the plan, this can be sorted once we are on the island and confirm the layout. One final point, if all goes tits up on the way to the operation base in the hills, the emergency RV is back on the beach. If nobody has any questions, let's head for the hotel and get some kip."

Chapter Eleven – Journey to Mano

Goes without saying that very little sleep comes my way. The night before any mission is always the same routine. Go to bed and then toss around all night with the plans rushing through the mind. At one point, while lying perfectly motionless so as not to wake Lucy, I was staring at the ceiling and wondering why I couldn't at least catch some shut-eye. A funny image came to the front of the noggin. One of the other idiots tied the sandman to a post and then placed a bullet in his head for getting sand in their eyes.

Across the room, the red glow of the digital clock is telling me it's 04:10. Fuck it, might as well climb out of bed and grab a brew, and sit on the balcony and watch the world waking up. As I sip on the freshly brewed coffee, over in the distance a small fishing boat leaves the harbour under the light of the moon flickering on the bay's calm waters. Let's hope the sea stays this way for the crossing to Mano this morning.

The next hour flies past, time to rise the rest from their sweet slumber. To give Lucy the first pass at the bathroom, make my way around to her side of the double bed and shake the body wrapped up in the white quilt. Seconds later, I'm held tight by the top of my sweater and a 9mm pistol inches from my head. "Morning, honey," I say in a low voice, not moving a single inch.

"Morning, sorry, was having a bad dream," comes the sweet response.

"You want to use the washroom while I rudely wake the boys up?"

She nods, then one body part at a time slid out from the soft, warm quilt.

Right, time to wake the others. As I enter the second bedroom, George is sitting on the front edge of the bed, "Heard you coming," comes a voice of something not yet awake.

"Morning, George, give Derek a kick. The kettle's just boiled."

Now for Simon, I learned not to stand close to him when waking him a long time back. Come within the danger zone, and you may receive a blow to the head. With that in mind, in one action, grab the bottom of his quilt, rip it off and shout, "Morning, Simon."

Back in the kitchenette area, grab another brew before giving my equipment one final check, while I wait for everyone to sort themselves out, ready for the off.

Once the whole team is sitting in the living room, their kit by their legs and sipping away on hot drinks, I run through this morning's plans.

"From here, we will make our way to the ammo dump and collect weapons plus the explosives. If Simon takes the Land Cruiser, then meets us there once he's hidden the vehicle. Then make our way to Paul and the trip to Mano. As per our standard operating procedure, once we reach sight of the vessel, we will stand off and monitor the situation for six minutes, to ensure we are not met with some kind of nasty surprise. Need to be in position by 06:40. Any questions?"

"Nope, but do you want Simon and me to make our way around the back and approach from a different angle?" comes the suggestion from George.

"Makes sense to me. In fact, stay there until you see me go inside the boat and come straight back out, just in case someone is waiting in the cabin," I reply.

Pick up my Bergen and throw it onto my back. "If you're all ready, let's make a move."

While Simon heads through the lobby to the parked Land Cruiser and drops off the keys, the rest of us follow the identical route as the journey to the fish restaurant yesterday.

There is a full moon giving plenty of light to highlight anyone moving around the resort. So as not to silhouette ourselves, we hug the bottom of the sandbanks, keeping to the shadows. Within 20 minutes, we are near to where we buried our weapons yesterday and span out, taking cover among the dunes. Five minutes pass, with no movement near or close by the weapons cache. I make my way first while everyone else watches out for any signs of unwanted attention.

After removing all sand from the top, I open the green wooden box and remove one of the assault rifles and two of the 30-round magazines. From one case, I take a 9mm pistol. While I'm loading the 5.56 bullets into the mag, Simon, Lucy, and Derek do the same. Meanwhile, George has uncovered the sniper rifle and is fixing his optical sight.

Once we all have our weapons, the wooden boxes are hidden. We move a short distance over the built-up piles of sand to the spot where our play equipment is buried, following the exact procedure as before. As expected, nobody is around.

I uncover the PE4 and give half to Derek and the rest to Simon. To be on the side of caution, all three elements of the explosives will be kept apart. George will take the detonator cord while I take the detonators.

Glance down at the glowing dial of Mickey, who is telling me it is 06:00. First light is at 07:00. We need to be in our positions close to the boat by then.

"Is everyone finished here?" I ask.

With four thumbs raised up, I lead off back to the Jebel Sifah to a point where Simon and George would leave us and take the alternative route. Once I reach a secure location within the resort, I stop and stretch my right arm out at shoulder height, keep it straight, and lower it down towards the ground. Do this twice to tell the team to take cover.

For several minutes I listen to the quietness of the night. The only noise is far away crickets rubbing their back legs together, producing a chirp-like sound. As I scan the area, the tiny rectangle lights appear on Paul's boat at the other end of the marina. In the distance, through the darkness, another small craft heads out on a fishing trip, its motor humming quietly, fading away as it leaves the shelter of the enclosed bay.

Well, at least they are still here and awake. Place my hand on my head to signal the others to close in on my location.

"OK, you two go around the back. We will give you 10 extra minutes to reach a place on the other side before moving from here." With that, George and Simon disappear into the blackness heading for the buildings.

After waiting the agreed time, "I'll lead, Lucy, take the middle – you can take the rear, Derek." I rise to my feet and move off towards the boat, scanning the whole area as I made my way, not only to spot trouble but innocent persons going about their daily business. The last thing they need is to catch a glance of an armed patrol tabbing across the resort.

So far, all is going as it should. We are now close to the target, where I once more stop and take cover in the shadows of the tall wall running to the right side of the harbour. From my vantage point, I witness Paul and John wandering along the top of the vessel, preparing for the crossing.

Give it another five minutes, to ensure Simon and George are ready at the back before standing up and walking the rest of the way. When I'm close, I shout out, "Morning, Paul, still on for this morning's trip?"

"Morning, Steve, yes, all ready when you are. Where is everyone... are they not coming?" says Paul, looking around.

"They will be here momentarily," I say, climbing onboard.

Hold Paul in the conversation for the next few minutes while I scan inside the central cabin through the extensive patio glass doors. "What's around here?" as I climb onto a narrow strip of a wooden deck to the left of the wheelhouse. Not that I give a flying fuck, this is the signal for Derek and Lucy to join me.

A couple of minutes later, I hear Lucy saying, "Morning, boys."

"Good morning," comes the reply from Paul, through a beaming smile at seeing a beautiful woman this time in the morning, even though she's dressed like a killer.

Leave them both on the deck at the stern and enter the cabin, decked out in a style that wouldn't look strange in a country manor. A teak coffee table bolted to the floor is surrounded by two green leather soft sofas that take up the space to the room's right. On the opposite side is an enormous glass-topped table. A teakwood bar runs along the back, complete with blacktopped stainless steel stools. My eyes are drawn to the cabinet behind, filled with bottles of spirits that any sailor would enjoy.

After a quick scan, I turn around, go back outside, stand at the aft, and peer into the green vegetation between us and the building 100 metres away. A few moments pass before, out of the corner of my eye, I catch sight of a figure emerging from the shadows. It's George.

"Well played, George, didn't even notice you there until you moved."

"Practice, mate."

Once all the people and equipment are on board, I turn to Paul, "All ready to go when you are."

Once John lets go of all lines securing the vessel, Kev pushes down on the control levers up on the flying bridge; the massive engines roar into life. Moving away from the dock, he steers the yacht towards the open ocean.

It would appear the breakwater is doing its job as the moment we pass the harbour's outer wall, the height of the waves increases, making the boat pitch and roll slightly in the swell.

I pivot to face Kev, "Bearing in mind the weather, how long do you think the crossing will take?"

"About an hour," comes the response.

Leave the bridge and enter the central cabin to find the rest tucking into a Full English breakfast, apart from George, who is looking a little green in the cheeks.

"Still not good at sailing then, George? One of those slimy runny eggs should sort out your gut," I say, taking the proverbial piss and occupying the seat next to him.

"You know where you can shove that, you wannabe sailor boy," comes the reply.

Seconds later, John emerges through a doorway that leads to the galley. "Thought you lot might have had an early start this morning, so decided to do you a fry up," as he slides a plate full of food in front of me.

"Thanks, looks fantastic," pulling my breakfast closer.

The following 25 minutes of the journey goes without any problems with the time spent eating, chatting and taking the piss out of George. We knew he isn't the sailing type from the crossing from St Bethanie a few missions back, but it passes the time.

Knowing that fresh air may do him some good, George heads for the open deck at the back with me tagging along. I want to confirm that we are still going the right way towards the island and have not made a diversion to the nearest Golden Camel outpost. Not that I believe they would, but not trusting people I've only known briefly is one of the conditions of my PTSD.

From the open deck of the stern, I peer up to catch sight of Paul and Kev up on the bridge at the controls and looking out to sea. For a better view of the surrounding area, I join them. In the distance, a small black shape appears over the horizon, "Is that Mano?"

"Yes, Steve, we should be there shortly," Paul confirms, looking over his left shoulder at me.

"Excellent, can't wait to land and start this party," I lie, turning to face the way we have come.

Stand doing nothing but watching the waves as they rise a few feet, peak with a splash of white water, and then disappear into the ocean. Brought out of my mini hypnotic state when I spot a vessel closing in at some speed from the direction of the mainland.

Shout down to George, leaning over the side and being sick, "You see that craft coming our way? Go inside and warn the others there may be trouble heading our way."

While I keep my eyes fixed on the boat approaching at a high rate of knots, I flashback to when the authorities pulled us up on the way to St Halb and almost boarded our boat. Could this be the Omani police?

Meanwhile, inside the central cabin, Simon breaks out the 9mm pistols from a bundle of Bergens to John's surprise, who's now stopped motionless in the doorway.

"OK, who are you and...what are the weapons for?" he finally manages to blurt out.

"I'll explain later, John... for now, just stay in the galley," Derek pushes him back through the door.

While George rejoins me outside, the rest take up defensive positions, looking through the windows with their 9mms hidden away from view, but easily accessible.

Back on the bridge, I can see the approaching vessel is now only 200 metres away from our current location. A few more minutes, and it is almost here. Confirm my 9mm is still tucked away down the front of my trousers by gripping the sweaty pistol grip with my right hand.

The boat is now on us. With a loud shout, George screams through the cabin's open door, "Make yourselves ready."

Everyone grabs their weapons and prepares to be boarded, and the fight that will undoubtedly occur if the needs dictate.

Several tense moments pass as it comes level with ours. Then without stopping, it speeds past in the direction of the island.

Release my grip on the pistol, "Thank fuck for that. It must be the fast ferry taking workers to the dock on Mano."

"Must be," declares Kev, now relaxing his hands that have been holding the wheel so tight for the last few minutes that his knuckles are now visible.

"Guess you have some questions on why we are heavily armed. Come with me inside, Paul—I will explain. You can relay that message to everyone later."

Once John and Paul have taken a seat at the table, "I'm not going to insult your intelligence. We are going to Mano to find an old friend and take him back to the UK. Our weapons are a precaution in case someone objects."

Not sure if they could be trusted not to utter anything to anybody, but I have no choice as they've seen the weapons and kit.

166

From the way I look at it, I now have three options. First, threaten them that we will hunt them down, sink their boat, and ensure they don't survive if any of this gets out. Second, blow them away once we land and throw the bodies into the sea. Third, play it nice and bribe them with even more money. Luckily for them, I choose the latter.

"Here is what I propose, so you don't blab to anyone why we are on Mano. Here is an extra 300 Rials to keep your gobs shut. Of course, it goes without saying, but I will say it anyway, so you comprehend the situation. If you say something before we leave the country, we will come looking for you and kill you." I say, looking at each of them in turn.

"No need for that—I'm ex-Royal Navy. None of us will say anything, but I will take the dosh. You have my word," says Paul, picking up the money I just placed on the dining table.

Ten minutes later, Kev, still outside, shouts, "We are approaching the coastline. Someone fancy coming out here and telling me where to beach?"

Along with Derek being our mountain goat, we start to head outside as we need a spot where he can lead us on a climb up from the beach. We return to the bridge. I scan the shoreline with my binos for the location we planned to land at the far end of mano.

"Over there, near the massive black boulders sticking out of the sea close to the yellow sandy beach," Derek points to an area on the island where it rounds a corner.

"No problem," Kev spins the ship's wheel hard to the right.

About 100 metres away from the landing zone, the boat comes to a halt facing the beach. "Sorry, the ocean is too shallow to go any further. You will need to go by our rubber tender the rest of the way."

"Not an issue, Paul and thanks again for the trip," I say, climbing down.

Within minutes, John lowers the smaller boat over the side and into the water. Once everyone has clambered aboard along with all the equipment, the outboard engine, with the flick of a switch, bursts into life with a loud humming sound.

Once we land and Paul returns to the vessel offshore, our first task is to secure the LZ. Seconds after landing, the team automatically spans out, facing different locations.

The LZ is about a 100 metre long sandy beach stretching another 50 metres down to where the waves are lapping at the shoreline. Lucy is laid flat at one end behind a sand dune, looking along a narrow strip of land that skirts the bottom of the steep cliffs off to the right. Crouched between two giant stones is Simon, looking at the small beach on the other side, which turns into a collection of small rocks before disappearing into the sea.

Under the vertical escarpments that back onto the shore, Derek is looking up, planning how to get the fuck out of here. The first part seems straightforward: a gravel patch that gradually slopes upwards for about 40 metres before turning into a steeper climb.

As the team goes over their respective fire zones, I search for the spot that will be our base for the next couple of hours before heading up the cliff later. I start to explore the beach, looking in every possible position some idiot could be hiding, ready to jump us when we least expect it.

The area is clear, so call everyone into a small indent that goes back about two metres into the solid rock. Deep enough to shelter us from above and behind, an outcrop of light brown sandstone rocks close to the cliffs should keep us out of sight of anyone cruising the coastline.

Once everyone is inside, I outline the plan, "The place where Lucy was covering is more than likely the potential contact point. So the four of us will rotate between one-hour sentry duty and weapon zeroing while Derek tries to find a way up. Suggest you take the first stag, George, as your rifle doesn't need a total zero, just a quick check due to the optical sight and the indicator thingy."

"I've no problem with that. At least I'm not last for a change," states George, gripping the sniper rifle.

"Remember to keep the noise level to a minimum — only use three rounds to confirm your aim. Only go to the makeshift range after your stag. This way, there will only be a burst of shots every 60 minutes. I'll set it up and go first. Questions?"

"Yep, one, when are we planning to go topside? Need to know how much time I have to locate a route."

"You have a few hours to discover a suitable pathway, Derek. I would like to be in a position on the top roughly one hour before last light."

"In that case, if everyone gives me some of their rations, I'll make my famous Army Chuck-in," declares Simon, grabbing his trowel from his Bergen, ready to dig a small hole to protect the flames from wind and view.

"About time you made yourself worthwhile, Simon. Besides, I'm hungry. Most of my breakfast went over the side of that fucking boat," replies George.

"You're always starving, fat boy," comes the instant reply from Simon.

Decide the best position for setting up the zeroing range is to the left of the location beyond where Simon was earlier. That way, if you miss the splash as the round hits, the calm water will indicate how far off you are.

Pull out a figure 12 target that, for some unknown reason, I routinely carry on a mission from my Bergen and head for the sandstone rocks with a bit of driftwood I found on the beach. The thought of walking around in wet boots and socks all day didn't seem appealing, so I removed them at the water's edge before wading into the ocean.

Place my right foot tentatively into what I expect to be freezing cold water to be surprised. The sun's done its job and warmed up the water surrounding the island. With the waves now lapping at my knees, I tread gingerly, not wanting an unseen stone to cut deep into my bare foot. Finally, I reach the perfect spot, a clump of rocks jutting out of the sea about 30 metres away.

Remove the printed target, secure it to the lump of wood, and lean it against a rock, ensuring the target protrudes above the top. This should stop any ricochets striking the stone and heading back and hitting anyone, with any luck. Once in place, I return to the warm sandy beach and my boots. Right, now time to fire my check rounds to find out if the bullets land where I'm aiming. As there is no place to adopt the prone position, I will have to use one of these sandstone boulders to give me a steady base.

With the rifle's stock resting firmly in the palm of my left hand and pistol grip in my right, I line up the rifle's barrel with the target. Then peer through the optical sight, ensuring the pointer is in the centre of the picture of half a man pinned on the driftwood. Now to control my breathing; breathe in, exhale, take one more deep breath, and exhale halfway and hold.

Feel for the first pressure with the index finger before squeezing the trigger slowly all the way home. The firing pin strikes the bottom of the case, causing an explosion of gases inside, hurtling the bullet out of the end of the barrel at 3000 f/s. A millisecond later, the recoil slams hard into my shoulder.

I see the bullet hit the intended target below and to the right through the optics. Make a tiny adjustment to the sight and fire another round. This time it hits the middle of the chest on the figure 12. With my rifle sorted, I head back to the cave-like structure to find Simon has dug a pit surrounded by small stones collected from the beach.

"Bit early for lunch, mate," I say, pointing at the fire.

"Just getting things ready, plus there is always time to have a brew going," comes the reply from Simon, as he put more bits of wood into the hole.

Not long after, Derek appears close to the bottom of the cliff, walking to join us. After helping himself to a fresh brew, "There is good news and some not so good, the good first; once you pass the shingle, the route turns left, just behind the rockface you can see from here. From here is a small stony trail that winds itself up towards the ridge. As it is still daylight and not wanting to risk being silhouetted against the skyline, I didn't peer over the ridge."

"What is the bad news, Derek?" asks Lucy.

"The track is worn, so if there are no animals such as goats up there that could make a descent like this, the tracks are made by humans, and we are not the only ones to visit this part of the island."

"Cheers — how long did the climb take?" I enquire.

"Didn't take that long, I would say, with all our equipment, we should be able to be at the rim in an hour," comes the reply from Derek.

Just placed my water bottle back after taking a swig of water when a shout comes from Simon, who swapped places with George not long ago at the stag post. "Look up on top of the ridgeline about 300 metres from my location. A person is standing on the front edge."

My first instinct is to grab my binos and focus on the individual. From what I can see from here, this is a lone man dressed in overalls very close to the rim. As I start to think he will fall if the idiot gets any closer, while handing the binoculars to Lucy, the man steps off.

"What the fuck?!" I shout.

"Better go and check if he is alive," yells Lucy, running towards Simon.

While holding her back, "There is no point. Nobody can survive that. Plus, he jumped. No one pushed him," says Simon in a quiet, subdued manner.

Take stock of the situation for a few minutes before calling everyone to my location. "First, it would seem that Nasir was right. These people are desperate and feel that chucking themselves off cliffs is their only option. Trust me when I say someone at the head of the Golden Camel will pay for this man's life once we get hold of them."

"They sure will, Steve," says Lucy shaking her head.

"But, before anyone gets killed, the man on the hill changes our plans. We can't stay here. Grab your kit together and be ready to scale to the rock face in 20 minutes.

We start our ascent with Derek leading, followed by me, with the rest spread out in a line about 40 metres apart behind. The small loose fragments of grey pebbles make the going hard. My foot slides, sending stones tumbling down, narrowly missing the person behind with every step. Up ahead, our mountain goat, Derek, has stopped below an enormous rock sticking out of the escarpment, waiting for us to join him.

The moment George reaches the spot, we take six minutes to catch our breath. Everyone appears knackered due to the heavy equipment they haul in their Bergens. But more importantly, we are all here and still uninjured.

"Don't worry—from here, the going is relatively easier," says Derek once more, heading uphill.

Once we round the corner, a grey, just about visible, worn-out track no more than a few feet across meanders back and forth across the cliff face as it makes its way to the top.

Our ascent has now become more of a climb than before. Three-quarters of the way up, with each breath scorching the back of my throat as I gasp for air, I reach a near-vertical three-metre spot. I turn to make sure everyone else is still OK. They have stopped, drinking from water bottles to quench the burning at the back of their throats and resting the aching limbs.

Not far to go, I think to myself as I reach up and grab a small rock indicated by Derek and pull myself up one foot and handhold at a time until I come to a ledge no more than four metres long and one and a half metres wide. About to move again when the sound of falling rocks can be heard below me. I turn quickly to see Lucy frantically grasping at another outcrop of rocks.

"You, OK, honey?" I yell.

"Yeah, just lost my grip for a moment," she replies.

"I'm OK, almost received a boulder to the head, but I'm fine, thanks for asking, lover boy," shouts George further down the cliff.

Wait for everybody to reach the ledge and take a deserved rest for the next fifteen minutes. After rinsing my mouth out with water, I glance up. The ridgeline isn't far, about another 100 metres of the winding pathway to go.

Once more, Derek leads off, heading for the ridge, before stopping a few metres shy of the ridgeline under a deep overhang. Finally, the climb is over, and we are all at the top. "Couldn't tell you what's on the other side as I didn't look," says Derek, coming close to me.

"Not an issue. I suggest we stay bunched up together here until darkness falls before sticking our heads over the parapet," I reply.

Chapter Twelve – Mano Day One

Receive a hard elbow to the ribs on the right side from Simon, sitting next to me on the ledge. With my eyes adjusting to the remaining daylight, I cup Mickey with my hand—it is now 18:45. From what I remember from working in this area of the Middle East, it directly goes from light to dark instantly. It's like the big man upstairs switching the lights off and saying, 'go to bed'.

Turn to face Simon, "Pass it down the line—we go in 10."

To my left, Derek is already at the ridgeline, ready to get the first view of what lays beyond. While the others prepare themselves, I throw my Bergen on my back and make my way the last few feet to the ridge to join Derek. "You looked over the rim yet?"

"Not yet, Steve, waiting for nightfall."

Due to the fact we don't know which part of the island we have landed on, for all we know, there could be people close on the other side; instead of risking the rustling sound of a paper map being unfolded, I remove the Splash Maps-printed Toob of Duhfa I have been using as a sweatband on the way up.

As the location is bathed in darkness and our eyes get their night vision, Derek and I ease our heads inch by inch over the ridgeline to get our first glimpse of the terrain.

Like I was taught as a Chosen Man in the Royal Green Jackets, I first scan the forward edge through the fading light, as far as I can in both directions. About 300 metres away is a perimeter fence of some type. Past that, I can make out the shape of several buildings lined up in a row leading away into the distance beyond the wire mesh through the hedgerow.

The next task is to survey the middle ground. To my right is what appears to be a pond with tightly packed vegetation running along the bank on one side. My attention now turns to the undulating sandy area to my immediate front. This could be a problem. From our present location, we must make our way to our planned base over on the jebel. But first, we have the task of getting over this dangerous ground and making our way silently to the fence without being detected.

Two people are better at scanning, as they might be able to spot something that you don't, even if it is staring you straight in the face. Turn my head slightly to whisper in a low voice that is only audible to Derek, "You see anything we can use as cover?"

"Yes, mate, about 10 o'clock halfway across, there is a clump of small trees and what I think is a brick building about a metre tall." To affirm I am looking in the correct direction, Derek indicates the location with his left arm.

"Thanks, I didn't spot that. Better go back down and join the others and work out where we are on the island."

Back on the ledge, I remove my torch from my jacket's inside pocket. Unfold the printed map. Then shine the red light of my torch through the gaps in my fingers to hide some of the light and direct the beam downwards to illuminate the diagram on the floor in front of me.

With my index finger placed on the cloth map, "I think we are here," I glance at Derek, who nods to confirm he is in agreement.

"From here, we need to make our way over to this fence through a small outcrop of vegetation about 150 metres from our current location." Once more, I draw my finger across the map to verify what I'm saying. "From here, we travel through Duhfa to our FRV in two separate teams...."

"Can you point to that?" asks Simon.

"Just here on the far side of the industrial zone," I place my finger on the spot.

"So what's the plan?" asks Lucy, moving in closer.

"We will all make our way to a safe place at the fenceline via the trees. From here, we will divide into two teams, with Derek and Simon going one way around the built-up area, the rest of us going the opposite direction. We will meet up at the FRV on the top of the jebel. Any questions? If not, we move in five."

Back on the ridgeline, I watch the dead ground while Simon heaves himself over and sprints in a zig-zag formation to the halfway point. I join him as soon as he is across while Derek covers me. Once half the team is on my location, Simon darts across towards the unlit cover at the base of the perimeter railings. Eventually, everybody is concealed in the long dark shadows created by the overgrown vegetation that intertwines the criss-cross wires of the fence close to the accommodation boundary.

Without saying a word, I set off at a gentle pace, following the border of the compounds, keeping to the cover provided as much as possible, as I still don't fully understand the lay of the land. To my front, about 50 metres away, the protection of the vegetation makes way to a sparsely populated yard with a few portacabins and containers scattered about.

The question is, do we continue our present course to the other side or retreat to the ridge and follow this, ensuring we keep the camp off to our right in view? At the edge, I drop down and signal the other two to close in on my position.

Once George and Lucy are alongside me, "OK, we have open ground to our right for the next 300 metres. We have two choices. You cover me while I sprint across. I'll turn around and cover you both across when I'm at the far end. Alternatively, we can divert back along the coastline and into the shelter of the darkness of the night and track the coast until we are past and then come back in. What do you think?"

A minute of silence passes before George speaks, "Why take the chance? It's not much of a detour, so might as well take it."

"What do you think, Lucy?"

"I'm with George on this one," she says, adjusting the rifle on her knees.

"The longer route it is then," adjust my Bergen as I stand up and lead off in the direction of the edge of the island and the protection of the darkness. After travelling a short length of time, I look back to glimpse a sight of Lucy spread out behind me and George 40 metres behind her.

As I walk, I count out 200 steps plus another 60. This should be enough distance, I think to myself before turning right and skirting the ridge. The ground is uneven with piles of sand, which make my feet slip a few inches on every step. So I add an additional 30 to be safe. On continuous undercover operations in the pitch-black back in my army days, I worked out that for every 100 metres I walked, it was equal to 110 paces.

Now following the coastline, I repeat the step count this time, counting an extra 70 to ensure we are well away from the open space when we find ourselves back at the perimeter.

Once we arrive at the edge of the motel compound, I stop, crouch down, scan the area beyond the fence, and listen for any sounds of movement. The only thing visible is the many lights scattered among the neat rows of the white-painted wooden accommodation buildings. Several people are chatting and laughing loudly in the far distance and out of view. Take a peek at Mickey, who tells me the time is only 22:00. Make a mental note, as this will be vital in the rescue phase.

After another 15 minutes, we reach the end of the second of the hotels. Signal for the rest to stop. Turn to see what I expected — George is facing the way we came with Lucy looking into the grounds. There is no point in watching the coast, as any movement will likely come from the hotel.

Adopt a kneeling position before taking a deep breath, as I need to be ready to act, in case I'm confronted by something or someone when I poke my head out from the cover of the metal upright of the border fence. When I peer around the post, to my front is a massive open area covered in a mixture of hard and soft sand. This stretches about 200 metres into the distance. Halfway along, close to a small sandbank no more than a metre high, are four vehicles, two ridged and two articulated trucks.

As I watch a car drives past the other side of the embankment, this must be the primary route running through Duhfa, the moving vehicle draws my attention to the opposite side of the road. In the dim light of the street lights, I detect a row of buildings.

From the glow of electric lights shining through enormous glass windows and a group of people sitting at long tables on a raised platform to the front chatting away, I conclude that these are probably two restaurants. To the left of the establishments is what looks like a parking area. From here, I detect the outline of at least 35 vehicles.

One thing taught in the military is that the best place to hide is in the open, so our route to circumnavigate the shops and our happy diners: go straight through the middle past the trucks, then through the car park onto the tarmac road behind.

Right, I have a plan, so turn back to face George and Lucy and signal for them to close in on me. Spend the next few minutes outlining the route, part of which is if it all went wrong, our emergency RV is back here.

Keeping the same formation, I lead off, hugging the back of what I'm now calling a truck stop and head for the far end. It's not long before we start to walk within 60 metres of the parked vehicles. Almost pass by when I feel a hand on my shoulder.

While staying almost calm and not jumping like a rookie soldier, I turn to catch Lucy holding a finger from her left hand against her lips. While I scrutinise what she's doing, she points to a space between two Man trucks. Laid out, encased in brown and white patterned blankets, the bulky shape of four people wrapped up against the cold nip in the night air, one of whom is starting to stir.

Nod my head to confirm I've seen them. Lucy then passes on the message to George. As George comes level with the gap between the trucks, one of the body masses escapes from his blanket and stands up. We immediately freeze — taking cover would make our movement stand out like a spare village idiot at a local fête.

With all of us holding our breaths, the man makes his way to the front wheel of one truck. A second later, the sound of running water breaks the silence. The twat is having a piss. Standing perfectly still, our gaze stays fixed on his every move as he returns to the land of slumber.

Now walking through the car park, I notice a Toyota Land Cruiser like the one I rented at the hotel at the end of a row of 10 cars. Maybe Simon can liberate this for our use later.

The question now running through the empty space between my ears is why are so many vehicles here? The reason rattles around for the next few minutes, like when you know something, but it will not identify itself. This is an island, after all. Then, it comes to me with a smack to the inside of the forehead.

The boat that passed us on the way to Mano had vehicles onboard. The workers must have their cars here to drive to the ferry and home when they finish work. From my time spent as a Health

& Safety Manager out in Oman, this is against the rules, not that the locals care about policies.

Around the back of the shops, a tarmac road separates businesses on either side. Like the open ground we witnessed earlier, the yards consist of a mixture of hard and soft sand. The only difference is that the yard on my left has several extensive workshop buildings and a vast array of vehicles, from massive articulated oil field trucks to bulldozers.

On my right-hand side is a less significant property consisting of a vehicle repair shop. Like the rest of the working spaces in the area, it's made up of corrugated metal sheets surrounding three sides, leaving the front open. A white portacabin is in the far left corner, probably an office of some sort. Lined up along the back fence are five white 4x4 SUVs.

Thinking about it, it might be better to liberate one of these vehicles rather than the Land Cruiser I saw earlier, especially if that gate is unlocked. Only one way to discover if it is or not. So signal for Lucy and George to close up on my position, then go to ground in the trench running down the right of the road.

Once we are all together and covering different arcs of view, I turn to George, "Go and inspect the gate, find out if it is locked. We may be able to borrow one of those vehicles later on a permanent basis."

After a quick check to see if anybody is around, George rises to his feet and slowly walks along the culvert before climbing up the bank to the two iron and mesh wire gates. I observe through the dim light as he runs his right hand down the gap in the centre from top to bottom, trying to find a securing chain. A minute later, he rejoins us in the ditch.

"It's not locked."

"Thanks, George. If you two are ready, let's make a move. According to the map, there should be a side street on our left that runs past a water collection point, not much further from here. From here, we can head cross-country to the jebel," I say, setting off.

We are about to cross the tarmac when I spot two lights breaking through the darkness down the far end of the road. Shit, someone is driving in our direction. Without saying a word, I dive back into the gully. My eyes are now fixed on the headlights approaching at a fast rate of knots towards our location. A glance to my rear confirms George and Lucy have also taken cover.

All different scenarios are now formulating in my head. Do we kill the person or persons if they detect us and then dispose of them in the desert, or do we simply restrain them? Or, with any luck, they will keep going. My fingers fidget nervously with my rifle just in case, ensuring I have a live round in the chamber. Just as it looks like I will have to make a snap decision, the vehicle turns left and stops on a small bridge crossing the culvert.

The shape of an SUV is now clearly visible in the dim light provided by the street lights spread about 150 metres apart. Moments later, a tiny glow of an electric bulb inside the vehicle bursts into life, followed by the noise of a creaking door being opened, which can be heard over the gentle rumbling of the engine in the stillness of the night.

Fuck, the driver must be getting out, so I press my body as flat as possible, pressing hard against the solid dirt bank to blend in. No point in checking the others — they will be doing the same.

With my head tilted to the right, scrutinise the man walking without a care in the world towards the fencing running along all the premises on this side of the roadway. Through the near silence comes a loud clanging sound of a heavy iron chain smashing into the criss-cross wire of the gates. This is followed a few seconds later by an even more audible scraping noise of metal on dirt as a gate is opened to its full extent.

After a long five minutes of us staying quiet and motionless in the ditch, the man reappears, locks the front gates and heads off, walking in the direction he came. Time is now getting on, and if we are to be in position at our FRV before daybreak, we better get moving. After scanning the area, I climb out from the location I've been lying in and head off down the tarmac road with Lucy and George spaced out behind me.

Several minutes later, we pass the water collection point with the dark shape of two supply hoses hanging mysteriously from a metal frame spanning the fence like elephants waiting to drink. Beyond the perimeter are four tall circular holding tanks illuminated by powerful spotlights. As the road bears left, we head out across the expanse of sand towards the jebels now becoming visible in the far distance.

At last, we reach the final physical obstacle before our trek to base camp, a significant dirt track. According to the map, this is the other major thoroughfare from the industrial area leading to the vast open desert. To be safe, I stop at the sandbank running along the edge and peer across to the other side, no more than 20 metres away. The opposite side is identical. Beyond that, the land slopes upwards into the mountains that overlook Duhfa.

The team has completed the next task more often than I can remember, so telling them what is about to happen is pointless. So after a final check to ensure no headlights are appearing in the distance, I spring to my feet and sprint as fast as my tired legs will take me across the dirt track. The ground underfoot is solid, so there is no need to worry about leaving a trail any idiot could follow.

Once across, I dive down into the sand, laying flat on my belly, looking in the direction of the main camp. The shape of Lucy is now visible as she races through the darkness to join me behind the bank, followed by George a minute later.

"Almost there folks, the RV is about 400 metres away." What I didn't say is the rest of the way is mainly uphill, but they more than likely already knew that.

"Wonder how Simon and Derek are getting on... hope they don't run into trouble or become lost," Lucy comments.

"Put it this way, if they are not at the FRV when we arrive, all we need to do is put a brew on – Simon can detect a fresh brew a mile away," George chuckles to himself.

"He wouldn't dare, being our recce troop. Plus, we will not let him hear the last of it if he does," I add before starting again off towards the top of the jebel.

Fortunately, I find an old dirt track that zig-zags as it makes its way through the grey sand-covered ground sloping up on both sides as it meanders through and up the mountain.

Soon we reach a narrow valley where the flanks are made of solid rock that shoots up vertically as high as the eyes can see in the darkness. Soft brown sand has been blown into the gap created by the sheer rockfaces, forming a steep slope stretching into the distance about 200 metres away.

Our RV is at the top on the other end, and this is our only way up from here. With the others close behind, I start the ascent one metre at a time. As I walk, each foot sinks a couple of centimetres into the sand, making the going hard. Halfway, I turn and look back to see Lucy not far behind, stopped and drinking from a water bottle. Behind her, George, with his head down, is closing in.

Not much further, I think to myself as I resume the climb to the top. Thirty gruelling minutes later, I crest the ridge onto a flat plateau backed by another sand-covered incline. On the leading edge is a rocky mound overlooking Duhfa. We have reached our FRV.

After dropping my Bergen under a small outcrop that protruded from the cliff, I arch my shoulders back and make circular movements to relieve the stress from carrying the heavy load. Shortly after, I'm joined by Lucy, and George, who'd caught up with her on the slope.

As I help her off with her own Bergen, "You OK, honey?"

"Yeah, that last climb was a fucking killer, though," she smiles.

Once George throws his bag down with the rest, we take up firing positions with George and his sniper rifle pointing towards Duhfa, while I cover back the way we just came. With only one other way here, a dirt trail off to the left of the location, Lucy covers this route. We stay like this for the next 20 minutes to confirm we are not followed.

A glance at Mickey confirms that we have made reasonable progress even with the delays, as the time is now 02:00. All we need now is Simon and Derek to come over the horizon, and the whole team is back together.

"While we wait for the other two idiots, fancy making a covert brew, George?" I ask, pulling back from my stand-to location.

"Sure, not a problem, could do with one myself."

While George digs a small fire pit underneath the overhang, I take out a two-metre square of light sandy-coloured canvas from my Bergen and attach two corners to the bottom edge of the outcrop. Make sure the other end touches the floor to block out the roaring flame of the gas burner.

While I do this, Lucy piles the bags around the open pit to stop my makeshift shelter from blowing into the flames, causing even more light as it catches fire. I walk to the cliff edge, turn around and glance back to ensure we are still in darkness.

****

Meanwhile, Simon and Derek on the other side of Duhfa have crossed the tarmac road and are now making their way across an expanse of flat sand-covered ground. A group of lights shine through the darkness at their two o'clock position.

"Take cover, something is heading our way," I shout as I jump to the deck and takes up a prone firing position facing the direction of the disturbance.

After leaping down into the loose sand on the floor, Derek crawls the 10 metres to join Simon behind a small sandbank, "What've you seen, mate?" enquires Derek in a quiet, barely audible voice.

"Spotted some movement at our one o'clock, halfway between our position and that clump of vegetation." To confirm the direction, I reach across my rifle with my left arm and point in the direction of the movement.

"Seen, and from what I can see in the available light, it's coming our way," says Derek, now trying to control his rapidly increasing breathing rate as excess blood starts to pump through his veins in anticipation of what's to come.

In the near distance, the ghostly figure continues to come closer as we both gradually raise our rifles into the firing position, ready to tackle anything that might come our way. Minutes pass, and my muscles become tense as they prepare to spring into action. Another agonising minute passes, followed by another. At last, the outline of the figure moving towards us becomes visible.

"What the fuck? We have a fucking camel, scaring the shit out of us," I say, snickering.

"At least it isn't a golden one," says Derek, also laughing to release pent-up tension.

"True. We better make a move if we are to meet the others at the FRV on time."

"OK, you're our recce troop, Simon, so guess who's leading the way, pathfinder," replies Derek, jumping to his feet.

Half an hour later, the route is blocked by a dirt road about 20 metres across with metre-high sandbanks running along both sides of the track. The same lights witnessed earlier are now glowing dimly to the immediate right in the distance. We may be in the absolute middle of nowhere, but this is not time to let standards slip, so our SOPs will come into play.

With my right hand on my head, I signal Derek to close up onto my position again. Once he is at the side of the road, without saying a word, I glance in both directions to make double sure no vehicle is approaching from either direction. Then spring to my feet and sprint across to the opposite side. Once I'm on the other side and covering towards the lights, I signal for Derek to join me. Across on the other side of the road, Derek leaps over the sandbank and darts across, joining me, lying flat against the compacted sand.

Time to take another bearing to ensure we are still heading the right way, so remove the SplashMaps Toob with the printed map from around my neck and lay it on the floor. Through the red lens of my torch, I shine a barely visible beam of light down onto the map, which is now being sheltered by Derek's hands.

"From my reckoning, we are here," placing a finger down on the cloth map.

Derek lifts his head and looks up at the jebel, "Take it we are now making our way uphill, Simon?"

"Afraid so, the FRV is here," indicating its position on the map.

Shift the heavy Bergen on my back before heading off, following the land's natural contours. After 25 minutes of trekking, our route becomes steeper the higher we find ourselves. Luckily we come across a well-trodden trail twisting backwards and forwards as it makes its way to the top through the vertical sand-covered slopes on either side.

Finally, the hilly ground starts to flatten out, forming a small plateau; time to recheck our course. As I crest the ridge, I narrowly miss standing in a massive pile of shit. Well, at least we now know what made this track: camels.

"Time for a breather, Derek, as unlike you fucking Green Jackets, I hate tabbing," allowing my pack to slip to the deck.

"Sounds good to me," throwing his Bergen to the floor.

After several mouthfuls of refreshing water, take the map out and line it up with the ground. "From what I can tell, we are here, from my reckoning... the final rendezvous point and the other idiots should be here. About one kilometre away."

"Roger that," responds Derek

Break over, sling my Bergen on my back, "OK, one more burst of energy, and we will be at the end of this little hike."

With that, we set off along another trail, skirting the ridgeline, but far enough away from the edge that we are not silhouetted in the night sky. Striking out, we follow the path for about 45 minutes until, eventually, the track drops down to a small plateau.

I turn around to face Derek, "Our FRV is about 100 metres away," I say in a quiet whisper.

We both knew this is the tricky bit. If the others are not here, it will not be an issue. All we would have to do is secure the location and wait for them to arrive. If they are here, we will need to approach with caution, as I don't fancy a bullet up the jacksy. So with the rifle at the ready, I continue down to the RV.

Close to the FRV, when a voice calls out from the darkness, "Stop, or I'll kill you."

Recognising the haunting tones of Steve coming out of the darkness, I reply, "A Donkey Walloper and some green numpty. And shouldn't that be 'who goes there?' you fucking idiot."

"Nope, I like my version better, Simon. Come in—George's got a fresh brew going."

****

Once in the FRV, Simon walks over to the cliff face, lifts the canvas sheet hanging from the rock, and sees Lucy and George sitting around a gas burner dug into the ground, drinking from mugs of freshly brewed coffee.

"I told you if I put a brew on, that he would sniff it out," says George, holding his hand out to grab the black mug now being held out by Simon.

"You know me too well, George."

Once everyone is comfortable sitting near the fire pit with a drink and Lucy is finished extinguishing the flame, I start to brief the team. "The time is now 02:20, and first light around here is at 07:00. However, nothing down in Duhfa will happen until at least 09:00, when the shops open and offices fill out. So there is no point in doing anything until the morning except getting our heads down for a few hours. As always, any questions or other ideas?" I suggest while sipping coffee from my mug.

"What about a sentry, Steve?" enquires Lucy.

"Of course, it is part of our SOPs. Suggest we post a lookout on the small bank over on the forward edge of the RV overlooking Duhfa. Instead of taking a stag, Simon, can you make sure you're awake by 06:00 and start a hot brew going. If you take the first one, George and then leave your sniper rifle in situ after your shift because it is the only long-range weapon we have."

"Not a problem, give me your mugs, and when you wake from your beauty sleep, and yes, some of you need it more than others, I'll ensure they're filled and ready for you when you open your little eyes," says Simon, already placing his stuff close to the pit.

While George sets up the sentry post, the rest of us grab some shut-eye.

Chapter Thirteen – Fact-Finding

For some reason, I ended up on the last stag duty of the night, and now find myself lying on the ground with the L96A1 sniper rifle resting on the floor in front of me, looking over Duhfa.

Over in the distance, evidence of life kicking into gear becomes visible, with several vehicle headlights busting through the early morning haze. It shouldn't be long before the place is humming with people heading for work.

A glance down at Mickey tells me it is 06:00; time to give Simon a rude awakening so that he can climb out of his maggot and get the morning brew on the go. All geared up to kick the shit out of his doss bag, but when I reach the sleeping bag, it is empty. Crap, the bastard has spoiled my fun.

Knowing Simon, if he isn't asleep, he will already have the water boiling, so I walk over to our makeshift shelter and pull the canvas back just enough to peer inside. To my surprise, Lucy is also awake and sitting with Simon around the gas burner, chatting quietly away.

"Morning, you two, you're up early. Didn't even detect either of you clamber out of your sleeping bags or starting the stove. You must have been as quiet as a desert rat."

"Either that, Steve, or you've been kipping on sentry, which is a killing offence... grab your rifle, Lucy, let's put the old dog down," proclaims Simon, supporting a massive stupid grin.

"Morning, Steve, don't panic—we were up before Derek woke you for your shift," comes the sweet female voice of Lucy, now handing me the first coffee of the day.

"That's a relief," I say, taking a seat next to them and blowing gently over the top of the drink in some sort of attempt to cool it down.

As first light is only minutes away, and most of us are awake and bushy-tailed, there is no point continuing with the sentry. We would detect anyone coming. Give it another 15 minutes before disturbing George and Derek from their beauty sleep. One bag at a time, I gently boot each green maggot in turn, to be greeted in unison, 'Fuck off!'

"That's not very friendly, gents. Simon's got your brews ready," I say, returning to the shelter.

A few minutes later, George lifts up the canvas sheet, "Morning all."

"Good morning, sleep well?" asks Lucy, handing him a black mug of sweet tea.

"Yeah, not too bad, thanks," comes the reply through the steam of his brew.

Not long before the whole team is sat cross-legged around the fire pit, engaged in idle chat and listening to the eerie silence of the desert. In fact, the only sound beside us is that of a gentle wind blowing grains of sand across the jebel.

With the big man upstairs turning the lights back on, it is time to organise the rendezvous point, which involves packing all our equipment away that won't be needed for today's recce and a fact-finding trip to Duhfa. This includes assault rifles. We would only take the 9mm pistols, as these are easy to conceal on our persons.

Once all our Bergens are packed and placed in plastic bags to stop sand from getting to places you didn't want it to be, George and I grab two shovels and extend the pit with sufficient room to place half the gear in. The last thing we want is some lucky bastard stumbling across our stash to find all our stuff in one place. So to be safe, Derek and Simon dig another hole at the far end of the RV and bury the remaining equipment.

Finally, everything is concealed out of view, and we are all standing at the ledge overlooking Duhfa. Time to discuss the plans for the day. "OK, this morning's activities will mainly depend on what happens when we arrive in Duhfa. Our first task will be to check out the row of shops George, Lucy and myself walked past yesterday on the way here.

"There are two restaurants in the line of buildings we saw yesterday; I suggest we grab some breakfast in any one that is open for brekkie. With any luck, it will be full of Indian workers, that might have information on where Joby is located and more info on the Golden Camel's operations on the island."

"Sounds like a good plan to me, Steve, especially the part about food," declares George, making small circular movements with his left hand on his stomach.

"For once, I'm with you on the food—I'm starving. What we do next is dependent on what we hear. If nobody has any questions, we will leave in five minutes," I continue.

"I have one—the two people we witnessed yesterday, the man at the truck and the one at the gate, were both wearing coveralls. If everyone is dressed identically, we will stick out like the accused at a hanging," states Lucy.

"If that's the case, we might have to relieve five people of their work attire, if we have no other option, of course."

"Let's hope it doesn't come to that, Derek. The place is full of businesses, and if the people down in Duhfa are like the ones I worked with, they will sell their grans for the right price. So we should be able to obtain what we need," I respond.

With me leading, we head down the jebel, following the same route we came yesterday until we reach the edge of Duhfa. From here, we walk in a group, as being in a single line would appear out of the ordinary.

The water point we passed on our way to the RV yesterday is a swarm of activity with two blue tankers parked beneath the filling points. On top, two men dressed in light blue coveralls are feeding the long hose through open hatches. After some shouting backwards and forwards to the man on the ground in a language I recognise as being Hindi, moments later, the sound of gushing water hitting the metal of an empty tanker could be heard.

As we stroll down the tarmac road towards the shops, we are passed by three huge articulated trucks carrying an assortment of oil rig equipment, some overhanging the sides of the trailer by at least three metres. Guess the Vehicles (Construction and Use) Regulations don't apply on island roads. Mind you, in the deserts of Oman, they didn't either.

The small vehicle repair shop near where we watched the man drive into last night is occupied, with both gates flung open and secured with a metal chain, and more importantly, the parked cars are still along the back edge.

"You might need to borrow one of their vehicles later, Simon, being the transport guy," I say, moving close to him.

It would appear Lucy is right about everyone wearing coveralls and us sticking out like a blind referee at a football match. "Appears we will need a change of clothing," I say, stopping short of the row of buildings.

Behind the rundown exterior of the establishments is a small collection of broken portacabins. Plus, a couple of breeze block structures no more than two by two metres and two-half metres high. Swinging open an old battered wooden door, I peer inside.

A tattered old porcelain tray lay flat on the concrete floor towards the back. A hole is located at the back with two foot-shaped imprints on either side. To the left of this is a bucket of water along with a plastic jug that's seen far better days. Plus, the stench is making my eyes water. Appears I just walked into an Arabic-style toilet.

Inside the portacabin, several interior walls have extensive gaping holes where someone deliberately put the boot in. All the windows, apart from one at the end are missing. With any luck, this should conceal the rest of the team from view as myself and George try to locate a store to acquire five sets of coveralls.

The floor is covered in rubbish and broken furniture. Worse of all is the overwhelming smell of ammonia, where people have used it as a urinal. But still a better stink than the actual bogs. But it will have to do for getting changed.

"You three wait here while George and I go and find out if we can find a shop that sells coveralls around the front. If you have to bug out, the RV is the dirt road running along the far side of Duhfa. But you shouldn't need to because we won't be too long."

Now that daylight has broken, my assumptions about the two intensely lit premises I witnessed last night are indeed two restaurants, while in the centre is a hydraulic pipe repair facility. Next door to that, from what I can detect through the expansive windows, is an outlet selling foodstuff. On the right of the row is a general store. This should be the place where I will find what we are after.

After walking up a set of grey stone steps which lead straight inside, on our left, as we enter, is a dark-coloured wooden cabinet about a metre high with a glass top full of mobile phones and other electronic equipment extending to the store's back.

To our immediate right, several rows of metal shelving sticking out about a foot from the wall, stacked with work boots of different sizes. The middle of the room is occupied by racks of civilian clothing that only Indians would find appealing.

On the first appearance, the storekeeper does his best to keep the desert out, indicated by two heaped mounds of sand near a stiff brush leaning against the wooden counter. An occupational hazard from the look of it, due to the front door being held open by a wedge of wood, probably to let fresh air in to mask the musty odour from stuff that's been here far too long.

At first, we can't locate what we are looking for, so I approach our Indian friend, who hasn't taken his eyes off us since we arrived. "Morning, do you sell overalls?" I ask in a polite tone of voice.

"Yes, sir, let me show you where I keep them," he announces, walking along the back of the counter and exiting through the gap at the far end.

He leads us to the back left corner of the store, where even more shelving lines the wall. On the top three shelves are piles of light brown coveralls. On the middle rows are several pots and pans and other cooking equipment. Three thick multicoloured blankets are sealed in clear plastic on the bottom row. Might need some of these, so put two aside.

Turn to George, "Remember, mate, these are sized for the Indians, and their 3X means something completely different than what you think. Suggest you try one on. You're probably a 4X."

Flick through the piles until I come to a size I think will fit with plenty of movement. "Can I see if this one fits me?" holding a pair above my head.

"No problem, dear," comes the response from our store-keeping friend.

Yep, that should do. Find a pair with long legs for the lanky git, Simon. I guess Derek and I would be the same size, with Lucy taking smaller coveralls.

Once we have what we came in for and paid the man a total of 50 OMR, we leave and head back to where the rest should be waiting.

Due to the fact I hate having a 9mm held against my head, when I reach the battered old cabin, I shout, "Hi, honey, I'm home."

"About time — I'm starving. My stomach thinks my throat's been slit," comes the reply from inside, from Derek.

Back in the portacabin, I toss everyone the respective coveralls and start to get undressed. It gets hot around here, so advisable not to wear clothing underneath apart from a t-shirt that helps absorb the sweat. Everybody is following suit when Simon glances up at Lucy, "You don't have to get changed in front of these hairy-arsed apes. There is a separate room at the other end," he points to the rear of the cabin.

"Not a problem, Simon. Plus, I would need exceptional eyesight to glimpse what you're packing," comes the response with a smile as she continues to strip off.

Turn my head to face George and Derek, laughing uncontrollably and flexing their little fingers in Simon's direction. After getting changed, I stuff my old clothes into my daysack and wait for the other four to get dressed.

"Time for breakfast, people," I say, after we have all finished sorting ourselves out.

The place reminded me of the one we used in Ruwi, with a few tables and chairs outside. As you enter, a cold drinks machine is against the wall. Beyond that, three more tables, each covered with a red and white chequered PVC table cloth. On top is a brown plastic water jug with a hot spice reddish sauce bottle.

Over to the right are two rows of three tables identical to the others, one occupied by a group of Indian workers, all tucking into a mixture of dhal, eggs and lentil dosas. Two white-faced men dressed in dark blue coveralls made them stand out from everyone else in the room. Both are drinking and eating what appears like filled pancakes, sitting at one table in the back.

Partially to listen to what the two westerners are talking about and the fact it's the largest of the tables, we sit at the table tucked away in the corner. Have not been waiting long when a skinny, scruffy-looking man wearing jeans and a striped t-shirt appears with a notepad and a fresh jug of water, which he places in the middle of us. "What can I fetch you, my dears?"

"Morning, can I have two parathas filled with egg and salad, please?" I enquire, putting down the menu.

The rest stare puzzled as they scan the colourful menu, "Have what I've ordered... trust me, they are tasty," turning to each of them, I'm greeted with four nodding heads.

Turning back to the waiter, to make sure he understands, I point at the spot in front of each person and state, "Two." He walks off towards the kitchen with a shake of his head that only Indians can do justice.

While we wait, mainly because most of the Indian men have probably only seen one or two white women in the last couple of years, due to them having to work every day for two years before they get a day off, unlike the locals who only work two weeks before getting two more weeks off, all their eyes are on Lucy. Not that it bothered her, she knew she would be able to use this knowledge to her advantage.

Out of the corner of my eye, I witness the two English men to my left crunching up pieces of paper and placing them on top of empty white plates. Sensing they are about to leave, I strike up a conversation.

"Morning, gents, I can't help but detect you're dressed differently from the rest of the people we've seen around here."

"Yeah, morning. From that, I would guess you're new in town," comes the reply from the man closest to me.

"You're right. We only arrived this morning. Over here for a meeting with ACM Drilling. Do you know where their office is?" I partly lied, as this is a company name given to us by Nasir as a likely place where Joby could be forced to carry out work.

"Sure do. If you leave here, take a right and cut through the car park until you reach the road, then follow this down for about 300 metres, you will find their yard on the right. The company is run by a man called Noor."

"Thank you, I'm Steve," hoping to obtain the response I want.

"I'm Joe, and this is Khalid. We work for Grover Sim and organise all the rig moves on the island. If you are around later, we can meet up at the boozer in the first motel you come to at around 19:00," standing up from the table.

"That would be great—see you in the bar tonight," I answer, after taking a sip of lukewarm coffee.

The scruffy waiter arrives, carrying a tray with our brekkie as the men in blue exit the restaurant. Wait until all the plates are down in front of us all, then thank him in my best Arabic, "Shukran."

The parathas taste as good as I remember them, I think to myself as I scoff down the second one. Then take a swig of coffee before grabbing everyone's attention. "Thanks to those two men, we now have something to go on."

"This is our first break in the mission, how do want to play it?" asks Lucy, after wiping her face with a paper serviette.

"Not sure, but give me five minutes to develop some sort of plan," I reply.

A couple of minutes of silence pass before Simon speaks, "While your brain slowly kicks into gear and you sit with a face like a chewed toffee, how's this for a plan? While you, Lucy and George visit our friends at ACM Drilling, Derek and I can try to hire some transport and then find a route up to the RV."

"Perfect, Simon. Plus, see if you can bribe someone into letting us borrow a vehicle for a few days. Two hundred OMR should do the trick, as for some of these poor fuckers that is more than a month's wages."

With breakfast finished and armed with information from Joe, we head for the workshop, where we catch sight of the vehicles parked last night. Leaving Simon and Derek to obtain our transport, the rest of us continue down the road.

The expansive yard is more significant than expected and stretches several hundred metres to the rear. A wire mesh fence runs along the front, only interrupted by two fully open gates to allow vehicles access. Off to our left as we enter is a group of containers, with truck parts laying on pallets on the ground outside. Beyond that is a tall corrugated workshop capable of taking three trucks.

An articulated lorry is being hosed down at the rear of the yard with a powerful jet wash by a man wearing a bright yellow jacket. Elsewhere more people are either on top of or underneath other vehicles. Over on our right is a collection of wooden buildings joined together to make one bigger one. To the left of that is another mixture of smaller portacabins. From what I can tell, the larger facility is more than likely where the local office of ACM Drilling is located.

No point in us all going in asking questions. Besides, if Joby is being forced to work here, they could have links with the Golden Camel. Then we could be walking into a nightmare where we may have to shoot our way out. With that in mind, George hangs around on the other side of the road close to another yard entrance, while Lucy and I head inside.

Before entering, I check that my 9mm is still in place and I can reach it quickly through the coveralls if the situation dictates. Glance over my shoulder to my right—Lucy is doing the same. Through the doors, people are sat at individual desks sectioned off by one and a half metre high dark brown wooden barriers. A room with glass windows on three sides is on our immediate left. Inside, an older man sits at his desk typing away on a computer keyboard.

A firm male voice comes from my right, "As-salamu alaykum, can I be of assistance?" I turn to face the direction of the noise. A young man sits at a small table behind a reception-looking counter. Behind him on the back wall is a Pakistan flag and an assortment of award plaques.

"Wa alaikum salaam, is it possible to speak to Noor?" I respond.

"One minute, I will find out if he is free," comes the reply from the Pakistani man.

A couple of minutes later, he returns from speaking with the man in the independent office behind us, "If you follow me, Noor can spare some time to talk to you."

You can tell this person is the boss; when you enter a black leather sofa is against the wall under one of the windows. In the centre of the room is a coffee table with a collection of rig moving magazines scattered haphazardly across the top. An ornate flask sits on a silver tray next to a bowl of dates and takes up room at the table's edge.

After standing up from behind his workstation, which is customary when someone enters your office in this part of the world, and telling the receptionist to bring fresh coffee, "As-salamu alaykum, how can I help you, my friend?"

"Wa alaikum salaam, my name is Steve, and the young lady is Lucy," I reply after shaking the man's hand.

He indicates that we take a seat on the couch while he sits in a black armchair. After sitting down, "Thank you for seeing us today. The reason for the visit is we are here on business, and a dear friend of mine who goes by the name of Joby works here in Duhfa. We would like to meet up with him, and someone told us he is employed by you."

"Not familiar with the name, but if you wait here, I will go and check for you." With that, Noor stands up and heads for the reception area. A short conversation follows between the two that is barely audible through the glass from our position on the sofa.

Being a nosy bastard, I continue to watch the other man as Noor disappears from sight before re-entering the room a couple of minutes later. The man behind the desk picks up a telephone, puts the receiver to his right ear, and starts talking to the person on the other end.

"Sorry, the man you are looking for, Joby, doesn't work for us, but my assistant, James knows him. He says he is working out on one of the hoists. He thinks it is Hoist 49. Give me a few seconds, and I can tell you where that is at present," Noor goes back to his computer screen and types something into the keyboard.

While his back is turned, Lucy grabs a sheet of paper from the table and slips it into her top pocket.

"Here it is, on the other side of the island," Noor stands up and places his finger on a wall map.

"Thank you so much for your hospitality, Noor. You have been very accommodating."

With that, we say our goodbyes and head back out of the building and head to meet up with George, still pacing up and down across the road.

"So, how did it go? Did you find any information that could be useful?" yells George, walking towards us.

"We've been giving a lead on where Joby might be," I say.

While we are talking, Lucy produces the bit of crumpled paper she took from Noor's desk and unfolds it for us all to see. "Took this because it looked like the same message about movements I caught a glance of in the Golden Camel's office in Muscat. Look at the name on the top. Isn't John Nair the man you said runs the organisation?"

"Fuck me, you're right. Mabe will be able to take him out as well," I reply, confused why a person such as him would come to a small island and not send his thugs.

****

Meanwhile, over at the vehicle workshop, Derek and Simon have entered the yard and are strolling over in the direction of what looks like the office. The identical vehicles they noticed earlier are still lined up along the fence. The bonnet of one is open with the shape of a person reaching inside with the rhythmic sound of metal striking metal echoing in the otherwise quiet workshop.

As they approach, the portacabin door swings open, revealing a middle-aged Indian man exiting the building wearing black trousers and a blue and white shirt. This must be the man in charge and the person we need to bribe, I think to myself as we walk over to meet the man halfway.

Before either of us can say anything, the man opens the conversation, "How can I help you two gentlemen?"

"Morning, my name is Simon. Are you the man we need to talk to regarding borrowing or hiring one of those?" pointing to where the man is still working.

"Yes, I'm the workshop manager. We don't rent vehicles from here. Why do you want one?" says the man in a questioning voice.

"We are new in Duhfa and need one to drive around in for the week. Shame you don't have any, so I might as well take my money and go somewhere else," holding 200 in 20 Rial notes in my hand in full sight of the now wide-eyed man.

As he rubs his palms together, "We might have one you can borrow off the record. How much are you willing to pay?"

Following Steve's advice earlier, these people love to barter, "Tell you what, I'll give you one hundred OMR, no questions asked," still holding out the wad of banknotes.

"No, that's not enough. Three hundred."

"My last offer, 200 and a tank of fuel."

"OK, done, but this is only for five days," the man holds out his hand to shake on the deal and take the money.

After taking the cash, the man walks over to his colleague, taps him on the shoulder and says something in Hindi. Moments later, he returns and says, "You can take that one once Vikas changes the battery."

"Thank you," Derek replies.

The last thing we needed is the damn vehicle to break down in the desert, plus being the team's transport guy—if it did, the others would take the proverbial piss for years to come. So while Derek engaged Vikas in conversation, simultaneously ensuring the mechanic didn't do anything untoward under the bonnet, I give the vehicle a thorough once over.

Nothing seemed to be out of the ordinary with the transport, so turn to Derek, "Jump in, mate, we need to find a route to the RV. I, for one, don't fancy fucking walking back up that hill we came down earlier."

The tarmac vanishes once out of Duhfa, turning into a hard-packed sandy track before hitting the major highway we crossed this morning. With the sand-covered jebel directly in front with no direct route up, I spin the wheel hard over and make a left turn before following the dusty track to a T-junction at the end about one kilometre away.

After a couple of twists and turns, the trail heads downhill. As we come around a corner, on the immediate right is another track leading off, contouring the bottom of the jebel. All we have to do now is keep the hills and the base camp on our right.

"Take that one as it seems to go in the direction we want," Derek shouts, pointing to his right.

"Why not? It appears to be going our way."

The new route meanders through the open flat desert sands as it weaves back and forth along its way into the distance. While dealing with the bouncing vehicle as it hit several dips in the uneven ground, Derek cries out over the racket of the engine and the deafening noise as the car strikes the deck hard, "Look over at our eleven o'clock. There's another vehicle coming."

In the far distance, a massive cloud of sand roughly 100 metres wide and 30 metres high trails behind the now visible truck heading in our direction. As it gets closer, and not wanting to play a game of chicken, we take the road off to the right on a sharp bend. In front is a sheer sandy rock face stretching straight up as far as the vision from the vehicle would allow. After five minutes of following this track, it finally leads uphill.

"You want something to laugh at," turning my head slightly to glance at Derek in the passenger seat.

"Go on then, Simon, what's funny?" replies Derek with a puzzled look.

"Look at the gap in the cliff. Near the bottom, the other idiots are about to start scrambling up the sand dune."

"If you head their way, you might be able to catch them before they reach a point too far for us to call them back."

"I could, but I don't feel like it. Besides, the exercise will do them good."

Eventually, the track levelled out on top of the jebel close to the FRV. After driving off-road for about 100 metres, we soon find a natural hollow in the ground to conceal the vehicle.

"That will do, as the only living creature likely to be up here, besides us, are camels. So no point in too much concealment—the dip should suffice."

"Sounds like some sort of a plan to me, mate, plus it gives you time to get the boys' and girl's brews going before the rest join us," replies Derek, heading for the spot where we spent the night, but stopping short.

Even though we might be the only ones here, we're too professional just to amble into the rendezvous point without first standing off and monitoring the location. Once the area appears secure, Derek retrieves all the Bergens from the hiding spots while I start on the brew and my famous Army Chuck-in while we wait for the other to return.

****

Meanwhile, on the steep climb up to the RV, George, Lucy and I are reaching the top; I stop just below the ridgeline, waiting for the others to catch up. Once everyone is together, I slowly move towards the ridgeline, ready to peer over to confirm the location hasn't been compromised. But stop short as the faint sound of people talking can be heard from the direction of the RV. After laying motionless in the soft sand and listening for a few minutes, I creep forward one inch at a time until my eyes are at a point I can peer over the edge. Turning to the others, I place the index finger of my right hand against my lips, indicating to keep quiet.

About 100 metres away, I detect the shape of a body moving around digging up our Bergens, so I slide my rifle into the firing position, keeping it near the ground. By this time, I've been joined by George.

"Over there, can you see him?" I point with my left arm.

"Sure can, you fucking idiot... it is Derek. That stupid laugh is Simon — I would recognise his voice anywhere."

With that, I signal Lucy to join us and make our way to Derek and Simon, who sit close to a pot of boiling water.

"You getting any better at that climb?" says Simon, pouring out several mugs of steaming water.

"Nope, still a killer. Take it you got us a vehicle and found a way up here?" I reply, adding coffee to my black mug.

"Yeah, it wasn't a problem. Didn't you notice us drive past below you before you started your climb?" answers Simon.

"Thanks for the fucking lift then, boys," says George, grabbing his own brew.

"Was going to, but Derek said you could do with the exercise, you fat bastard," Simon grins once more, laughing out loud.

"You lying piece of shit," says Derek proclaiming his innocence.

Chapter Fourteen – Interrogation

Time is passing by quickly, and if we are to gather more intelligence before extracting Joby from the hoist, we need to take Joe up on the offer of drinks in the motel bar. As we have never been there and didn't know if coveralls or civvie clothing are in order, it's decided to go with the latter.

I've just finished re-packing my Bergen when Simon shouted from behind our makeshift shelter. "Grub's up, folks, and like your mother always told you, you can't go drinking on an empty stomach."

Hold out my mess tin while Simon scoops a dollop of cooked stew from the pot and dumps it inside. After taking a mouthful, "Tastes good, mate, thanks."

"You're welcome," comes the reply, as he shares the rest between the team.

While we are sitting around in a tight group eating and drinking a fresh brew Simon also made, Lucy glances up and declares, "My first time with your famous Army Chuck-in — tastes not too bad."

"Thanks, you're most welcome, unlike them three ugly bastards," replies Simon, packing away the cooking equipment.

Once everyone is ready, with the kit packed in the back of the Land Cruiser, George, Lucy, and Derek clamber onto the rear seat with me in the front. Simon turns the key, and the engine bursts into life. With his right foot easing down on the accelerator pedal so as not to spin the drive wheels in the soft sand, he eases the vehicle from the dip in the ground.

As he moves off, George in the back cries out, "To the bar, please driver, and make it snappy."

"Of course, sir, shall I wait outside for you to become pissed or can I take the night off?" comes the sarcastic response from Simon.

Down in Duhfa, a two metre-high wire mesh fence similar to the one at the rear runs along the entire length of the front of the motel, complete with several man-sized holes near the row of shops and restaurants. Guess people didn't want to walk around to the front entrance, which consists of a sentry box sitting in the centre of the road.

After turning right off the street, Simon stops at the gatehouse. Inside, the interior is in darkness, with nobody in sight. The red and white barrier is up and embedded in the bush to the left of the entry point, so we continue to the right to locate a parking space.

The workers' motel is busy, and the car park is packed with works vehicles of different makes and models. Eventually, we find an empty spot in the corner, close to a sandy-cloured square building with an enormous red cross on the wall. Parked under a plastic and wooden lean-to is an ambulance. That's good to know if any of us require any medical treatment after or during our rescue attempt.

With no idea where the motel drinking establishment is situated, stop the first person I find, "Evening, sir, can you tell us how to find the bar?"

The man I just asked points to another substantial sandy-coloured building about 50 metres away, "Follow this footpath, and it will take you straight there."

"Thank you," I say before walking with the team down the winding path to the entrance. Outside the two glass doors, a man, a local from the look of him, is checking the IDs of the Indian men before letting them inside.

We don't have any IDs to prove we work here, so thinking on my feet, I turn to Lucy, "Time you use those stunning looks of yours and smile at the bouncer on the door."

"No problem," as she walks past me to take the lead.

Once we are close, Lucy breaks out a vast, beautiful grin that would melt any man, followed by "good evening", and the man opens the door for her and lets her in. Wasting no time in seizing the moment, the rest of us quickly follow her inside. Beyond the door is a corridor with a set of double heavy brown doors on our right, just as they are swung open to reveal the drinking establishment.

The interior is the same as I remember from my time working in the oilfields of Oman. Several tables with a soft multi-coloured fabric bench running along the wall to our front. Off to the right as we enter, a long dark brown-wooded bar complete with barstools occupied by a combination of locals dressed in white dishdashas and white-faced westerners.

As the sitting area turns right, a cluster of men are playing pool at the far end. Another small group of Indians take residence at the tables in front of the only bar and drink from small glasses containing some dark mixture.

While the others sit at a table close to the people we are about to tap for information, I head towards the man busy serving drinks from behind the counter to fetch our own refreshments. When I notice Joe and Khalid sitting at the end closest to the door, I head over to say hello.

"Evening, gentlemen, can I buy you a drink?" I say, standing in the gap between them.

"Hi, Steve, see you found the place OK. I'll have a Stella," comes the response from Joe.

"Yeah, it wasn't too hard to find, but I didn't think the man on the door was going to let us in as we don't have passes."

"That wouldn't have been a problem—you're wearing your pass, a white face," Khalid points to my face.

Stand with them for the following 15 minutes, letting the conversation and several drinks flow while listening to the background conversations, trying to detect a whisper of the words Golden Camel.

When I return to join Lucy and Simon, "Where are the other two idiots?"

"Over there playing pool with a group of people, and by the sounds of it getting on well," Lucy states, pointing towards Derek, leaning over the green fabric-covered table with the cue in both hands, ready to take his shot.

Out of the corner of her eye, she sees a young man sitting close to her counting out money under the rectangle table in an attempt to hide it from view. She grabs the opportunity and moves closer to him, "What's the matter? Can't afford another drink?" The man shakes his head.

"How about I buy you and your friends the next round?" says Lucy in a quiet, friendly voice through a huge smile.

Not believing his luck that a pretty white woman is talking to him, he replies instantly, "Yes, please. Everyone is drinking rum and Coke."

After using her charm at the wooden bar, she soon returns, joins the men at the table, and starts a conversation. As I stand up to leave and find out what is around the far side, I overhear Lucy say, "How come you're short of money? Are the wages that bad here?"

As I pass the pool table, I witness Derek miss-potting a striped ball. From experience, I knew that Derek is, in fact, a fantastic player, so he must be losing on purpose to gain their trust. A scan of the room finds George standing at a tall circular table, chatting away with four people.

A grin of confidence spreads across my face as I chuckle silently to myself — the team are working well tonight. Time for me to get in on the action when I spot a group of men playing darts at the end of the room.

Once more, I let the conversation flow as I purchase round after round for deliberately losing each game. It may be costing money, but every minute the info we require for the mission escapes from the unwitting mouths of my fellow players.

A glance down at Mickey tells me the time is now 23:00 and time for us to move back up to our base camp and consolidate all the information gathered tonight, ready for any required action in the morning.

The instance Simon crosses the dirt highway, he turns off the vehicle's headlights. Then using all his experience as a Recce Troop Commander, he finds his way along the twisting sandy tracks up the jebel to reach the dip in the ground where we left from earlier in the evening.

The moment the Land Cruiser comes to a halt, everyone jumps out and dives to the deck, each of us facing a different direction and waiting in the silence of the night, listening for any unwanted sounds.

Stay this way for the next 10 minutes until I'm sure nobody followed us or are preparing to attack once we enter our camp. Everyone meets under the overhang after the equipment has been removed from the rear storage area of the vehicle.

Take out my notepad to make any notes on this evening's events, "I'll start. From my conversations, I found out that the Indians have a short two-week window after getting paid to cough up the money to the Golden Camel representative. They wouldn't tell me where, due to being scared of reprisals. What did you two world champion pool players uncover?"

"Same as you. These people are terrified of what will happen to their families if they say too much and the wrong person overhears them. Apparently, they have spies among the workforce who relay info on anyone who talks in exchange for money off their next payments," says Derek, with a confirming nod from George.

"What did you manage to find out from the young man who thought his luck was in, Lucy?" I ask, turning to face her.

"Again, the identical type of stuff as you lot. However, I did find out where this money is paid. It's a small building at the front of the motel — we passed it earlier. Plus, the men from the organisation will be there by 07:00 tomorrow morning," comes the reply from Lucy.

"Excellent work, team... from the sounds of it, we need to snatch one of these men in the morning, and our trained interrogator, Lucy, can ask him a few questions. So while I try to sort out some type of agenda, can you four work out the stag roster?"

The rest of the night went without a hitch. So the following morning, over a hot brew, I gather everyone together and outline the plan for this morning's abduction of our local Golden Camel member. "Once everybody is packed and the equipment loaded, we'll head for the buildings outside the motel and take up positions surrounding the place. With the information gathered last night, he should arrive any time before 07:00, which means we need to be ready by 06:00 at the latest."

"Any idea on how we recognise the individual is our man? Would hate to kick the shit out of the wrong person," says George, packing his Bergen.

"From what I obtained, he is the only one who works there that will be wearing a grey suit and turning up at that time. The rest do not start until 09:00," I reply.

"You want me to stay in the vehicle, ready for a fast exit?" Simon suggests before heading for the Land Cruiser to give it the once over.

"Good idea. If Derek takes the left of the building, looking at it from the street, and George goes into the grounds to cover any escape to the rear, Lucy and I will hang about at the front in case he arrives from this direction. Remember not to do anything until he enters the office."

"Take it the emergency RV... if everything doesn't go to plan, is back here," Derek enquires.

"Yes, mate," I reply.

Once everyone is seated inside the Land Cruiser, Simon accelerates away from the location, again with the lights switched off so as not to attract attention as we skirt along the ridgeline.

Down in Duhfa, the place is still in the grips of darkness, with the only light coming from the streetlights lining the street. As the time is merely 05:30, only a handful of people are about walking at varying speeds up and down the central road in some vain attempt to carry out their morning exercise before work.

A couple of minutes later, Simon pulls into a small dusty parking area to the right of the money collection office building, surrounded by a metal barrier painted yellow and black about half a metre from the ground. By the looks of it, in the morning light, it's just big enough to accommodate four vehicles.

With the engine turned off, we sit and listen in silence and glance around the surrounding area for movements out of the ordinary. I signal everyone to take their assigned positions to ensure we are all in place and ready.

Forty-five minutes later, a white Jeep enters the car park and parks close to our vehicle right on time. Simon must have seen him coming in his rearview mirror as he is not in sight when I glance over, as I want to see which way the target person will enter the premises.

A few minutes pass before he alights from his vehicle. Without knowing what is about to happen to him and the fact that this might well be his last day on this earth, he heads in my direction.

Positive George will have spotted him, so grab Lucy's hand to give the impression that we are a young couple taking advantage of the moonlight and cover of darkness for a private liaison while strolling towards the tarmac road.

Once there, attract Derek's attention to ensure he is aware our man has turned up. At the edge of the road, I grasp both of Lucy's hands and manoeuvre into a position where I can see the man entering the building through the front glass door that swings inwards as he pushes it with his right hand.

As I continue to watch, the man makes the worst mistake of his short life by not relocking the door once he is inside. With the man probably feeling protected and secure in his office, this is our time to ruin his day. By this time, Derek has joined us, "You ready?"

They both nod in agreement. There are times when you would enter stealthily, but this isn't one of them. So when I signal to the others to make a move, we all storm the door and rush inside.

A wooden counter painted white about one and a half metres high runs the length of the back wall. Behind that is a row of wood shelving filled with black files stretching from one end of the room to the other.

Off to the right is a smaller separate cordoned off room you enter via a solid brown door behind the counter, while the front is made of thick glass with a silver serving hatch at the bottom, similar to the ones you see in a post office. Hanging from the ceiling on a single white cord is a single lightbulb. More importantly, our man is nowhere to be seen.

Frantically I scan the room. In the left corner, close to the rear exit, is a small boxed off area with a slightly ajar door. The fucker must be in there. As I race over, Derek leaps over the counter while Lucy blocks the front entry point in case he tries to escape that way.

Moments later, a scared-looking man emerges from the office, fearing for his life, rushes towards the back door, slides open two large sliding bolts that secure the door, pushes it open and starts to run for it. He only makes it a few feet before being hit by an unmovable force, George, who knocks him down onto the blue painted wooden floor just inside the doorway. On hearing the commotion, George had clambered through a hole in the fence and had raced to join us.

The man is now starting to get to his feet and throwing punches in all directions to break free from the current vice-like grip I had around his neck.

Eventually, we gain control and have him on the deck, and Lucy is sitting on him, preventing his legs from kicking out; we manage to turn him onto his stomach. One arm at a time, George twists his arms into positions that don't come naturally to a body and forces them behind his back. Now that the other two are holding him firmly to the wooden deck, I pull out several thick cable ties and bind his hands at the wrists. While I'm doing this, Lucy places a wet hessian sack over the man's head.

Now on his feet, I whisper into his right ear, "Listen very carefully... if you do as I say, you might come through today unharmed... If you don't, you will feel more discomfort than you could imagine."

To make sure he gets the message, he receives an assertive punch to the area of his kidneys from Derek. He cries out in pain and tries to double over due to the excruciating agony shooting through the lower part of his torso.

Outside, with George and Derek pulling up on his bound arms and me pushing his head down, make our way to the Land Cruiser while Lucy keeps an eye out for any would-be heroes.

When we arrive, Simon is standing, holding the back door wide open, ready to launch the man in the rear footwell where we can keep control.

Before we leave the building, there is one more surprise I need to put in place for our friends at the Golden Camel. Reach into my Bergen and pull out the light bulb I rigged earlier to explode wrapped in several layers of cloth out of a plastic container to stop it from breaking.

"I know what that is... but where are you going to put it?" asks Simon.

"In the money intake room, when some numpty enters and switches on the light, boom. Then the next thing the person will be doing is taking harp lessons," I reply, grinning.

"And you know they will not be innocent people, how?" comes the response from Simon.

"Do you really think the Golden Camel will allow anyone not part of their organisation to handle the money?"

"Good point, Steve, well made."

Once everyone is back in the vehicle, and with our new friend occupying the limited floor space behind the front seats with three sets of boots keep him securely in place, we drive to the unassuming building, half-hidden between the tall brown bullrushes blowing gently in the breeze, surrounding the pond on three sides. The same one we first encountered when we crested the ridgeline after the climb from the beach.

Close to the spot where Lucy will carry out the interrogation and with the light starting to break over the horizon, Simon brings the vehicle to a halt. "OK, time for you three GRUNTS to go and recce the joint and ensure nobody else is about," says Simon, clambering out and making his way to the back to take George's place, stamping on the groaning, disorientated body stretched out on the floor.

Don't expect to see anyone around here this early in the morning, but better be safe. While Derek and I go one way around, past the clumps of green and brown reeds that line the water's edge, making our way to the pump house, George takes the longer route to the building, following the opposite bank.

With one ear close to the orange painted half-rotten wooden door, I stand listening for any sound coming from within while waiting until we are all in situ. There aren't any. So far, on the mission on Duhfa, we haven't needed to draw our weapons, but now we have taken one of the Golden Camel's people. This situation has drastically changed. With that in mind, I remove my 9mm with my right hand while placing my left on the door handle in the exact instance.

About to fling the door open when the noise of a motor bursting into life comes from inside. After confirming the other two are ready, I throw open the battered door. George races in, followed by me, with Derek bringing up the rear. We don't have any more time to waste as someone will undoubtedly come looking for their missing colleague. Immediately scan the interior for any unlucky person who has unwittingly stumbled into an awful day for them. The place is clear.

While Derek and George go and help the others to fetch the representative of the Golden Camel from the vehicle, I search the room to find the switch, which I locate close to the door.

Now the room is illuminated by a single light fixed to the wall near the entrance. A huge water pump on the grey concrete floor with big rusty iron pipes leading through the structure to the exterior becomes visible in the dim glow of the artificial light.

Another substantial metal tube reaches for the roof before crossing the room and back down the other side prior to it disappearing outside. Over on the back wall, someone has fixed a few rusty old spanners, a coil of nylon cord, along with a stiff bristle brush.

As I remove the length of rope from its hook behind me, I detect the unmistakable sound of feet being scraped across the floor. Turn to see the man from the Golden Camel, still wearing the bag covering his head, being dragged through the door by George and Derek, with Lucy and Simon close behind.

The team doesn't say a word in order to disorientate, confuse, and hopefully fill him with total anguish of what might happen to him. Without removing the thick black cable ties, his whole body is pushed through the gap between his two arms, still keeping his wrists tightly bound, resulting in deafening screams of agonising pain echoing throughout the tiny space of the empty pumphouse.

With his hands bound at the front, I attach one end of the rope around his wrists. Throw the other over the pipe running along the top of the building. While Derek and George lift the struggling person from the ground, Simon and I pull down on the cord until our new friend is balancing on the balls of his feet, arms just short of the ceiling. While we are doing this, Lucy throws a bucket of freezing water from the pond over the man's head.

Still, without saying a word, we all exit the pumphouse, turning the light off, leaving the man alone in the darkness with nothing but his thoughts to keep him company.

Back over at the Land Cruiser, "Fancy making a brew, Simon? I'm parched." I make a cup symbol with my right hand, putting it to my lips several times.

"Who do you think I am, some sort of brewmaster?" comes the reply from Simon.

"OK, you two kids, leave it to me. I'll make the brews," says Lucy opening the vehicle's back door.

Thirty minutes later, with the drinks finished, we head back inside to start our interrogation or, more to the point, see the expert, Lucy, at work.

My eyes are drawn to the person hanging down from the ceiling, as he starts to twitch as he can hear us moving around, still not communicating among ourselves or with him. We leave the situation like this until he finds the courage to blurt out, "Who are you? What do you want from me?"

Another five minutes pass before Lucy walks over, places her head close to his ear and whispers, "I will ask the fucking questions," as she grabs his bollocks and squeezes hard, resulting in another deafening scream.

Once more, she pours a bucket of freezing water a little at a time over the man's shaking body and steps back to watch his head vigorously move back and forward, gasping for air as the wet hessian sticks to his face. Through a gurgling mouth full of water, "Please let me go?"

"Now, what did I say about who asks the questions?" as she grips his throat, tightening her hand one painful inch at a time.

Once Lucy lets go, through a fatigued voice, the effort of trying to balance on his feet and not hang on the rope is starting to take its toll, "OK, what do you want to know?"

"Now that's better," Lucy declares, walking back to join us at the back of the room.

Again a few minutes pass before Lucy finally asks her first question, "Let's start easy... what's your name, and why were you in the office?"

"My name is Arun, and that's all you're getting, bitch," comes the agonising reply.

Not liking the way he just answered the last question, I walk over and land several strong punches into the side of Arun's body. He tries to curl up from the pain by lifting his legs from the floor.

"That's not nice—you don't even know me. Shall we put the question another way... what is your role in the Golden Camel?"

There is a moment of silence before Arun answers, "All I do is collect the money and then hand it over to senior people who travel from Muscat once a month."

To lead him into a false sense of security, "Now, that's better, someone let him down."

This is what separates a person asking questions from an interrogator. Lucy wasn't requesting he be cut down to be friendly. No, she didn't want him to pass out. Now she is getting somewhere. Once Arun is down, George and Derek take him outside and over to the Land Cruiser, where Simon has been keeping a lookout for anyone approaching the location.

After being helped into a sitting position on the sand in front of Simon, Derek removes the bag from the man's head. With his eyes blinking rapidly as they try to adjust to the bright lights, his head darts around, trying to orientate himself to the surrounding area to find out where he is.

"Good morning, here have a drink," Simon holds a plastic water bottle to his lips.

With the bottle tipped up at 45 degrees, Arun takes several fast gulps of water before pleading with Simon, "Please let me go."

"Would love to, mate, but like you, I'm scared of that psycho bitch," Simon points back to the pumphouse.

From the look in his wide-open eyes, you can tell the ploy of bringing him outside is starting to work, with the fear of having to go back in now etched in his scared-looking face as he is helped back up to a standing position.

"Don't send me back in there... I'll tell you what you want to know," comes a trembling voice.

"Tell you what, you answer that nasty bitch's questions, and when you come out, I will personally cut them cable ties for you so you can set yourself free," proclaims Simon, grabbing the man's hands.

Still struggling and digging his feet into the sand, George and Derek drag him back inside where the nylon rope is tied, and he is once more hauled back up towards the ceiling.

With her face centimetres from Arun's face, "Hope that idiot out there didn't offer to set you free," Lucy asks, knowing what was said as it is all part of the plan to give him the false belief he may make it out of here unharmed.

No response comes from Arun, so I grab the live electrical cable I had released from the wall socket when he was outside to ramp things up. Place it on his arms to allow the electricity to flow down to the floor, sending an agonising pain down the entire length of his body. Arun's body jerks several times intensely as he yells out in unbearable pain, filling the room with the sounds of a man who believes he is about to die.

Lucy continues with her interrogation, "I have a couple more questions for you, Arun. Respond to my first one correctly, and I'll give you a wooden stool to stand on. Answer it incorrectly, and... my colleagues will pull the rope tighter, resulting in you hanging from the roof. Nod if you understand."

The man nods his head backwards and forwards in slow motion, along with a hardly audible "yes", as the mixture of fear and hope he may still come out of this situation alive if he answers the questions sinks in.

"OK, for a stool, when are the members of the Golden Camel coming over from Muscat to the island?" This is a question Lucy already suspected she knew — it was written down on the piece of A4 paper she saw in the office in Muscat, again on a scrap of white paper liberated from Noor at ACM Drilling.

Five more minutes of silence pass before Arun says, "They will be arriving on the afternoon ferry tomorrow."

From the corner of the room, I pick up a small, battered old, four-legged stool about 30cm tall and just big enough for two feet to stand precariously on. "See what happens when you answer the nasty woman's questions adequately," I say, sliding it under his feet.

Once Arun's feet manage to find a footing and the pressure from the rope on his arms is lessened, he lets out a sigh. Before he can become too comfortable, Lucy asks him her final question for now. "Regarding someone who has been forced to work for the Golden

Camel against death threats, we would like to know the whereabouts of a man called Joby?"

Now, believing things might be going better for him, "I don't know."

"Try thinking harder," as I hit him with the electricity again.

He lets out a thunderous scream as his body once more jerks violently. "OK, his name will be in my bag, which I left in the office before you bastards abducted me."

"Language, there are ladies present," says Lucy, hitting him in the bollocks.

Turn around to witness George opening the light brown briefcase and taking out a black A4 sized black hardback notebook. After flicking through the pages, his finger rest on a page, "Got it, he is on Hoist 50 and not on 49 like some people let us believe."

With all the information we need, for now, it's time to vacate from here and recce Joby's location, which Arun has kindly indicated in his black book. There is no way we can afford to let our man free until after we have extracted Joby, so we have no choice but to leave him here.

Before we depart, I unscrew a valve, start flooding the place with water and leave the electric wires I had used to electrocute the man dangling down the wall below the height of the step by the door. Once the cold water starts flowing over the concrete step, the cables will be underwater, causing an electrical circuit and a nasty surprise for any wannabe rescuers.

As a secondary backup, I use a trick learnt from terrorists as ordinary people can't help themselves. If they see something valuable, they cannot fight the urge to pick it up. So I grab another toy from my collection in case that fails. This time, the explosive mobile phone inside a leather case is fitted with a light-sensitive trigger. Now once the nosy bastard opens the cover, the light will set off the switch sending an electrical circuit to the detonator, and the phone will explode in their face.

With the interrogated man yelling for us to allow him to go free and water slowly filling the room, I yell out, "Don't worry, you will be safe as long as you don't touch the water."

As we depart the location, the team's voice of reason, Lucy, says, "Nice work, but what happens if an innocent worker wants to go inside?"

"Just to keep you happy," I clamber back out of the Land Cruiser, use a black marker pen I found in the vehicle, and write, 'No Entry, Golden Camel Property' on the door. If the workers here are afraid of this organisation like we are led to believe, this should ensure anyone who enters will be people nobody will miss."

Chapter Fifteen – Recce

As we still have several hours of daylight left, the decision is made that instead of going back to our makeshift base in the jebel, we will go and try to find Hoist 50 camp. Hopefully, once on location, we will be at long last able to confirm the whereabouts of the missing Joby.

Simon drives cautiously along the uneven sandy ground from the pumphouse, weaving between the small clumps of dead foliage for about 200 metres before turning right on the dirt road leading out of Duhfa, heading out into the open desert.

Follow the route for the next 15 minutes as it passes through a level landscape with the occasional small sand dune, nothing on either side but the rare glimpses of camels walking in the distance across the sandy terrain.

A short time later, the compacted ground of the trail makes several turns as it winds its way up a slight incline before flattening out at a T-junction in the middle of nowhere, with nothing but a flat lifeless desert all around.

On the opposite side of the road, crossing our path at right angles, a single wooden board painted black. The words 'Hoists & Camps' are printed in large bold white writing at the top. Under the heading, a list of hoists and rigs in the area runs down the centre.

A thick white arrow on both sides of the name points to either the location of the hoist or its associated camp where people eat, sleep and work on broken equipment.

"Which way, boss?"

"Drive to the camp first, Simon—with any luck, this will be where Joby could be working. From the information given to us by Nasir, he is an administrator."

"Left it is then, Steve."

After another left turn, in the distance, a few hundred metres away, the outline of a rig camp comes into view on the horizon. A narrow dirt road leads up a small jebel overlooking the base to the right.

"Take that track, Simon," I point with my right arm to confirm the direction.

Near the top, a rusty-looking metal oil pipe runs from left to right along the ridge, dipping underground as the road passes over it. This should give us a perfect place to scrutinise all movements in the collection of portable buildings.

To be safe, in case someone is looking this way, Simon continues to drive over the crest of the hill to a point further along the track where the Land Cruiser can't be seen by people down on the campsite who might look our way.

Once the vehicle is parked close to two sets of metal pipes following another sandy route, to give the impression to any nosy bastards we are working on said pipeline, we all clamber out.

"Grab your sniper rifle, George—we can use the optical sight to gain a closer view of the target," I say, removing my own binos from my Bergen.

"Roger that," George responds.

"If you stay with your vehicle, Simon, and cover the rear, the rest of us can make our way back to the ridge and scrutinise the workings of the hoist camp using the pipes as protection."

After our interrogation of the man from the Golden Camel earlier, I remind myself it's now prudent to be armed at all times, so I pick up my rifle. Then without saying anything else, I set off with Lucy behind me, followed by Derek, with George taking up his usual position at the back.

Once in place along the pipeline, all four of us space out a few metres. Too much would make us stick out like cucumbers at a sausage fest. Scan the ground to my front with the binos on the lookout for our man, Joby. Spot several people milling about, going into one of the white neatly lined accommodation blocks.

Each set of three is mounted on a thick black metal subframe so they can be hoisted onto a vehicle when moving the camp. A closer glance confirms they are similar to the ones I used to live in when I worked in the oilfields of Oman.

The rest of the Hoist campsite is in the same layout, which is a standard formation on all Hoists in the local area or even country. From the direction we are looking at it, there are four rows of living accommodation blocks, dining rooms, and stores on the left. The smoke escaping from a vent on the roof means the kitchen is at the end of the first row. An enormous light blue water tank beneath a wooden shelter to protect it from the rays of direct sunlight is on the far end.

To the camp's right, the area appears to be a makeshift office running perpendicular to the others. Beyond that, a person is welding metal sheets together under a small canopy, probably made by the welders themselves as protection from the hot sun.

As I continue scanning, watching people's movements as they go about their daily work routine, I'm tapped on the shoulder by Derek. "We have a vehicle coming down the road trailing a cloud of sand from our nine o'clock," he points in the general direction.

Moments later, the white SUV turns into the camp and pulls up outside the office block, a few feet past the open door. Monitor the situation as all four doors swing wide open. Pick up my binoculars for a closer view of who is climbing out.

From the rear left passenger side, a short, overweight man with dark hair and wearing light blue coveralls clambers out and walks around the back of the vehicle. It's Joby. Well, at least he is alive, which should make getting him back home a hell of a lot easier. To confirm, I keep crouched down so as not to skyline myself, and head to where George is observing through the sniper rifle's scope.

"Is that our man down there?" I say quietly, not that people down there can overhear what I'm saying, out of habit, I suppose.

George turns to face me, "From what I can remember from the photo Nasir showed us, I believe it is."

Return to my previous position, and relay to Lucy and Derek that our man is down there as I pass them. After observing for the next hour without anything out of the ordinary happening, a grey and cream coloured minibus pulls up at the office.

Within minutes a group of men start to appear from one of the portacabins, possibly a dining area and stroll unenthusiastically over to the bus. A few more minutes go by before they are on board, waiting for the driver who had walked inside the building earlier. It must be time for a shift change.

Five minutes pass before he re-emerges, followed by Joby. The two men climb on the transport before it does a complete 360 in front of the welding shed and leaves the camp. Signal the other three and sprint back to the Land Cruiser. An educated guess is they will go straight to the hoist, but now we have found Joby, I don't want him disappearing again.

By the time we arrive at Simon's location, he has spun the vehicle around with the engine running. Fling the front passenger door open and jump in. "Quick, drive down to the T-junction. Need to follow a bus — Joby is inside. "

When we reach the junction, the target vehicle has turned right on the same track we came in on, indicated by the enormous plume of sandy dust kicked up by the wheels that mark its location, like a moving arrow on an electronic map. There is no point in getting too close as the sand would indicate the way, so Simon keeps a short distance behind.

Soon we pass the marker board we saw earlier, which is now on our left. Perfect, the transport must be going directly to the hoist location. Confirmed ten minutes later as the tall metal mast appears over the horizon. Simon stops short of the site so we can survey the surrounding area. The hoist is erected between two massive sand dunes encircling it on two sides. The dirt track winds through a narrow gap on the leading edge, from what I can see from my vantage point.

"Need a way to the back of that dune, Simon," I say, looking at the open ground to my immediate left.

From the rear seat, Lucy declares, "I've been scanning the environment... there appears like there is a route about 40 metres behind us."

"Good enough for me," replies Simon, selecting reverse gear and easing the Land Cruiser backwards until he is past the track.

With all the skills he can muster from his army days as a tank driver, Simon drives across the uneven, loose sand to a point at the back of the location. Once everyone is out of the vehicle, "OK, here is the plan. George and Lucy, go straight up from here to the ridge and locate a favourable sniper position. Be careful — halfway up the mast is a platform called the monkey board. There could be someone working up there who might spot you.

"The rest of us, by which I mean Derek and me, will make our way around to the side," I point to my left. "As always, Simon mate, can you stay with your vehicle ready for a swift exit, if required?"

Before we depart, Derek reaches inside the rear of the Land Cruiser and pulls out three PRC 350 radios. "Best we make most of these, just in case."

"Remember folks, this is a recce, so try to avoid contact if possible... we will meet back here in 30 minutes. If it's needed, the emergency RV will be back here with Simon."

With that, I head off with Derek to find a suitable place on the other side to gain a better view of the target area. Once there, I scan the ridgeline for the best place. Soon find ourselves at the base, ready to climb the 40 metres to the top. Due to the soft sand on the dune underfoot, the going is a little challenging, but nothing that can't be overcome.

About 50 metres from where we are standing, the main ridge dips down before making a steep incline and continuing to a point just past the row of trailers down on the hoist. This will be perfect, as we can scrutinise the entire area to our front without skylining ourselves.

We stop and turn around, to ensure nobody is following us before sitting down and sinking a few inches into the soft ground near the ridge. Once the grains of sand rolling down the dune have stopped, we make our way to the left and peer around the edge to get our eyes on the area surrounding the pad.

We must have caught them on a maintenance day as there is no drilling up on the drill floor. The only people visible are working on pipes on the running board, while another is on the side, standing close to an enormous red Blow Out Preventor or BOP.

On the far side of the place, immediately opposite the rig, is the Company Man's white metal office mounted on a trailer for ease of moving. Pick up my binos to peer through the front window to detect if anyone is there. Inside, two men are sitting looking at what I would guess is a computer screen.

A detailed plan of the whole area will be needed if our extraction of Joby will be here for any reason, rather than the more accessible camp. Before taking out my notebook, I turn to Derek in a whisper, "I'll be concentrating on making a drawing, so you're our eyes and ears until I'm finished."

"No problem, off you go, Da Vinci," comes the reply as he turns to face back down the slope.

With my notepad lying on the sand, I start to sketch the layout of the entire location, beginning with the three trailers lined up in a row. If memory serves me right, the first should be the tea/meeting room, and the other will be a store for all the gear. Next, I make a rough outline of the derrick, drill floor, shakers, water tanks and other associated equipment. They are not that important because if Joby is here, we will be removing him from one of the trailers.

The next task is to mark the approximate distances to the front entrance and any other escape routes if things go badly on the extraction on the paper. As I'm putting things away, I sense a hand on my shoulder, spin around to face Derek. He speaks in a near whisper, "We have company — a white Jeep is coming down the track towards the hoist."

Turn to monitor the entrance as the vehicle disappears behind the dune, following the route into the location. With us both observing the rig pad, the car comes to a halt outside the Company's Man's office. Two hefty looking men wearing blue jeans and grey t-shirts climb out. They are joined by the man I saw earlier sitting at the computer through the window. He is sporting different coloured coveralls than the other people working here — I guess he is what the oil industry calls a Company Man.

From what I can tell from my location, there is a brief conversation between the group before the man points in the direction of the last trailer.

Still observing, we watch the two men stroll over to the welding container. Whoever they are, this can't be good news for someone, as I glimpse sight of one man walking towards them, but on spotting the men, he turns and goes back to a spot beyond the water tank.

Moments later, they ascend the steps and enter the metal container used as a welding workshop. This is followed by sounds of heavy items striking the sides from inside. A minute passes before a man dressed in light blue coveralls clutching a red welding mask is thrown five feet down to the compacted sandy floor through the open door, hitting the ground hard as he lands.

What happens next makes people like me want to go over and put a bullet through their fucking brains. Survey the scene to my front as the men start landing several decisive kicks in quick succession to the body and head of the man on the deck. Turn to face Derek, who is shaking his head.

While listening to the many painful screams from our friend, trying his best to curl up in a tight ball to protect himself from the continued onslaught from the two men, glance to my left to witness the Company Man standing about 10 feet away, just watching everything as it happens, with no attempt to stop the beating of one of his crew.

Even though my heart is saying go down and kill them arseholes, the brain is telling me this is not the time or place as we have a job to do. With any luck, they will stand in my way when extracting Joby, and then I'll be able to completely waste the bastards.

The attack on this poor man lasts for another few minutes before they stop the assault, climb back in their Jeep after saying something to the Company Man, and drive off.

Give it a while before turning to Derek, "Think we have everything we need here... you ready?"

I could tell by the tone in his voice that I would need to join the queue to waste them fuckers if he sees them first. "Yeah, let's get the fuck out of here before I do something about that fucking man who stood by and observed."

As we begin our walk back to meet Simon, I hear from behind me Derek send 'Leave now, out' over the radio to let Lucy and George know to start making their way back as well.

Rounding the corner at the very bottom of the sand dune is an empty space where Simon and the Land Cruiser should be parked. He must have seen the Jeep arriving and took cover, hiding himself and the vehicle somewhere close by.

After a scan of the area, we still can't find him. 'Where can the fucker have got to?' I think to myself, still scanning. A few minutes pass when I detect the sound of someone or something coming towards our location. Without thinking, I sprint across and dive behind a slight dip in the ground, about four feet to my rear, without saying anything. Slowly, I raise my rifle to the firing position, and take the first pressure on the hairline trigger as I'm joined by Derek.

While we wait, the sounds of people trying to keep quiet but making more noise than a hippo on the rampage to the trained person. A second later, they finally came into my view... it's George and Lucy spread out about 10 metres, with George leading the way. Gradually I release the trigger and remove the rifle from the aim.

The moment George arrives, "So where is the lanky streak of piss?"

"Haven't a clue, mate; I'm still looking for him, " I respond.

"Don't panic, boys. He is over there," Lucy points in Simon's direction about 200 metres away.

Still keeping a space between us, we walk over to meet him and the Land Cruiser parked in a hollow between several mounds of sand. When we arrive, Simon climbs out to be hit with, "What's the matter, Donkey Walloper... get scared of a couple of thugs punching the crap out of an innocent man?" comes a sarcastic voice from George.

"Nope, just wanted you to do more walking, fat boy," Simon retorts.

Back in the vehicle, I turn to Lucy and George in the rear, "You witness that man receive a beating from them two fuckers?"

"Sure did... bet they are from the Golden Camel," replies Lucy, placing her rifle between her legs.

A glance down at Mickey tells me the time is 16:00, so it's a toss-up whether to go back to base camp or to the restaurant we used yesterday for breakfast to grab some nosh. The unanimous decision is to chance food at the eatery.

We still don't know if Arun has been recovered from the pumphouse, so to be safe, Simon parks on the open ground across the road facing the row of shops. Not having much time to waste before we lose the light, we only monitor people entering and leaving for 15 minutes.

"That should be enough time. If Lucy, Simon and I go inside first while George and Derek wait here in case we are followed, then if you don't detect the sound of gunfire or witness us being dragged out of the premises by our short and curlies after five minutes, come in and join us."

"No problem, Steve, mine's a tea," says George, climbing out the rear of the vehicle to let Lucy out.

Not to appear too conspicuous, we walk together in a group the brief distance from the Land Cruiser, through the car park, out the front of the shops and enter the restaurant. Unlike the last time we visited, the place appears deserted until I notice Noor sitting at a table in the far corner. This is the bastard that tried to dispatch us to the wrong hoist. With our eyes interlocked and to make him uneasy and intimidated, we stroll towards him without saying a word, pull out the remaining seats at his table and sit down.

A few seconds of awkwardness follow before Noor starts to speak, "Did you find the man you were looking for... Joby, isn't it?"

Before I could reply, the same scruffy waiter that served us last time appears with a jug of water. "Would you like tea?" he enquires.

After confirming with the others, "Yeah, four coffees and one tea, please."

With that, he wobbles his head and disappears back to the kitchen. My attention returns to Noor fidgeting in his chair. "Yes, thanks. Even though you attempted to send us to the incorrect place," I reply, staring straight at him to once more make him feel uncomfortable.

A slight delay of time elapses before both Derek and George enter the place and come over to join us after a quick scan of the room.

"Did we miss much?" asks Derek, looking directly at Noor.

"Not much... he is about to explain why he fucking lied to us," grabbing my coffee from the waiter, who's just reappeared.

Once the man is out of range of our conversation, Noor glances up from the table, "Yes, I didn't tell you the truth. Wanted to find out if your reputation is as good as I have heard."

Glance around the team to witness the same expressions on their faces that expressed what I'm thinking, "OK, don't know how you know who we are, but now you do, you must realise we do not let anything get in the way of a mission including killing the ones who try."

After taking a gulp of a milky liquid that appears to be something like tea from a glass in front of him, Noor resumes what he was saying. "No doubt you know ACM Drilling is a physical front for the Golden Camel here on the island."

I nod, "Yes, we knew that already — that is why we came to your office."

"What you do not know is, like most people here, I work for them, but being a Pakistani, I hate being under the control of an Indian organisation and therefore I'm cynical about what they do to people I work with. Plus, I had to lie to you as my office is bugged, and spies are everywhere."

"Interesting... anything else we should know?" Simon moves in closer to trap Noor in the corner, in case he now tries to make a bolt for it.

After a short pause, Noor continues, "You and your team may be exemplary at what you do, but have you realised you have been set up right from the beginning?"

Not believing what my ears have just heard, I interrupt, "What the fuck? When and by who?"

"People were following you right back from when you left your home on the Isle of Wight. Their job was to make sure you attended the meeting with Nasir in Southampton and took the bait. The Golden Camel is not stupid enough to kill you in the UK. They needed you in a remote place where your deaths wouldn't be noticed."

Take a deep breath and stop him again, "So does Nasir work for them as well? Do you know who set us up?"

Noor took another mouthful of his drink, "Like me, Nasir is an honourable man and has witnessed two close friends vanish, so he is also disillusioned with the organisation and wants out. When it comes to who, I don't know, but from the whispers I've been hearing, it was from a drugs syndicate originating from the Caribbean."

Glance across to Simon and George, who look like they have just been whacked with the butt of a rifle, like me. Not showing any reaction to Noor's last gobsmacking comment, "Very interesting, how do we know we can trust what you've just said?"

Even though he is right, still need to make sure he is speaking the truth. I was followed on the island, and we were tailed in Southampton, plus when I arrived in Muscat, thinking about the man I stuffed down the pipe near McDonald's and the envelope with the blue stripe we first encountered on St Halb.

"Do you swear on Allah that what you're saying is correct?" Remember he welcomed us with As-salamu alaykum, the Muslim greeting.

"Yes, I'm risking being killed for telling you this information. Take it you found Joby, so ask yourself this. If he is in danger, would he not be locked away rather than moving freely between camp and hoist?"

"Excellent point, Noor," I reply.

As Noor stands up to leave, "Just one more thing. Witnessed a man getting the crap kicked out of him while the Company Man watched from the front of his trailer. Any idea what that was about?"

After looking around once more to confirm nobody is listening, in a hesitant voice, "Yes, Steve... the two men are the enforcers on Mano who work for the Golden Camel. They come under the control of the people running the money transfer office opposite the motel. If people don't pay on time, they get a visit from these people who beat the poor sod to ensure the person complies in the future."

"Cheers, we will be in touch later if we need more info," I shout as he starts to walk away.

With our own meals finished and only two hours before last light, we clamber aboard the Land Cruiser and head back to the base camp for the last time. Tomorrow we extract Joby whether he likes it or not, then make a run for the boat off the island.

Chapter Sixteen – Planning

Once we are back at the top of the jebel and sitting under the overhang, we discuss how the removal of Joby will happen and from which location.

As I'm the group's planner, the rest leave me to develop the plan while George strips and cleans his sniper rifle and Lucy and Derek sort out their own weapons and distribute the ammunition equally among the team. Meanwhile, Simon gives the vehicle a thorough once-over to ensure it will not let us down when we need it the most.

Remove my extendable car aerial I carry for all briefings from my Bergen. Not knowing if Joby would be on Hoist 50 or at the camp, I need to make two models on the flat open patch of sand close to the side of our location.

My first task is to smooth out a couple of two-metre squares for each target area. First, I draw an overview of the campsite in the light covering of loose sand using four rectangle blocks to represent the rows of living accommodation, and write 'portacabins' in the centre.

Next, collect several rocks from around the base camp and place them on the diagram to symbolise the office and welding shed.

Along the far edge of the map, I draw the road leading up to the position we observed from earlier, with two lines sketched in the soft sand to demonstrate the pipeline running across the location. The last step is to show our individual starting points. Once the strategy has been established, I will use stones from the rockface above the firepit.

Right, on to the Hoist. Once more, I sketch out the site, piling up piles of light-coloured sand representing the dunes surrounding the place on two sides. In the centre, I draw the rough silhouette of the rig equipment. This doesn't need to be detailed because Joby will either be in the Company Man's office or the restroom trailer. If, in fact, he is actually here, that is.

With the extended aerial, roughly sketched in the shape of the two trailers and the welding area, on the leading edge, make two squiggly lines to indicate the route in from the track. Then use a small twig to act as the derrick because if we come up with any resistance, they could utilise the monkey board as a firing position.

Once the outline plan of both locations is finished, I spend the next 20 minutes staring at each one, running all possible scenarios through my head until a rough agenda of attack is formulated in my mind.

Then walk over to the rest who are sitting in a group drinking a brew. "Got our extraction plan sorted—if someone grabs Derek from the stag post, we can run through it. Plus, pass me a coffee."

"Here you go, mate, and as per SOPs on the night before a mission, get some of this down you," Simon hands me a drink and then pours a tot of whiskey into the black mug.

"Cheers. Come and join me at the plans when you're all ready," walking back to my diagrams in the sand.

Once everyone is sitting around and checking out my handiwork, "The first problem we are faced with is we don't know where Joby will be. We would have completed several observation posts on any other mission to determine his movements, but we can't do this due to lack of time..."

"Can we count on Noor? He might be able to call Joby and tell him he is needed on Hoist 50 first thing," enquires Lucy.

"Best not to let anyone know our movements and I, for one, don't entirely trust him."

"Me neither," Derek adds.

I continue, "Let's leave Noor out of the plans for now. From what we witnessed yesterday, Joby is going along in the bus on shift changes, so we can work on that. A calculated guess says he will do the same on the changeover from the night crew. If he does, we will gain the advantage of only a few people to deal with."

"Why don't I drop you lot off at the hoist before driving to the campsite where I can observe what's happening. If he heads in your direction, I can alert you over one of Derek's radios and then drive over to meet up with you."

"That's scary, Simon, you are starting to read my mind," picking up one of the smaller stones on which I write the letters 'TS', his call sign and place it down next to the two lines indicating the pipeline.

"Would say great minds think alike, but you're a fucking idiot, Steve."

"Thanks for that, Simon—as I was saying, if Simon conceals himself here and watches the camp, paying particular attention to the office area, then if you see Joby clambering into the bus, broadcast the following over the radio, 'TS, Joby out'. If he does not board the transport, send 'TS, Joby in.'"

"Roger that," replies Simon.

"In the first scenario, our target leaves the campsite. After sending the message, you need to drive to this point," I indicate with the aerial.

Simon leans over the map to get a better understanding. "Where is that...?"

"Same location you tried hiding from the two bad guys," George chuckles out loud.

"Go fucking clean a rock," comes the instant response from Simon.

Turn to see Lucy and Derek trying their best to hold back laughter through huge grins.

"Back to business, boys and girls. After being dropped off at the hoist, George and Lucy will set up a sniper position on top of the first dune, where you were earlier, and cover the whole area."

With two more stones, one slightly larger than the others, write 'GD' and 'L' before indicating the place on the front of the first of the two dunes...

"One question, why is my stone bigger than everyone else's?" George asks with a pissed-off look, knowing he already knew the answer.

"Matter of scale, mate, you're rounder than all of us," I say, trying hard to keep a smirk from crossing my face.

"Look who's talking, fat boy," George responds.

"Hope the rest of the questions are that easy to answer. Derek and I will make our way around the dunes and approach from the rear," I draw the route from the Land Cruiser's potential concealed location to the bottom of the dune and up to our start point in the sand.

"Suggest once we are all in our positions, we confirm over the radios using our call signs and OK," Derek adds, tapping one of the PRC 350s.

"I don't have a call sign."

Thinking for a few seconds, "How about 'LK'?" Derek announces.

"Go on, then hit me with it. What does LK stand for?" says Lucy, turning to face Derek.

"L is for Lucy, plus as you are an assassin, the K stands for Killer, so simple," replies Derek expecting some sort of retaliation.

With that all sorted, I continued with the briefing. "Once Simon has joined us and is protecting our escape route, and everyone is ready, I will make my way with Derek behind this trailer." With my aerial, I point and place two more stones marked with S3 and DR at the back of the rig pad to confirm we all know which one I'm referring to.

After a swig of his brew, Derek gives me a raised thumb to say he understands.

"From here, we will enter and snatch Joby, bring him back to Simon's location, taking the same route as the one we went in on. From here, we make our way to the beach we landed on to be picked up. If for any reason, we encounter resistance, first remember there will be a lot of innocent people about, so try not to kill any."

"Guess you want me and Lucy to dispatch any armed Golden Camel people?"

"Yes, George, and if you two can stay in position to cover our retreat with Joby until we arrive at the Land Cruiser, we will then protect your own withdrawal."

Gave everyone a few minutes to let the information sink in before asking, "Has anyone got any questions on plan A?"

"Just the one. Are we sure Paul and Kev will be there waiting for us, or do you have alternative arrangements?" Simon enquires.

Take out a small piece of paper from my pocket with a mobile number written across the page. "With any luck, the boat will be there, mate. But here is our contingency plan. Once we are finished here, you can call him and arrange to pick us up. His name is Carl, ex RAF. Say you're a mate of Tony's."

"Not a problem, Steve," says Simon, reaching out and taking the note.

"OK, on to scenario two, in case our friend doesn't climb on the bus and remains at the campsite. As before, everything will happen after receiving the appropriate radio message. While Simon stays with his eyes on the target, the rest of us will make our way by foot as fast as possible to his location. Shouldn't take more than 30 minutes."

George glances over at Simon for some retort about him having to tab. "Any comments, Donkey Walloper?"

"Nope, not from me, mate," says Simon, holding back a chuckle.

Taken aback by lack of any sarcastic comment, I resume, "When we arrive at the pipeline, Lucy and George will swap places with Simon and set up their sniper position. The remainder of the team will jump into the Land Cruiser and drive past the campsite along the road until we are out of view. From here, Derek and I will make our way on foot towards the camp office approaching from the rear.

"Again, once we all confirm by radio we are all in our positions, we will make our way inside, extract Joby and return to the vehicle and Simon. Any questions so far?"

Everyone shakes their heads, so I continue,"If for any reason we come under live fire, first Simon will drive to the back of the office and pick us all up. While this is happening, the snipers will dispatch any armed people dropping them dead facedown in the sand..."

"Take it the escape plan is the exact same back to the coastline?" Lucy asks.

"Yes, the same. Any more questions?" I ask.

"What happens if everything goes wrong on the operation and there is no boat waiting?"

"Just moving on to that point, Derek. The emergency RV is back here if we need to abort the mission. In the unlikely event we do not lay eyes on Joby, we will go with plan B. Now, if Joby doesn't want to come willingly, we will bind his hands, gag him, and drag him along if needs must. So make sure you take a few cable ties, Derek. On the matter of our way off Mano, if all goes well and no shots are fired, and there is no transport waiting at the coast, we will use the ferry that passed us en route to the island."

"And if the idiot on the hill," Simon peers over at George, "puts a bullet up our arses or if anybody gets injured?"

"Don't panic, Simon... I'll aim for that ugly head of yours," replies George, picking up his sniper rifle and aiming at Simon.

"In the unlikely result any of us does manage to become hit, then stay where you are, and we will fetch you at the end before moving for the coastline. And George is right, Simon, he won't miss. Before we wrap up, if we are under attack and making a hostile retreat and no boats are waiting, we will conceal ourselves on the far side of Mano until transport can be arranged or alternative plans are made."

Leave the maps up for 10 minutes until everyone is familiar with the target area and their start positions before wiping the whole place clean, so no trace of our plans is visible if someone should stumble across our base camp. As I walk back to my own kit, "One last thing, folks, Zulu hour tomorrow will be at 05:00, as we all need to be in position by first light."

A glance down at Mickey on my wrist tells me the time is now 18:50, it will be dark in the next few minutes, and this is not the time to become too relaxed. The camp will need protection until we leave in the morning. But first, time to continue with the team tradition already started earlier by Simon, reach in my Bergen and produce a one-litre bottle of Southern Comfort.

After cleaning my rifle and ensuring my stuff is packed away, I join the other four sitting around the fire pit, drinking hot brews. "Here you go, get this down you." I pour a large amount of alcohol into each cup held out at arm's reach.

The following few hours went far too quickly, with us all joking and laughing about everything imaginable apart from tomorrow's mission. With the mugs now containing pure booze and hot drinks being something of the past, the three boys got up and walked a short distance into the darkness for a piss.

Take the opportunity to move close to Lucy, grab hold of her hand, and stare into her eyes. "I'm glad you're here, and I know you can handle yourself, but for me, can you stay alive tomorrow? Don't think I can manage to lose you."

"You won't," she smiles and kisses me on the cheek. "If you get shot, I'm not patching you up again, did that on the previous mission, remember?"

Grab the quarter-filled bottle and pour us a little more Southern Comfort just as the boys, complete with empty bladders, return.

"More booze, boys," I say, holding out the Southern Comfort.

"Might as well—I'm getting used to this," says Derek, holding out his mug.

With all the booze gone, it is time to call it a night and get some kip before the early morning light breaks through the darkness of the night. With only six hours until the off, we split the night's stag up into parts, each doing one hour and 20 minutes. So I can get the brews going in the morning, I take the last sentry, with Lucy taking the first one.

Chapter Seventeen – Extraction

Woken up 20 minutes ago by Simon to take over from him on stag, and I'm now lying on the cold ledge overlooking the motionless settlement of Duhfa in the distance. A glance down at Mickey tells me there are only 30 minutes left before I need to wake the others and start the mission's next stage.

While the rest remain in the land of nod, I pull back the canvas sheet still hanging down from the rockface. Empty the contents from my black plastic bottle into the mess tin perched on a small burner at the bottom of our fire pit. Time to start the water boiling for the hot brew before we leave.

With the index finger of my right hand, I push the igniter button on the side, which makes a loud clicking sound as the spark ignites the gas now silently escaping from the canister. Instantly the stove roars into life, sounding like a jet engine ready for take-off in the silence of the night.

Within minutes the water is bubbling away in the metal container. Pour steaming water into the assortment of mugs the team had left out overnight, adding coffee to four of them and a teabag to the other for George.

A glance down at Mickey on my wrist confirms it is time for everyone to leave the relative safety of their slumber. So amble over to each one, in turn, giving a gentle nudge until their eyes are wide open and staring at me, ready to say 'fuck off, I need more sleep'. Once everybody is awake, I return to the shelter, pack everything away, including the sheet hanging from the cliff face, and wait for the rest to join me.

As I sit sipping on my brew, I monitor everyone as they stuff their sleeping bags in their Bergens and walk over to the back of the Land Cruiser without saying a word. In fact, the only sound that interrupts the morning air is that of the rear door being opened and closed as they pack away their kit.

"Morning, honey," it is Lucy — she takes the brew I am holding out for her and sits on the sand next to me.

Shortly after, we're joined by Simon, Derek and George, picking up their hot drinks before sitting in silence for the first few minutes, sipping away on their brews. Like me, they are probably running through the plans for the day and brushing aside the notion that this may be their last day on Earth if they are killed in action.

When it appears like everyone is finished, "Come on then, let's go and fetch our man and head off this fucking island," I say, standing up and throwing the dregs from my cup over the ground to my right.

"Right behind you, mate," comes a quiet response from Simon.

Moments later, we are all in the Land Cruiser, and Simon fires up the engine and pushes down gently on the accelerator. We drive with the lights turned off as it is still dark. The last thing we want is to highlight our movements to anyone who might be out for an early morning walk. Instead, Simon senses the vehicle's slight movements up or down and presses the gas pedal accordingly. He would have picked up the same skill as a tank driver. A knack I also learned as an FV432 armoured personnel carrier in Germany in my army days.

As Simon drives to the drop off location, we double-check our weapons, ensuring there is a round in the chamber. It's not long before we pass the black hoist marker board, where Simon steers off the road and heads cross-country to where he took cover yesterday and our starting point.

In an attempt to make the attacking force seem more significant than it actually is, if for any reason, we are discovered, he deliberately drives off his previous tracks in the loose sand to make two fresh ones trying to make it look like there are two vehicles.

Just before Simon comes to a halt in the dip between two high piles of earth, I swivel a little in my seat, "I know everyone knows the plans, but to confirm: once out of the vehicle, we will head off one behind the other to the bottom of the dunes surrounding Hoist 50. Once there, Derek and I will cover you until you reach your sniper position. Then we will move towards the far side of the dune but stop short. Remember, don't show yourselves until the message from Simon that Joby left the camp comes over the radio."

Once the Land Cruiser comes to a halt, we all pile out, each taking up individual firing positions surrounding the location, facing a different approach and staring into the darkness, looking for any movement on the flat open ground. The instance Simon departs, I cautiously stand up and walk in the direction of the hoist. There is no need to glance to my rear as the people behind me are professionals and would be following me.

A few minutes later, I arrive at the base and crouch down, facing the entrance to the rig pad where I'm soon joined by Derek, with Lucy and George reaching me seconds afterwards. The sniper team head upwards to the ridge without saying a word while Derek turns and covers the way we just came.

Peer up to witness George and Lucy stop just short of the ridgeline. Watch with some interest as George reaches up with his right arm, grabs a handful of sand, and drags it back towards him. He does this several times, moving a small amount each time until a dip appears in the sandy ridge just big enough to rest the 7.62mm L96A1 sniper rifle, while doing his best not to expose too much of his head. Once he is finished, Lucy follows the same procedure to make another hole to monitor the area to her front and spot targets for George.

When they have completed setting up their position, tap Derek on the shoulder and lead off around the base, stopping short at a point where the sand dune starts to dip back down.

In the distance, I detect the voices of people working on the drill floor and pad, along with the intermittent sound of the powerful winch bursting into life as it drags the heavy pipes the length of the running board and through the V-Gate and hoists them up high up the derrick.

From the noise of clanking metal higher up the mast, I can make an educated guess they are stacking them in the monkey board near the top of the derrick, ready for a run later.

A glance down at Mickey confirms that it's been 15 minutes since Simon drove off. All we can do is wait for a radio message to let us know if Joby is staying on camp or heading our way.

Spin around to face Derek, "Take it you have already sent the transmission that we are in position?"

"Of course, and have received messages from Simon and Lucy saying they are also ready."

"Cheers, mate," I reply, turning back toward the dune's edge and glancing around the rim, working out where we go from here.

Feel a hand on my shoulder, "Lucy's just reported the minibus is coming towards the hoist. Wonder why Simon hasn't sent his message?" says Derek, looking puzzled.

"Fuck knows, with any luck, he hasn't been compromised," I respond.

With that bit of information put to one side, I position myself in a spot where I can see the small bus pull up outside the Company Man's trailer to observe who gets off. As I scrutinise every person clambering off the transport, I can't determine if any of them is Joby.

Once more, I turn to Derek, "Radio Lucy and find out if they have spotted our man."

After his fingers press the transmitter, he sends the following message, "Can you confirm the presence of Joby? Over."

A second later Lucy replies, "No, he isn't on the minibus. Do we start heading for the camp? Over."

Now thinking on my feet, do we abandon this and head for plan B or wait? I grab the mic. "Hold fast for a few mins. Then if there is no sign, we head for the campsite. Out."

Several minutes pass, and my attention returns to the hoist where the night shift is boarding the bus, which leaves once everyone is on board. Shit, where is Joby? More importantly, what's happened to Simon?

About to give the order for everybody to head for the RV and begin tabbing back to the hoist camp when the familiar tones of Simons's voice breaks radio silence, 'Joby, out'. Perfect, Joby is heading our way and should be with us soon, so there is no need to start walking.

Several nervous minutes go by before a white Jeep arrives and parks up at the far end of the location close to the entrance, out of my line of sight, so I can't see who is in the vehicle. Is Joby one of the people inside, if not, who just arrived?

To my relief, a short time later Joby appears, strolling across the rig pad, chatting to another man who I don't recognise, and heading for the restroom trailer. Now our man is where we want him. Time to stick to our original plan, which is the most favourable to us. Here, fewer innocent people could get injured if they wander in front of any crossfire.

There is only one more element to be set before we can start the next stage, Simon covering our rear and ready with the Land Cruiser to facilitate our withdrawal to the coast and, with any luck, a boat.

Minutes later, everything is in place as Simon broadcasts, 'TS, OK'.

Give it another five minutes for the sniper team to settle into a firing position before Derek and I head off, making our way around to the far side of the restroom trailer and our final start location.

There is about a 50 metre space between the dune and the first clump of machinery, a gap we must cross to the rear. At the back of the hoist, there is nothing but open featureless sandy ground with the occasional bump in the terrain. Bearing in mind this is my first glance at this part of the location, I stop, lay flat down on my belly and peek around the corner.

Once I know that nobody is watching, I sprint across the gap with Derek covering my move. When I reach the other side, I turn and glance back while Derek does the same and joins me.

Not far away, a man is sorting through a pile of scrap metal. Recognise him as the man who got the beating from the two thugs from our friends at the Golden Camel. Now within a few feet of him, when he turns and peers straight at us. You tell by the impression on his face that his brain is deciding whether to fight or flee.

Grasping at the opportunity, I raise my index finger to my lips, "Shush, we are not here to hurt you. Only here to deal with members of the Golden Camel," I say in a low voice, just a little more than a whisper. I'm sure he will be compliant as I know he doesn't have any allegiance to the organisation.

As the man strolls off into the desert away from any possible danger, we crawl underneath the restroom trailer from the rear before proceeding to a position close to a set of solid iron stairs leading into the trailer to listen and scrutinise what's going on to our front.

Directly in our line of sight, two men are rolling drill pipes from their metal stand on the far side of the running board and connecting the lifting eye. I can't see up the derrick from our location, but from how the winch cable came back down empty, someone must be on the monkey board to disconnect the drill pipes.

Over to my immediate right at three o'clock, two mechanics are working on the Blow Out Preventer and choke manifold. Apart from that, there is no sign of the rest of the crew or Company Man. Let's hope it stays that way for the next 10 minutes.

As I turn to face Derek to signal him to move, above us, I can detect the footsteps of someone walking from the area closest to the door towards the far end. Seconds later, the distinctive sound of the legs of a wooden chair can be heard scraping along the metal floor. Perfect, we now know where the people inside will be seated.

Tap Derek on the shoulder and mouth the words, 'Let's go.' We burst out from beneath the trailer, sprint up the stairs, and enter. To our immediate front is a white-painted cabinet that's seen far better days, on which stands a large silver boiling vessel and several dirty-looking mugs.

Without pausing, I spin around to my right, facing a row of three bare wood-looking tables piled high at one end with a mountain of paper and cardboard folders.

Three men still coming to terms with what is happening are sitting at the back on one of the white-painted wooden bench seats that occupy the space on each side of the old battered-looking tables. With Derek covering from a position near the doorway, watching for unwanted attention, my 9mm held out in front of me, I approach the back of the room where Joby is now standing with his back resting against the wall.

In a loud, firm voice, "Don't panic. We are not here to hurt you unless you try something stupid. The team are only here to take that man, Joby." I point in his direction. "Both of you sit back down and stay quiet," I indicate by flicking my pistol in the direction of the tables.

Once the others are sitting back down and not in the way, "Come on, Joby, you are coming with us back to the UK."

"No, I'm not going," comes the unexpected reply from Joby.

"What did that fucking idiot just say?" shouts Derek from the door.

"Sorry, but you don't have a say in it, mate. There are two choices, you can either come the easy way or the hard way, but you're coming with us," I say, grabbing hold of his coveralls and pulling him to the exit.

Joby grasps the table with one hand, "You don't understand. If I leave, the Golden Camel will take revenge on my family back in India."

"That's already been taken care of... your immediate relatives have been flown back to England," I don't know if they have or not, but I need to make him move before anyone puts up a fight.

"Don't believe you," Joby protests.

"Actually, mate, I couldn't give a flying fuck what you believe— you're coming," I yell, now getting pissed off with the idiot.

While I hold Joby's hands out, Derek fixes two thick black cable ties around his wrists before grabbing them and dragging Joby towards the door. I am about to step out and descend the stairs when I spot two white SUVs driving onto the rig pad and coming to a halt outside the Company Man's office.

Still in the doorway, I monitor four men exit the leading vehicle. The individual who clambers out of the front passenger side is about six feet tall with short brown hair and wearing grey trousers and a similar coloured jacket. As he turns to walk to the back of the vehicle, my heart skips a beat. This whole situation just got nasty — the man is John Nair, the person who runs the entire organisation.

Two other men sling open the doors and climb out of the rear, and another four from the second vehicle, now parked at the edge of the pad. They all appear to be armed with assault rifles. The question is, are they to scare the crap out of the workers to keep them in line or are they for our benefit. Whatever the reason, we can't stay here.

After making a snap plan, "OK, once we get the chance, we can leave via the same route we came in on. You go down first and cover Joby and me while I protect you from here."

Once Derek is in position, I turn to Joby, "Right, shut your fucking gob and come with me, or I'll put a bullet in your head... you understand what I'm saying?" Joby nods in agreement and starts to follow me down.

As my right foot lands firmly on the sandy ground, I detect the distinctive sound of bullets flying past my head and the thud as they strike the exterior of the restroom trailer behind me. Before I can scan the entire area to discover where the rounds came from, another lands a few inches from me. Instinctively I dive to the deck, pulling Joby with me.

Derek yells out, "It came from the mast," then a single shot rings out, followed by a body bouncing off the metal structure of the derrick as it plummets to the floor. It would appear the sniper team is doing its job.

Within seconds, armed men are racing towards us across the rig pad, firing wildly as they come. At the top of my voice, I shout out to Derek, "Four men, three o'clock, you take the ones on the left, I'll take the other two."

While letting off two rounds in quick succession at the first of my attackers, I scream at Joby, "Fucking get under the trailer and stay there."

My next shot strikes the man still running at a considerable speed towards me in the chest, dropping him to the deck, lying motionless with thick red blood now oozing out from under him and saturating the loose sandy ground. My attention turns to the second of my two targets, still heading my way at a fast rate of knots.

It's when all your training comes into play as you calmly, like you're moving in slow motion, adopt a kneeling position, take aim, control your breathing and squeeze the hairline trigger. The result sends a solo brass bullet spinning along the barrel's rifling, exiting in a puff of white oily smoke as it hurtles towards its target, hitting the person in the head. A nano-second later, another lifeless body hits the ground, sending up a cloud of dust high into the air.

With my targets dispatched, I turn to witness Derek placing his own 9mm on the forehead of a half-dazed man and pulling the trigger, scattering blood, bone fragments and brain matter across the sand.

The fourth assailant has taken cover behind the blue mud tank and is firing blindly in our direction. With the heart pounding under the sudden exertion sending life-giving blood pumping around my body, I spring to my feet simultaneously with Derek sprinting towards the tank, zig-zagging to make it hard for the man to obtain a fixed aim on us.

Now metres from him, I leap over the end of the choke manifold, land and continue trying to stay away from stray flying bullets. As we reach the target, the firing stops and there is silence. Once more, our sniper team had seen the danger and dealt with the situation. To be safe, I empty two rounds into the body, in case the idiot is playing dead.

Right, time to grab Joby and get the fuck out of here, but when we turn around, he is gone. While I check the inside of the trailer, Derek makes his way around to the back to see if he is hiding there.

After a few minutes of searching and not finding the bastard, Lucy's voice comes over the radio, "Joby is being dragged over to the rear of the site and the other vehicle."

Shit, in the heat of the moment, we forgot about John and the other three members of the Golden Camel. Seconds later, the SUV is hurtling towards me as I stand firm in its path with my 9mm aimed at the windowscreen. I haven't come this far to go home empty-handed.

With the vehicle now only metres away, I raise the pistol and fire at the driver. At the last moment, the motor vehicle swerves violently to the left, and my round hits the screen and strikes the centre mass of the passenger sitting in the front seat.

Thinking on his feet, Derek presses the button on the mic, "Simon, block the exit to the hoist, prevent that car from leaving."

As it races away from our position, George fires a shot smashing the rear window and hitting one person in the back, hopefully not Joby.

Our prime objective now is to stop that vehicle, so Derek and I sprint as fast as our legs will take us to the entrance. With my lungs feeling like they will burst any second, we reach the small dirt track leading away from the location. About 50 metres to our front, Simon is waiting with our own transport.

"Sorry, wasn't quick enough and they have got away, but not too far. That cloud of dust in the distance, off to our one o'clock, is them,"

"Not a problem, Simon — once everyone is on board, drive after them and don't spare the donkeys."

A minute later, the panting figures of Lucy and George clamber into the back. Not wasting any time, Simon bangs down the accelerator, which slams the rear door shut, and races off along the track, chasing the escaping vehicle.

With some of the best offroad driving I've seen in a while, Simon proves why he is our transport guy and is soon only a short distance behind. They may be ahead, but this is where our recce and planning come into play.

The trail we are following will do a 90 degree turn in a few minutes, forcing the other vehicle to cross our path at right angles about 500 metres away. Formulating a plan, I spin around in my seat to face everyone.

"Our prime objective is to stop that vehicle; be prepared to jump out, George, with your rifle. This will have to be the finest shot of your life. While George and I are getting in position and bringing that SUV to a halt, the rest of you catch it up and don't let anyone get away, especially Joby."

With that, Simon slows the Land Cruiser down to about 60 kilometres per hour. Push the door slightly, ready with George to leap out. As we crest a small ridge, I shout, "Now!" fling the door fully open and launch myself out of the moving vehicle. Hitting the ground hard, I go into a roll with my rifle tucked close to my body to protect it. Once I've stopped rolling, I crawl several feet to the ridgeline of hard pack sand overlooking our new target area.

As I lay there waiting for George to join me, my mind flashes back to Northern Ireland training, where our platoon sergeant made us do this type of thing repeatedly, wearing our complete kit, including our 100lb Bergens. Sure, the bastard got some twisted kick out of us getting injured.

Brought back to the moment by George lowering the legs of his sniper rifle on top of a patch of a rock-solid raised pile of sand about 10 inches tall. "OK, mate, make this count and stop that vehicle."

While George starts to control his breathing for the killer shot, remove my binos to act as a spotter if the first doesn't hit the target. Seconds later, the loud crack as the bullet leaves the barrel rings in my ears. George has taken the first shot at the precise moment the SUV with Joby inside rounds the corner about 500 metres from our present location.

He misses with the first round, "Dropped short about six metres, speed smack on," I relay the information of where the shot lands.

After a quick alteration in his aim, George fires the second. This time it hits home and enters the driver's window in a hail of shattering glass. Immediately the vehicle swerves harshly to the left, striking the built-up edge of the road and rolling over in slow motion twice before coming to a standstill, resting on its roof in a massive cloud of dust. Within seconds, the Land Cruiser pulls up nearby, and the team bail out and rush over to grab Joby.

"Come on, George, time to get them fat little legs running and join the others, " I shout, springing to my feet and starting to run.

Over at the crash site, Simon has already pulled out the blood-stained Joby from the wreckage. He has him sitting on the floor with his hands still bound together when I arrive at the overturned vehicle, panting like a deranged idiot trying to get my breath back six minutes later, closely followed by George.

To the right of the SUV, Lucy has dragged John Nair out from the debris. Thick red blood pours from a large gash on the front of his head, running down his face and drenching his grey suit, while a lump of metal protrudes from the right side of his lower abdomen.

Observing that he is drifting in and out of consciousness, Derek gives John a forceful kick to his ribs to keep him awake, ready for any questions we might have. By the time I'm prepared to ask any, Lucy is standing over him, asking her own question.

With her 9mm only inches from his face, "Don't suppose you know how the man you ordered beaten up on the hoist is recovering? In fact, you probably don't even know his name, do you?" Lucy yells.

A dying man's faint, desperate whispering voice comes from John's lips, "Help me... I'll pay you whatever you want... Just take me to a hospital."

"Nope, don't fucking think so," Lucy replies angrily as the pistol recoils upwards a nano-second after she squeezes the trigger, sending a 9mm round into the centre of his face, splattering crimson red blood in all directions.

"Well, that put a stop to the questioning. Might as well search the arsehole to find out if John has any information about the Golden Camel on him," I say, bending down and reaching into his jacket.

Inside the silk-lined pocket are a flash drive and a mobile phone that managed to come through the crash unscathed. With any luck, this will contain a list of contacts, not that I'm holding out any hope as this man didn't rise to a position where he could run a crime syndicate by being careless. But let's wish he got cocky and overconfident in his standing, like most people in his position often do.

While examining what I found, Simon asks, "What shall we do with the body? We can't leave it here and don't want the bastard's blood staining the seats in our nice clean Land Cruiser."

"Pour some fuel over him and burn the fucking arsehole and the vehicle," I reply as I walk over to our transport and place the stuff in my Bergen.

Monitor the situation as Derek and George cram John's body back in the SUV and toss two gas cylinders from our cooking equipment inside. Need to ensure it burns and explodes so no remains can be found by the untrained eye. Before the bottles ignite and the whole area becomes a massive fireball, we clamber back into the Land Cruiser. Simon slams the accelerator to the floor, and we depart at speed heading for the central coast and the boat or boats waiting to take us back to the mainland.

Once we are away from the scene, Simon slows down so as to not attract any unwanted and unwelcome attention to our movements. In fact, the journey to the spot on the coastline where we entered the island a couple of days back goes without a hitch. The only vehicles we notice on the route are two white cars heading towards Hoist 50 at some speed, followed by a brown-coloured one complete with blue lights fixed to the roof flashing in the bright sunlight.

Behind the motel near our exit point, we halt and ditch the transport along the edge of a small building close to where we climbed up from the shore. Off to our right are the pond and pumphouse, which still seems intact with the door tightly shut—I guess they've not missed Arun yet.

There is no time to fuck about, as the whole area could soon be swarming with people looking for whoever killed the people on the hoist. So once everyone is out of the vehicle, we head for the ridgeline and the waiting boats before starting the dangerous descent. Take out my binos, search along the length of the coast, and out a few hundred metres to sea for our transport off this island. Only one slight snag, neither Kev and Paul in the boat we came in on, nor Carl with his yacht are anywhere to be seen.

Chapter Eighteen – Withdrawal

Now thinking on my feet, from what I can see we have two options: stay and wait for one of the two vessels to turn up or run for the vehicle ferry and hope nobody is waiting for us at the dock.

Once the whole team have joined me on the ridge, "OK, as you can see, we have a change of plan. As our transport away from the island hasn't shown up. I suggest we go for the ferry, which, according to Kev and our friend Arun, leaves at 14:00," I check my watch, "which is one hour from now."

"Agreed, the sooner we depart, the safer," comes Lucy's voice of logic.

"Sounds good to me," says Simon, heading back to the Land Cruiser.

"Yep, let's go," George replies, following Simon.

No doubt if the word's gotten out that the people who snatched Joby from Hoist 50 under gunfire, the Golden Camel will be looking for five men and a woman once they've gathered information from people like Noor and his colleagues. With that in mind, some team members will need to be concealed somewhere in the vehicle with me driving, and Lucy will sit in the front passenger seat.

Before we clamber in, I turn to face the others. "This is how it will play out. We need to separate to limit the chances of being prevented from boarding or detained by the Golden Camel's thugs. If Simon and George board the vessel on foot, you two are less likely to have been spotted by anyone on the hoist.

"No problem," says Simon.

Once I receive a raised thumb from George, I continue, "To keep Joby out of view, we will conceal him beneath the equipment and the blankets I purchased from the store in the back. To ensure our friend doesn't try to do something stupid, Derek will be on the rear seat with his 9mm hanging over the back seat and pointing at Joby. If nobody's got any questions, I suggest we drive to a point close to the ferry and wait until boarding is about to finish, then board."

The place is a swarm of activity when we arrive at the dock, located roughly one kilometre north of the shops and restaurants we used previously. About 30 cars of different types are lined up in rows facing a concrete slope of the loading area on the ground to our front. On the other side are two 12 metre grey portacabins, one of which has its door open, in which several people are entering before re-emerging, grasping what looked like a green coloured card.

Spinning in my seat, "We don't have much time before the vehicle ferry arrives, and we need tickets. While George and Lucy purchase all the boarding passes, the rest of us can cover them from here, ready to drive over if they get into any trouble."

"Roger that, give us some dosh then, tight arse."

Reach into my jacket pocket and pull out a 50 Rial note, "Here you go, George. That should be sufficient... in fact, here's another twenty to make sure."

The instance Lucy and George start walking over to purchase the tickets, I jump out and take up a defensive position behind the door with my assault rifle sitting on the seat in easy reach, just in case.

A few minutes later, they are past the cars and are about to enter the main ticket office. Before entering, Lucy turns and glances back in our direction to confirm we are still watching.

Two local men in white dishdashas and a third man dressed similarly to the goons from the Golden Camel also enter. My heart sinks before the head takes over from the slight flapping. A couple of anxious minutes go by before George exits, grasping the same green-coloured card we saw the other drivers carrying. Several more tense seconds disappear before Lucy also comes out and joins George in walking back to our location.

"Here you go," she hands me the vehicle ticket.

We need this part of the plan to go without a hitch or attract unwanted attention. So I hang the boarding pass from the rearview mirror. Turn the key in the ignition just enough for the lights to come on the dash to check the time. Only 10 more minutes until the ferry arrives. But saying that, this place is probably comparable to Oman, so anywhere in the next 30 minutes will class it as being on time.

I detect in the silence the rear door open, turn my head to the left to glimpse sight of Derek standing by my window, and declare, "Back in a minute, just going to recce the area."

"Great idea, I'll come with you," declares Simon, getting out of the vehicle.

After another nervous look at the Land Cruiser clock, I detect the sound of people behind us. Scan the mirror hanging down in the centre of the windscreen, can't see anyone, but I'm not taking chances this late in the game. Without saying a word, I grab my Browning 9mm, disembark with George, and head for the noise source, an old dirty brick building about 20 metres away.

To move undetected, we hug the midday shadows caused by the structure. Close to the closed, rotten, blue wooden door, I raise my pistol vertically until it runs along the front of my chest, being held in both hands with my back pressed hard against the brickwork.

On the opposite side of the doorway, George is doing the same. From inside the building, I can detect the sound of people shuffling around with the occasional sound of wood being hurtled across the room. I turn to face the door and, in a quiet voice, announce, "Now." With my right foot, I kick the door open and rush inside, followed by George.

In the dimly lit room, over in the far corner, highlighted by a narrow beam of light coming in from a broken window high up on the wall, two men dressed in torn t-shirts, dirty black trousers, and shoes that have seen far better days are trying to hide behind an old battered desk.

From the fear etched across both of their faces, I can tell they aren't a threat to us, so I ask, "Who are you — what are you doing here?"

In a faint, slightly trembling voice, the older-looking of the two yells, "Don't kill us. We are just looking for stuff to sell so we can make our way off the island."

"Why is that? Surely you can jump on the daily ferry like everyone else," I enquire in a non-threatening tone and lower my weapon.

"We were sacked by our employer, so we can't pay back the Golden Camel, and fear for our lives. Therefore we have no money to buy tickets," comes the response to my question.

Due to a rare sensation of empathy for their plight, I find myself reaching in my jacket and pulling out 100 Omani Rial. "Here you go, that should help you in your plans. Suggest you go and purchase your ticket out of here as the boat will be here soon."

The oldish-looking man grabbed my hand holding the money with both of his and repeated "thank you" several times before disappearing outside.

From my right, "Don't fucking believe what I just saw with my own eyes... you've gone soft on us. Only seen you show that type of kindness once since I've known you," says George, pretending to hold himself up by resting his left arm on my shoulder.

"To use one of Simon's saying, the second word is off, guess the first," I respond, heading for the door.

As we arrive back at the Land Cruiser, Simon and Derek are walking back from the coastline direction. "Ferry's on its way in," shouts Simon.

"Thanks, mate, everyone, head for your positions — we will meet up again once on the ferry, and it's left the harbour, " I say, climbing into the driver's seat.

Wait until the last line of vehicles starts to drive onto the vessel and our foot passengers have boarded before firing up the engine and going over to join the queue.

Halfway down the concrete slope, the ferry's massive metal loading ramps are rubbing up and down the hard surface, groaning as they slither along with the flow of the tide. At the base of the ramp, two men dressed in jeans and t-shirts are checking and collecting tickets while sticking their heads into every vehicle to ensure they aren't conveying people who haven't paid.

Four metres away from the checkpoint, I say in a firm voice that could only be heard by only the people inside our Land Cruiser, "This is it, folks, time to play along and pretend to be nice if stopped. Make sure Joby keeps perfectly still, Derek."

As expected, we are brought to a stop by the man on our left and his outreached hand. As we come to a complete halt, I press the down button and lower the window, allowing the sea breeze to blow gently inside alongside the salty aroma of the ocean. Of course, you're never too far from the stench of crude, this being an oil facility.

"Morning, can I see your tickets?" comes a firm, stern voice of the man now with his head half in our vehicle.

"Good morning to you as well. After a long two-month stint, the three of us are heading home," I reply in a laidback tone, trying to distract the man from paying too much attention to what is inside, especially the rear.

After a quick scan of our documents, he waves us onboard the ferry, where another person directs us to the back of the third line of vehicles. Once out of the Land Cruiser, I complete a brief check to determine if anyone is paying any interest in our activities. So far, we are not attracting attention to ourselves, and all is going to plan. Poke my head through the open rear door, "You can let him up now."

Derek pokes Joby, still concealed under the blanket, with his 9mm, "Out you get, and don't try anything silly."

Once we are all out of the Land Cruiser and standing on the car deck, I head for a point approximately halfway along, through the aroma and a faint cloud of exhaust fumes wafting along the wide-open decks. On both sides are weighty metal red sliding doors, behind which are the stairs leading up to the passenger lounge one floor up.

The seating area is similar to what you find on most short crossing ferries. Four rows of blue imitation leather seats are on one side, and two lines of tables and chairs are opposite on the port side. A small counter selling the usual drinks and snacks is off to the rear.

We make our way through the lounge, through the ambient chatter of conversations that fill the room and the rays of light flickering across the floor from the huge windows surrounding the lounge on three sides. Off to the right is a double glass door leading out to a small outside space, probably for the cancer addicts among the passengers.

It isn't hard to spot Simon and George sitting at a table close to the front of the half-empty room. In fact, bearing in mind the number of vehicles on board, this room should be fuller.

Maybe this is because this is only a one-hour crossing, even though several signs displayed through the boat state that no person is allowed on the car deck during transit. The locals have undoubtedly decided the signs don't apply to them and have stayed in their vehicles.

As I sit across from George and Simon, "Take it everything went OK with your boarding?"

"Yeah, no problems our side. We were the first on board, so we took the liberty of getting you three numpties a brew — not sure what you wanted, Joby, so got you a milky tea," states George, pushing one of the mugs towards Lucy.

"Thanks, George," after sipping on her coffee.

Through a mouth half-filled with doughnut, "You have a plan of action for when we disembark, or is it a dash to Muscat airport with our friend here?" enquires Derek.

"Been thinking about that. The other vehicle is still parked in Jebel Sifah, and it would be prudent to swap our transport over to keep people off our track, so I suggest we go straight to the hotel and do a changeover. Then it's a sprint to the airport to catch our late evening flights home."

"Sounds like some sort of a plan, Steve," replies Simon, after taking a sip of his brew.

The next 35 minutes go without a hitch, with the conversation flowing about what each of us will be doing once we got home. While Lucy and I will be going on another cruise, Derek will be heading back to St Bethanie. The other two don't have plans, apart from making the most of the money from the job.

The ferry should arrive in Muscat in about 20 minutes, so I use the time to stretch my legs before driving to the hotel at Jebel Sifah. Besides strolling around the central lounge, there is only one other option, go outside and experience the hot sea breeze out on the open deck with the smokers.

Only one other person is on the small outer area, leaning on the chest-height metal barrier when I push the double doors ajar, but he goes back inside once I step outside.

I stand looking out to sea for a few minutes before I feel a hard blunt object in my lower back. Realise straight away what it is. This is not the first time I've had a weapon poked in my back, so there's no need to panic immediately. In the short nano-second between me working out what action to take and the sound of a voice behind me speaking in an Indian accent, "You know how this works, Steve, do what I say," I realise it must be someone from the Golden Camel.

Right, snap plan—once he eases the tension of the weapon in my back—and he will, that will give me time to swing around fast, grab the pistol, and knock him to the rigid metal deck, with any luck knocking the wind out of him, giving me time to better understand the situation.

Another few tense seconds pass when I hear the unexpected sound and rush of air as something passes within millimetres of the back of my head and strikes something or someone close to me. The pressure of the weapon being held against me immediately dissipates and hits the metal floor with a loud clanging noise as it bounces several times.

Waste no time spinning on the balls of my feet to catch a glimpse of what just happened. To my pure amazement, one of the two men I'd given money to in the old building before we boarded is standing in front of me, holding a fire extinguisher. Stunned, I say, "Thank you, I guess one good deed does lead to another."

Kicked out of the 'what the fuck' frame of mind by the brain telling me we can't leave the concussed body lying on the floor for everyone else to discover and start asking stupid questions. Fortunately, a red lifebuoy storage cupboard is behind my new friend up against the bulkhead, and it isn't locked.

"Help me move him in there," I point to the emergency locker.

Place both my arms under his armpits and pull the torso upwards, while the person who I may just owe my life to grabs his feet and lifts him over to the big red metal box. Inside are piles of life vests, leaving sufficient room to stuff the body, ready for him to be found later, or when he comes round after the smack in the head he just received.

Back in the lounge, "You took your time," says Lucy, looking at me puzzled.

The mainland ferry terminal is coming into view. "I'll explain once we are in the Land Cruiser and on our way."

Now back in the vehicle, I describe the events that occurred on the open deck. By my reckoning, nobody else would try something like that—plus, going by his accent, he must be from the Golden Camel.

"Fuck, you think we were followed onto the boat?"

"Nope, don't think so, Derek. No way that would have happened, as we took all the necessary steps to ensure we weren't. He must have been on here already and fancied his chances," I say, as Simon drives down the ramps and into the dockyard.

Due to the ferry landing on the far side of Sultan Qaboos Port, we drive past tall industry warehouses and multi-storey brown stone-clad office buildings that line both sides of the winding road. After two roundabouts and a couple of turns, we finally reach the main entrance to the docks. Apart from a few customs officers and

Royal Omani police, the place appears quiet, and we depart without being stopped, forgoing any unwanted checks.

Soon we are speeding away down Al Mina Street, heading for the hotel and our other vehicle. Once the highway passes through Ruwi, Simon takes a right turn off the major road and follows the same route we took less than a week ago, through the high rocky mountains towards Jebel Sifah.

One hour later, we are driving through the last small village with its dust-covered buildings, before the roadway turns from tarmac to compacted sand, then winding its way to the Sifahwy Boutique hotel.

As we arrive close to the fish restaurant we used to meet the arms dealer, George comes up with an idea. "It doesn't take everyone to fetch the vehicle, so how about Steve and Simon do that while the rest of us go and order some nosh?"

"Trust you, fat boy, to think of food at a time like this," comes the reply from Simon.

"Do one, you skinny twat," George retorts.

"Tell you what, that sounds a good idea—nobody followed us here, did they, Simon?" asks Lucy.

"Not that I can detect."

"As I can't refuse a beautiful woman, I'll drop you four off before Simon and I pick up the other Land Cruiser... talking of vehicles— where did you conceal it?" I ask, as my stomach starts rumbling.

"I was going to stash it in the dunes but decided the best place to hide it from view would be in the wide open, so I dumped it in the hotel car park," Simon replies.

"Makes sense, mate, I suppose."

Once we've dropped Lucy, Derek, George and Joby off close to the restaurant, we continue to Sifahwy Boutique Hotel, arriving several minutes later. Apart from a few other cars scattered about the place, our vehicle is the only other one in the car park. After the events of the last couple of days, aligned with the information from Noor about us being followed from the very beginning, we need to be positive the vehicle isn't being monitored.

With that in mind, Simon reverses into an empty space on the other side of the car park directly opposite our hired Land Cruiser. We stand off for the next five minutes and scan the whole area visible from our location. As we didn't detect any people moving around, it's time to make to leave. The first job is to ensure none of the cars located here has any members of the Golden Camel, or any of their hired thugs, sitting and watching.

While I walk past and check every car individually, Simon waits in the vehicle with the engine running, ready to get the fuck out of here if events go in the wrong direction of perfect. Doesn't take long to confirm the area is clear, so signal Simon to drive over and park next to our motor vehicle.

One last step to be 100 percent nobody's been meddling with our ride to the airport, I examine every part without touching it to determine if anything is not as it should be and could indicate tampering. When I reached the driver's door, Simon climbs out of the Land Cruiser and joins me.

"Is the foliage I placed between the door and frame still in place?" Simon enquires.

I run my eyes along the narrow outline of the door until I notice a small brown leaf wedged in the structure close to the underside of the door. "Yes, mate."

"In that case, help me transfer the team's equipment so we can get a few drinks with the others."

With everything moved over, we drive off to meet up with the idiots at the restaurant. By the time we reach there, Lucy, George, Joby and Derek are sitting at a brown wooden table on the veranda, drinking glasses of what looked like cold beer, from the colour and moisture running down the outside of the glass.

Take a seat next to Lucy, "Have you ordered any food?"

"Not yet, Steve. Take it you had no issues retrieving the vehicle?" placing her hand on my knee.

"Nope, all went to plan, and I take it one of those beers is mine?" I declare, reaching out and grabbing one.

While gulping down half a glass of beer, the same waiter from our last visit comes over. "Are you ready to order now?" he says, with a notepad and pen poised to take down the orders.

Everyone finishes ordering their food, several more rounds of beers, and soft drinks for Simon as he's the chauffeur. The last thing we need on the way to Muscat international airport is to be pulled up by the ROP for drunk driving. Usually, this wouldn't be an issue as we would somehow blag our way out, generally with plenty of money, but we must try to avoid unwanted attention this time.

After a scan to ensure nobody is trying to overhear our conversation, "Our flights are open-ended, so I think we should go to the airport straight after the meal and grab our flight home. If none are available with BA, we can pay for alternative flights. What're your thoughts on this, ladies and gents?"

"I, for one, agree with Steve—we ought to get out of Oman as quickly as possible before the Golden Camel tries to block us from leaving by paying off some unscrupulous officials," says George, putting down an empty glass before picking up a fresh beer.

"Yeah, think we should depart ASAP— Steve and I are on a cruise on Norwegian Prima next week and still have packing to do," replies Lucy.

With Derek and Simon agreeing, we turn our attention to the plates overflowing with the array of food we ordered that has just arrived at the table with our friendly waiter. Like our last visit, the meals are beautifully laid out and taste just as good.

A glance down at the time confirms we better make a move to Muscat airport and our 23:59 BA flight, especially if we are to be at the airport three hours before boarding, and it's a good two-hour drive from here.

"When you're ready, boys and girls, let's get going," swigging down the last of my beer.

The route to the airport is straightforward. We soon reach the central short stay car park, where we dump the Land Cruiser among the other abandoned vehicles after leaving a note on the windscreen for security to tell them where the car belongs and the hire company's phone number.

On arrival at the terminal, through the enormous glass sliding doors, you enter a vast departure hall with a few scattered coffee shops and, most importantly for us, multiple airline ticket offices. After walking up and down the counters, we finally find one that deals with several airlines because British Airways didn't have a separate desk.

In a square booth, no more than six feet across, a young Indian lady is sitting behind a counter, typing away on a computer. No doubt she would want to take a look at all our passports. No point separating up, so the whole team approaches the desk.

" As-salamu alaykum," I wait for her to reply.

"Wa alaikum salaam, how can I help you?" comes the response from the young lady, who I can now see from her name badge is called Deepti.

"Hi, Deepti, we have flights booked for tomorrow night but would like to travel tonight instead for family reasons," I use the same excuse every time I need to switch flights.

"No problem, sir, just let me find your details,"

After 30 seconds of tapping on her keyboard, "Here you are, six people in business class on BA6373 on tomorrow's flight. One moment while I find out if there is room on tonight's departure for you."

"Thank you," being polite as possible, as you're more likely to obtain what you want this way.

Once again, Deepti taps away on the keyboard before looking up, "You are in luck—only six more seats available for tonight... would you like me to modify your tickets? There will be a small charge for this?"

"Yes, please."

Pay the 100 Omani Rial for the change, and head straight for security. The airport is bustling with people eager to progress through and make their flights, so there is a long queue. Once we have navigated security, we should be safe. Not that I'm expecting the Golden Camel to have people working at the gates as they are all locals, so not under their control, hopefully.

Once through, I catch sight of the distinctive blue of the BA counter. On both sides are rows of airline check-in desks. Up to this point, the team's been deliberately quiet so as not to attract attention to ourselves with our British accents. Plus, we might accidentally say something about the mission.

Due to the fact we had left a lot of the equipment buried in the sand near Jebel Sifah, along with the weapons we destroyed, making them inoperable and scattered across an extensive area, we didn't have any baggage to check-in. Each person only carried their Bergens with their own personal kit inside.

We still have three hours to waste before boarding, so I ask the others, "Anyone fancy some cold ones while we wait?"

"Do bears shit in the woods?" comes the response from Derek.

"Count me in for that," says Simon, looking around to spot the nearest bar.

"Hey, we are flying business class, so we might as well use the lounge," comes the response from Lucy.

"You're right, of course, honey," I reply, "Where is it?"

The area inside the lounge is bustling with people. Some line up to indulge in the hot and cold buffet before grabbing drinks for the bar, while others relax in the soft furnishings lined up in neat rows.

From the look in Joby's eyes, you can tell that he's never been in a business lounge before, and unlike the rest of us, he doesn't know what to do first, eat or drink. He soon starts to get the hang of it and sits with the team as we while away the few hours before our flight departs back to England.

Chapter Nineteen – Home

The last week has been hard on us all with the lack of sleep and the mental concentration, so it goes without saying we spend most of the flight sleeping, only waking up for food and drinks. But now, the captain is informing the crew they've got 30 minutes until landing. Time to collect all my things together, ready to leave the plane.

Thankfully, the line for passport control is short, and we manage to make our way through it quickly, thanks to the electronic gates. Once everyone is past immigration, we head for customs. This should be a quick process as we didn't bring any bags. Therefore no need to waste time waiting for cases to arrive.

It would appear the customs officers are either bored or are having a 'let's piss off every passenger' type of day. Lots of random people are being diverted to the red lane to go through extra checks.

It must be Derek's unlucky day, probably as he isn't from the UK, because as he starts to exit the baggage hall via the green channel with the rest of us, he is directed to the goods to be declared one to be checked.

The rest of us make it through with no problems. As we exit, immediately in front of us is a small Caffé Nero consisting of the serving area and several tables cordoned off with dark red removable barriers.

"Tell you what, while we hang about waiting for Derek, let's grab a brew and sit over there," I point to a table directly opposite the exit.

While Lucy goes off to fetch the drinks, the remainder of us drop our Bergens on the floor before taking a seat to wait for the numpty to come out. It isn't too long before Derek emerges through the doorway, looking around like a lost schoolboy on a field trip trying to find us.

After standing, I raise my right hand before yelling, "Over here."

"Didn't expect to see you so quick. Take it there was no rubber glove or internal search required. Positive, the customs officers would have found some dodgy-looking stuff in your bag," says Simon, supporting a vast stupid grin.

"Not a chance, Simon—I put them all in your Bergen before we left," Derek responds as he sits down with the rest of us.

"Wish you had told me that earlier... I would have spoken to immigration as we came through and got him strip searched," cries George, trying not to laugh.

"Do one, tick-tock, haven't you something to clean?" Simon responds, as quick as a shell from a tank turret.

"Joking aside, boys and girls, we are now almost home and dry, but we can't put this mission in the 'Done' file yet. One last thing to do before we call endex is deliver our parcel to Nasir. With that in mind, can you call him and arrange a meeting for 14:00 today for delivery, Simon?" I ask, before picking up the mug of coffee.

"Will do it now, before heading for the long stay car park to pick up our vehicle." Simon takes out his mobile phone and dials Nasir's number.

After a few rings, someone answers, "Hello, this is Nasir. Who am I talking to?"

"It's Simon. The package you requested is with us. Can you meet us in the same place as last time at 13:00, with the rest of the payment?"

"Yes, no problem," comes the excited voice on the other end.

Within two hours of leaving the airport, we pull into the multi-storey in Southampton, attached to the West Quay shopping centre.

"Park on 7B, Simon, as this is usually quiet, we can use the stairs to move down to street level, one floor down." As predicted, there is only one other car parked neatly in between the white-lined bays about halfway down.

Just because we are at the end of the mission, this is no time to become complacent—seen too many missions fail because people took things for granted, because their task was coming to a conclusion.

So with that in mind, Simon, Joby, and I head through the centre, exiting on the high street before turning left and making our way slowly to the meeting point, thus giving the other team time to get in position. This leaves Lucy, Derek and George to take the longer route via the new part of West Quay, along the main road, right at the Civic Centre, to join the street running past the public house from the top end.

Once we reach the boozer and the arranged rendezvous point, Lucy and Derek will enter, purchase drinks, and sit close to the front door. Due to the fact, out of the whole team, these are the only people that haven't been seen by Nasir, their role will be to watch for Nasir's arrival, hopefully alone, and deal with any people he might bring along.

George will conceal himself across the road, looking for anyone Nasir might have brought with him who didn't enter the place, and act as a backup while remaining out of view of people entering or leaving the building. Plus, he will give us an early warning that our man is approaching. My team will buy drinks from the bar before heading upstairs and sit by the window.

I glance down at my watch—only 30 minutes before the scheduled meeting time, so I turn to Joby. "Tell me, are you glad to be out of the control of the Golden Camel and a reunion with your family?"

"Yes, Mr Steve, thank you for getting me out. But the moment we go back home to Kerla, they will come, and the punishment will be severe... some people may even be killed," comes the quiet voice of Joby, still coming to terms with his new surroundings.

"No need to worry about that, my friend, everything's been taken care of. You're not going back to India, and neither is your whole family," I say, after investigating the noise of feet striking wooden boards as someone walks heavy-footed up the stairs.

"What do you mean?" Joby looks puzzled.

"I believe you are moving in with relatives somewhere in England," I reply.

"Where?" Joby requests.

"Don't..." I am interrupted by my phone vibrating in my pocket. The message from George read, 'target and two others strolling towards the pub'. A few seconds later, another text, this time from Lucy, 'the two men that came with him have stayed downstairs — Nasir is walking up on his own'.

Put the telephone away as my attention is drawn to more distinctive sound of footsteps coming up the wooden staircase. A few tense moments pass before Nasir steps onto the first floor, carrying a brown leather briefcase. His eyes dart around the room before he spots us by the window and walks over.

As he gets closer to the black veneer-covered rectangle table, I stand up, "Hi Nasir, I hope you're well," I hold out my hand to shake his.

"Fine, thank you, Steve, and good afternoon, Simon," comes the reply, as he occupies the seat across the table from me and next to Joby. "Namaste, have these people been looking after you?"

"Namaste, yes, I am OK. Do you have my family?" questions Joby.

"Don't worry, they are safe back at my house. We will go there once we've finished business here."

"Sorry to break up this little reunion, but did you bring the rest of our money?"

After putting the leather briefcase on the wooden table, "Yes, Steve, what you are after is in here," pointing at the case.

"Thanks," I slide the briefcase over to Simon, who opens it and removes two bound banknotes piles. To ensure he selects a random sample, he takes one from the top and one from the bottom row and holds them beneath the level of our table out of view. I watch as he flicks through each stack to make sure all the notes are genuine and Nasir isn't trying to rip us off with blank inserts.

"Don't you trust me, Steve?" Nasir says with some sort of annoyed look that I even thought about not trusting him.

"Yes, of course. Besides, we have already dispatched several members of the Golden Camel, including their leader, John Nair. One more won't be an issue."

"Not sure what you mean," replies Nasir, who is now looking uncomfortable and fidgeting in his seat.

"Really? We met a friend of yours in Duhfa, a man called Noor, who became very chatty about your involvement in the organisation, and the fascinating fact that you set us up from the start." I stare straight into his eyes, looking for any visible signs of acknowledgement that he's been found out.

"You're right, Steve, but did he also explain that I'm planning to leave, as I'm not happy with their methods?"

"He did—that is the only reason we are handing Joby over to you. What you don't know, while we've been away, I had you followed and know exactly where you live. So if we receive any information that harm has fallen on Joby or his family, we will be coming after you, plus your wife and two kids."

"There will be no need for that, I can assure you," Nasir replies, standing up from the table.

After looking at the message on my mobile phone, "One more thing before you and our friend Joby leave, Nasir. Do not forget to take your two thugs sitting at the downstairs bar drinking beer," I wanted to let him know all the details, so he realises people are watching his every move.

After saying goodbye, Simon and I remain seated and watch as Nasir and Joby disappear down the stairs. Our plan is to stay in position for at least 10 minutes, giving time for them to disappear and for George to inform us that nobody is waiting to follow us once we vacate the property.

With Simon holding the briefcase, I type a message into my phone, 'meet at the transport', before rising to my feet and heading for the exit. Once we've left, Derek and Lucy will stay inside the pub for a short time after. We must ensure we are not followed by anyone who might have been planted there by Nasir before we arrived. At the same time, George will depart his location and take a different way back to my car.

When we arrive back in the multi-storey, George is leaning against my vehicle's bonnet, "You get all the money OK?" he shouts out as we close in on his position.

"Yup, right here," Simon holds up the brown briefcase.

A couple of minutes pass before Lucy and Derek appear through a vast blue door at the far end and amble over to join us. Once everyone is in the Suzuki, we head off to the ferry and my place on the Isle of Wight. All that remains of the mission is to sort out equipment and, more importantly, do the accounting. I need to take away the job's costs before splitting up what's left five ways.

The crossing is the same as usual, one hour of boredom broken up by good conversation and a few beverages to celebrate another successful mission where we all came home, with the added bonus that nobody is supporting a new battle scar this time.

Back at my home in Shanklin, we are not taking things for granted because the task is complete, so Simon drives to a spot in the park away from my haunt. Once the vehicle comes to a halt, George and I clamber out and walk the short distance to the lodge. Each takes a different side, looking for signs that someone might have tampered with, including checking the grass to see if it's been trampled down close to any entry point, or anyone who might be waiting for us nearby.

With the outside clear, I turn my attention to check all the telltales are still in place in the door and windows. With all the leaves and tape still in situ, it would appear nobody's been fucking about, and the area is safe, so call Simon to drive around with Lucy and Derek.

Once inside, George and Simon head for the rooms they were staying in before we left, dumping their mission equipment into orange waterproof bags and repacking their Bergens for the way home later.

"Dump your stuff with Simon's, Derek. I'll give you some dosh to take back to buy some new civvie clothes," I yelled, heading for my bedroom.

After disposing of mine and Lucy's Bergens in my room, I grab my notebook and pen before joining the rest at the table where the cash has been piled up on one end.

For the following few minutes, I scribble away on a blank sheet of paper in my notepad. With the aid of a calculator, I work out all the expenses for the mission and subtract that from the £250,000 we've been paid to bring Joby back to the UK.

Eventually, I announce, "OK, folks, we are left with 40 grand each after I've taken out all the costs."

"Sounds like a good week's assignment to me," declares Simon, fondling one of the stacks of cash.

"And me," George agrees, also grabbing a pile of dosh.

"Before we all start helping ourselves, remember I've still got some of the money in my bank account. Therefore, the best thing is for everyone to take 20 grand now, and I will transfer the rest to your banks in two payments in two days to stop any nosy bastards from getting interested in your bulging accounts. Apart from you, Derek. If you take nine thousand now, that should keep you under the limit of having to declare it when you land in St Bethanie. Will transmit your share in three different amounts."

"Good thinking, Steve, that's fine by me. But you're buying us all food down the Barley later," says Derek, holding his hand out.

"The boozer thing sounds interesting, far better than Steve's shitty cooking any day," states George through a stupid grin.

"While you lot head off to drink far too many beers, I will stay here and get a shower," declares Lucy, leaving the table and heading for the bedroom.

When we enter the pub, the joint is almost empty. The only other people are a small group at tables to the left, close to the back door and one man sitting alone on a barstool at the long bar which runs across the back wall.

Love the place when it's like this, as our favourite spot on the leather sofas near the fire with its flickering flames and the sounds of crackling wood is free.

Been reclining on the sofa for a couple of minutes, looking through the menu when from behind the bar, I detect a man's voice yell out, "Afternoon, gents, you finished that job already?"

Lift my head from the list of food options and glance over in the direction of the voice—it is Gary. "Hi Gary, you still serving grub? The fat boys here are hungry," I point at Simon, Derek and George relaxing on the soft cushions of the sofas.

"Yes, mate. "

"Rather than you three numpties wasting time deciding what to eat, shall I save time and order the food?" I suggest, grabbing the menus.

"Yeah, why not. And I'll have a Stella as well," states George, raising a cupped hand to his mouth.

"Same for me, " comes the response from Simon and Derek.

"Four gigantic grills heavy on the dead pig coming up," I walk over to the bar to place the order.

With his hand placed on the handle of the John Smith's pump, "Take it you're having the usual?"

"Yes, and three Stellas and four of your mixed grills please, Gary."

Over the time spent drinking here and making it my local, I've got to know him quite well and found out he is an ex-British Royal Marine and someone who can be trusted to keep information to himself when required.

"Here you go. Will give you a shout when your food is ready," says Gary, plonking four glasses down on the counter in front of me.

"Cheers, mate. And thanks for doing that track and trace job in Southampton for me. It did the trick. The man from India will think before trying anything silly."

"Not a problem—that's a beer you owe me."

"Can do better than that," I slide three £50 notes across the bar. "Keep the change."

"Thanks, Steve — any time you and the boys need some work doing, just let me know," replies Gary, taking the cash.

Back on the sofa, the conversation flows almost as fast as the beers goes down on everything, but primarily celebrating the success of another mission. Then I detect the squeaking of the extensive wooden front door being flung open behind me. Turn to see four young men in their early twenties enter the room. At first glance, I thought it might be the youths we stitched up before going away.

"That's not them, wonder what happened to the numpties," proclaims Simon, waving an empty glass to say 'whose round?'.

At that moment, Gary appears carrying a grey-coloured tray containing our food order. "Don't become accustomed to the waiter service, either — this is a one-off."

"Thanks, mate. Do you know what came of the idiots we were sitting with some time back?" asks George.

"A while back, there was an attack on a property in America Woods. Lots of people were killed, including the owner. I believe his name was Dennis. Of course, this has nowt to do with you lot," he replies with a knowing grin, as he knew it was us.

"Yep, not our handiwork," I declare, trying not to smile at a mission that mainly went without a hitch.

After picking up the empty glasses, Gary continues, "Well, whoever it was, when the constabulary arrived and searched the house, they found three young children unharmed and hiding in a back room. The reports say they are Dennis's grandkids and saw the event unfold."

"Glad the little ones are OK," says Simon.

"The boy gave a description to the local police that fitted your profiles. That is why you were taken in for questioning,"

I turn to face Simon, "What did I say about...."

"Don't fucking look at me, I'm still against killing kids."

"Thanks for that, Gary, but what about the four men we encouraged to go down to America Woods?" I ask.

"This is where you idiots catch a break. While they were in the woods, someone called the emergency services and told them where to find them and when they were located, the police found them with a Browning pistol. Of course, that also wouldn't have been you." Once more, Gary looks at us all with a knowing smile.

"So, where are they now?" I enquire.

"Just getting to that bit. The authorities did a ballistics test on the 9mm and matched it up with the spent cases and bullets in the deceased. So they are in prison on remand, waiting for a court case. You're out of the line of sight for now."

I turn to face the others, who do their best not to laugh at the numpties that tried to jump me on our first encounter. Maybe they will think before acting next time.

We stay for a few more beers and finish the meals before heading back to my place. Lucy is sitting on the decking at the battered round table that I keep meaning to replace, by the time we arrive.

"You boys have fun?" she enquires, while sipping on a steaming hot mug of coffee.

"Yes, thank you, honey. Brought you some food back as well," I place a tin-foil wrapped package on the circular table, like a drunken squirrel making an offering to their mate.

"I placed several beers in the fridge, if you want any more?"

"No, thanks, Lucy, A brew will do me," Simon enunciates, heading indoors to put the kettle on.

"About time you came in useful, Donkey Walloper, make us all one," yells George, after sitting down next to Lucy.

Not sure if the excursion or the mission has caught up with us or the amount of alcohol consumed, but by 21:00, everyone is starting to act like nodding donkeys and falling asleep where they sit.

Staggering to his feet, "I'm calling it a night and off to bed. See you all in the morning."

"OK, Simon, see you tomorrow," I yawn.

Within 40 minutes, everyone's gone to the land of nod, so I drag my knackered body to the bedroom and join Lucy under the warm quilt that covers my double bed.

The time is now 05:00 and been lying wide awake for at least an hour. Unable to return to sleep. I wonder why I find it easier to grab some kip in any woods or on some clifftop than in my own bed. In the end, I slide gently out of bed so I don't wake Lucy and make my way to the front room.

First, I need my morning coffee, especially as my mouth tastes like a camel's flip-flop. The noise of the switch on the kettle switching off with a loud click must have woken Simon, as he joins me a couple seconds later.

"Did you not sleep either?" I ask, working on autopilot. "You want a brew?"

"Yes, please, mate."

After sitting in silence for a few minutes, I glance up from my mug and ask, "What time do you and the rest want a lift to the ferry?"

"We'll be off once the other two are up and ready. Need to set off for home to the other half. Best I let wifey know I'm still alive," replies Simon after swallowing a mouth full of hot steaming liquid.

About an hour later, everyone else is up and kicking, drinking the brown liquid of life, coffee, including Lucy, who is standing in the kitchen with her head in the fridge. "Anyone want breakfast before you depart?" she asks.

"No thanks, Lucy, we will purchase a Full English on the boat," declares Derek, finishing his brew.

Shortly after, I'm pulling into a parking space outside the Red Funnel terminal in East Cowes in time for the boys to catch the 09:00 ferry. Once out of the car and standing at the top of the slipway, I can see the ship as it enters the Medina River.

"OK, you lot, fuck off. Hope your flights go OK, Derek. Give us a call in a few days, and let me know if you reach home without any issues. Say hi to Claire from us all. Will speak to you two other numpties sometime this week," I yell, as they disappear into the terminal.

Thirty-five minutes later, I arrive home to find Lucy sitting outside, soaking up the bright morning sun. She gives off an enormous, beautiful smile when she spots me walking toward her from my parking spot.

"You appear stunning sitting there with the morning rays of light dancing off your face," I express, smiling back at her.

"Thanks, honey—what do you want to do today, apart from nothing?" comes the sweet female tone of her voice.

"That about sums it up for me, do bugger all," I respond.

We spend the next hour or so sitting outside in the warm sun, chatting away and planning for our cruise when the mobile phone rings. "I'm going to ignore that thing, as I'm contented doing my bugger all and enjoying your company," I state, annoyed.

"You better answer it. There could be a problem with one of the boys," Lucy says, with a grin I can't neglect.

Remove my phone from my trouser pocket and glance at the screen. It's Simon. "What the matter, fucking miss me already?"

"Never, sorry to interrupt your busy day, but I just received a call from someone who's got a job we might be interested in.

Glossary

Army Chuck-in	Stew
Bergen	Backpack
Binos	Binoculars
Call Sign DR	Derek Radio
Call Sign GD	George Dog
Call Sign S3	Steve 3(RGJ)
Call Sign TS	Tanky Simon
Call Sign LK	Lucy Killer
Chimp	Mind / Anger Management programme used in the treatment of PTSD
Click	Kilometre
Donkey Walloper	Tank Driver
Dhobi Dust	Washing Powder
Egg Banjo	Egg Sandwich
Endex	End of Mission
Escaped Librarian	A term used in the treatment of PTSD
FRV	Final Rendezvous
Grunt	Ground Reconnaissance Untrainable
LZ	Landing Zone
Maggot	Sleeping Bag
Mickey	Cheap Wristwatch
OP	Observation Post
PAYG	Pay As You Go
Pit	Bed
Polo Donkey	Horse/Donkey
Range Card	A drawing or sketch used in OPs shows potential locations and distances to targets.
RV	Rendezvous – Meeting Point

Shanks' Pony	Walking
SLR	Self Loading Rifle
SOP	Standard Operating Procedure
Stag	Sentry Duty
Tab	Walk or Hike

Codes

#	State	#	Sub State
01:00	All OK	01	Car
02:00	Followed	5	Boat
03:00	Situation Dealt With	10	Coach
04:00	Travel with Caution	15	Plane
05:00	Don't Travel	20	Taxi
06:00	Contact Not Made	25	Dispatched
07:00	Contact Made	30	Being Watched
08:00	Golden Camel Located	35	Located
09:00	Golden Camel Not Located	40	Confirmed
10:00	Transport to Mano Arranged by		Waiting On
11:00	Transport to Mano Not Arranged	45	Contact
12:00	Airport Pick Up Confirmed	50	On Time
13:00	Get Taxi to Hotel	55	Delayed
14:00	Target		
15:00	Joby		
16:00	Meeting		
17:00	Explosives		
18:00	Weapons Collection		
19:00	Flights		
20:00	Are you OK		

About the Author

I was born in 1962 in Farnham, Hampshire, in England. Lived in several places before moving to Southampton near the south coast where I lived before I joined the British Army.

I left School in 1979 and within a month joined the Royal Green Jackets in Winchester, after completing training joined 3RGJ in Cambridge. Continued to serve until 1989 in which I saw service in Cyprus on the UN, Germany, Ireland, Falklands, Canada, and of course the UK.

In 2017 after many years of suffering, I was diagnosed with PTSD from three life-threatening events during my service. Part of my recovery at Combat Stress someone suggested I should begin writing.

I had always written short pieces of work which never go past the printer. I have a love of cruising and have completed 28 in total to date. Therefore it was natural to write the first two books on cruising. I have now published two other books called 'The Lighter Side Of Cruising' and 'The Lighter Side of Cruising Part two.' Both available on Amazon. Both of these books look at cruising through my eyes, which is not as others see cruising — some times with humous effect. So if you want a funny look at cruising they are for you.

During my last two week stay at Combat Stress in April 2019, I started to write Poetry. Have now published my first ever book on poetry called 'Poetry from the PTSD Mind,' which takes you on a journey from the bad times to the good.

Other Books by Steve:

Covert Ops: Danger in Paradise

Covert Ops: Danger on the Island

For more information about our books, or to submit a manuscript, please visit

www.green-cat.shop